Death of Connor Sanderson

Prequel to the Fire & Ice Series

By

Karen Payton Holt

Copyright - Karen Payton Holt: 2018

If you are here, you are about to read my book and to start out on an adventure.

Think 'Twilight' meets 'Game of Thrones', with a dark twist, and you are in the right mindset to enter the world of Fire & Ice.

AVAILABLE NOW:

BOOK ONE in the Series:

Fire & Ice: Awakening
Available in Paperback on Amazon
Paperback and Hardback available in bookstores:
A5 Paperback ISBN 978-1-9996614-0-3
6x9 Hardback ISBN 978-1-9996614-1-0
Available on Kindle & FREE on Kindle Unlimited

BOOK TWO in the Series:

Fire & Ice: Survival
Available in Paperback on Amazon
Paperback and Hardback available in bookstores:
A5 Paperback ISBN 978-1-9996614-2-7
6x9 Hardback ISBN 978-1-9996614-3-4
Available on Kindle & FREE on Kindle Unlimited

Three upcoming releases are:

BOOK THREE: Earth Walker

BOOK FOUR: Heart of Stone

BOOK FIVE: Invasion

Death of Connor Sanderson:
Prequel to the Fire & Ice series

is also available on Kindle & FREE on Kindle Unlimited

For the latest news on the publishing dates visit my websites:

karenpaytonholt.com
Karen Payton Holt on Facebook.
@karenpaytonholt on TWITTER.

The epic journey continues, and I hope you enjoy the book.

Please share your thoughts and feelings in reviews – I welcome
your support!

I dedicate this novel to the people who believed in me.

They drove me forward, and, at times, gave me a much-needed kick up the posterior.

This is for my mum, Sylvia, and my friend of forty years, Steve.

With special thanks to my Uncle Michael and my Australian friend, Craig – both of whom read the first four chapters of an early draft, and kept asking, "When can I read the rest?"

8

Death of Connor Sanderson.

London, 1910. *Bram Stoker's Dracula had made barely a ripple in the pool of human consciousness, and it would be another 12 years before Nosferatu breathes life into a vampire on the big screen.*

Chapter 1

Doctor Connor Sanderson rolled over in his trestle bed, hearing the creaking beneath his weight and not knowing for certain if it was the juddering of bed springs, or his bones grating through his skull. It seemed louder than usual. The sweat-stained padding of his cot fell far short of being comfortable. The meager hospital accommodation encouraged a body to keep moving until exhaustion was complete.

Settling his shoulder blades back onto the sagging mattress, he peeled tired eyelids open and stared at the mustard-colored ceiling. The cracks decorating it appeared to have laid down a labyrinth of new shoots overnight. They reminded him of a family tree. He always thought of himself as a ripe plum hanging on the thickest branch, but, this morning, he felt drained and more fitting to a prune. *I feel so lethargic, what the hell is wrong with me?*

The thought percolated. A memory danced around the edges of his tired brain, but, the more he tried to capture it, the faster it raced away. His mother's adage, along with a sepia-tinted picture of her delicate features, came to mind. "Memories are like love; stop looking and they'll come and find you." *Complete rubbish, but heck, what else have I got?*

Connor heaved a deep sigh and trapped the breath inside, along with the word 'OUCH'.

Swinging his legs over the side of the bed and moving awkwardly to a sitting position, he lifted his cotton lawn nightshirt and craned a stiff neck to peer down the length of his hard, ridged abdomen. Everything looked normal – an edifice of boulders covered in the velvety texture of peach-toned skin – but the process of breathing had pressure inside, as though his lungs were already full and trying to burst.

T.B., pleurisy, pneumonia? His speculation was tempered with the certainty that the symptoms did not fit. *I can't become ill now, I'm just getting somewhere with Sir John. He has just noticed me.*

Planting his feet hip width apart, he put his palms on his knees and straightened his spine. Closing his eyes, he ran over the familiar territory of his body, attending to the tension in every muscle, in an inventory of how he felt. *Everything feels... unusual.*

Connor laughed gently and shook his head. *Get a grip. What did you expect?* He had just worked sixteen hours straight and spent the remainder of the night on a cot that only allowed sleep when he was too exhausted to think anymore. By the time night had fallen and he rolled onto the down-filled mattress, his thigh muscles were aching as though he had been wading through molasses, and his bones felt like heavy rods of iron.

The Royal Eye Hospital in St George's Circus had only been a teaching hospital for four years and competition was fierce. Connor would be twenty-five next birthday and was too busy *operating* on eyeballs to gaze into any with romantic intent, but, he at least had a promising career. *Home and hearth will come later. I'm not losing my place on the team, not now.*

Opening his eyes, he manipulated his neck, digging his fingers in hard to ease tight muscle as he stretched out his shoulders and rose to his feet. Suddenly six-foot and three-inches seemed far too lofty a height for the pumping station of his heart to manage. Flecks of burning ash, like white-hot wisps dancing around a bonfire, clustered in front of his eyes.

He sat down again, fast.

"Damn. Low blood pressure? Vertigo? What on earth-?" Connor dragged his hands down over his tight face, freezing as his fingertips faltered over a hardened network of capillaries under his skin.

Confusion drove him towards the mirror for a closer inspection. His fingernails dug into fists when he pushed himself up from the bed more carefully this time. He moved forward, testing the ground as though he feared his world would drop away from beneath him.

Nothing behaved like it should, and he felt like a paraplegic rediscovering the use of a forgotten limb. When his hands gripped the chipped rim of the small porcelain sink, he felt a spike of satisfaction at having made it.

He looked into a mirror, finding a clean spot on the tarnished silver-foil trapped between two sheets of glass.

The early dawn of another gray day in London struggled to break into the room through the rippled, hand-crafted panes in the window. Finally, Connor got the angle right, and enough rays of light reflected in the mirror for his eyes to gather them and build an image.

Turning his cheek to one side and then the other, the silver threads under his skin taunted him as they etched and faded when he moved. He leaned closer, stretching his cheeks in a ghoul-like expression. He peered hard into his rattled gaze, unnerved by the brittle jet-black glitter of anxiety in his pupils, and a cold sweat broke out on his clammy skin.

"Are they paler?" he muttered, feeling foolish at the thoughts escaping his mouth.

Mr. Banks, the guy with the hemorrhage inside his eyeball, the blood clot darkened his eye-color to navy, tinting the lens. Connor had also seen pigmentary glaucoma. *That disease made eyes appear lighter, but the onset would not be this fast.*

He stared at his irises, assessing their startling light-blue color, with striking cobalt rims, and wondered aloud, "Are they lighter?"

His black hair lay in a disheveled mess across his forehead, and his chin was dark with stubble that needed the urgent attention of a cut-throat razor if he was going to make it to Sir John Creedy's study by seven a.m. The longer he stared at his tight, blank features the more ridiculous he felt.

"For goodness' sake man, pull yourself together."

He sucked in a huff of frustration which made his ribcage ache, straightened, and yanked his nightshirt off over his head. A puzzled frown cut into his brow when he noticed a greasy brown stain smeared over his chest and shoulders.

Striking a match to light a candle, Connor held it aloft and rubbed at the space below his clavicle with a wet finger. A cleaner patch confirmed it was not a shadow. "What in God's name?" The hole in his memory rattled like bones in the closet. *What happened last night?*

A surge of panic felt like a cold wet flannel on the back of his neck. A grimace cramped his features when needles of pain shot up through the base of his skull, and sweat erupted on his brow as a vise gripped his temples. With an agonized groan, he dropped to his knees and vomited over the hard flagstones. When the retching spasms faded to dry heaving which burned his throat, he rocked forward and rested his hot brow on the cold stone floor.

The respite was short-lived as his muscles jerked violently, and he keeled over onto his side. He clutched his stomach, feeling like a fist of pain had reached in, twisted his guts, and was trying to rip them out. Connor's last conscious thought was, *'am I dying?'*.

His slack body lay where it had fallen until the hot-ash burn of pins and needles penetrated, and the black clouds parted. His face was stiff where his cheek had pressed into the hard cold flagstone. For a moment, opening his eyes and seeing the fallen extinguished candle embedded in a puddle of cold wax, his disorientation was complete.

The confusion dissipated when his nasal lining burned with the bile of his stomach contents, and his guts ached. *How long was I out?* He felt like a coach and horses had driven over his body. His stiff limbs ached when he fought to stand up. Avoiding the urge to look in the mirror, he walked with a labored stride through to the small bathing room and, finding relief in routine, he mindlessly kept moving.

He wound open the faucets to fill the bath, listening when the pipes clattered with more ferocity than he had ever heard before. Stripping his vomit-soiled clothes from his body, he stepped into the water, and recoiled at the biting pain of the scalding liquid. His nerve endings danced on that point where ice and fire felt the same and he looked for the steam which should be condensing on the mirror. *Nothing.*

With a scowl, he directed a blast of ice-cold water into the tub. *How can it be boiling? Great. The tank must be rusted up again. Must get Baxter on to it.* He ignored the worm of discomfort which suggested that maybe, it was his flesh that was *cold.*

Uneasy and disgruntled, but not understanding why, he tried again. Stepping into water that was merely hot now, he lowered himself down, reclined back onto the slope of metal. Billowing clouds of pink stained the water, before the eddying currents of his body movement swept them away. *What on earth?*

Puzzled, he rubbed his fingers over the stain on his collarbone and inspected them in the dim light. *Blood?* He sat up fast, the water sloshing over the side of the cast iron bath and soaking the floor.

A wave of disgust drove him under the water again, submerging him completely. Then he surged upward like a deep-sea diver rushing to the surface, sluicing both hands through his saturated hair. Grabbing the bar of carbolic soap, he frantically rubbed it over his neck and shoulders. He stood and continued the harsh treatment down over his abdomen, which felt tender beneath the rigid girdle of muscle. After he scoured every inch of his skin, he stepped out, snatched a white towel from the wooden rail, and repeated the brutal scrubbing, drying himself with the rough cotton fabric.

Without pausing, naked, he strode across the small room back to the basin and stood in front of the mirror. Driven by the distraction of perpetual movement – if he didn't stop, he didn't have to think – using a soft bristled brush, he lathered his jaw and neck with shaving soap. He frowned in fierce concentration while he focused on each grazing sweep of the cut-throat razor. Running the blade methodically up his neck, he leaned his head to one side and then the other. *Ouch.*

He pressed his fingertips to his jaw, inspecting a line of small bruises that formed a crescent shape on his neck. He leaned in closer, rubbing harder, and picked at the scabs he found. They came away easily, with no bleeding. *So, three days old?* Staring hard into the mirror failed to jog his memory. *Three days? Nothing to do with last night, then. And the blood?*

Connor shrugged, shaking off the confusion. He at least felt clean when he pushed his arms into a starched white shirt, buttoned the fly on his high waisted charcoal-gray trousers, and pulled the suspenders in to place. He donned a V-neck waistcoat, and threaded the chain of his pocket watch across his chest from one button hole to another, leaving it hanging in plain view over his breast pocket.

Running a tortoise shell comb through his hair smoothed the raven wing sweep back from his forehead, forming a sleek black skullcap which accented his chiseled features. Most of the nurses considered him handsome, with a streamlined nose, full lips, and high cheekbones that arrested their glances. But, the most compelling aspect of his attraction was that he was oblivious of the effect these attributes had on female hearts.

He filled his mind with the day's grueling timetable of lectures and surgical rounds, and ran from the puzzle pieces inside his head which were fusing into pictures he did not want to look at.

Snatching up his jacket, he pulled open the door and fled down the gloomy hallway. His footsteps rang out, bouncing from the walls, and a headache that he had not registered before, amplified the sound to an eardrum piercing volume. Pushing both arms into his jacket at once and jerking the thick flannel fabric up over his shoulders, he headed purposefully to his morning meeting with Sir John Creedy.

Chapter 2

Connor descended the steps which led down into the public area of the hospital, opened the door at the bottom, and stepped into the whitewashed corridor. He paused abruptly when a harsh cocktail of carbolic soap, uric acid, and antiseptic stung his sinuses, as if he had walked into a wall of stagnant water. Distaste curled his lip, and he glanced at the high-level vent in the wall opposite and cursed softly. He expected to face the odors of stale sweat on fevered brows and the soiled bedding of the incontinent on the wards, but not here in the students' quarters.

"The damn place is falling to pieces. The ventilation shafts from men's' surgical must be blocked."

Closing the door behind him, he hung onto the door handle to steady himself. His head jerked around – a sickly sweet aroma clung to his nasal passages and flooded his mouth with saliva. The familiar rustle of cotton under starched linen whispered through his head, but he waited a seemingly interminable time for the young nurse to finally appear.

As she approached, he focused on her delicate features. A frown flitted across his face when her softly gasped breath, ricocheting from the white walls, curled a knot of inexplicable excitement in his stomach. Most of her brown hair was demurely swept back and hidden under a starched cap, secured like a bonnet under her chin. Her throat was covered by an impeccably-starched white detachable collar, which formed part of her crisp white apron, and her back was ramrod straight, and yet, he could almost taste the air of agitation which surrounded her.

Connor battled with confusion as her footfalls were accompanied by a galloping beat, like a mallet tenderizing a bloody steak. When she drew closer, the wet pounding sound separated into four harmonized hammer strikes, and an accompanying shushing descant note. His gaze darted around the corridor. *What is that sound?*

"Are you feeling unwell, Doctor Sanderson?"

"Not at all. I am quite well, thank you, Nurse Ramsey." Connor forced a calm response, deliberately turning his head to look back along the corridor in the direction from which she had come. His heart galloped in his chest and vibrated through his ribcage with the thudding of a jungle drum beat.

"Well, if you are sure," she said. She seemed unwilling to tear her gaze from his stony expression. Her apron swished when she busied herself, brushing an imagined speck of dust from the fabric.

His jaw clenched as the symphony of the wet clattering sounds became faster, and a rouge flush stained her cheeks before she moved slowly away.

Connor remained rooted to the spot, swallowing the sudden taste of citrus which filled his mouth, and waiting for the palpitations to subside. *I must get checked out. Vomiting, and now, palpitations.*

When the corridor came back into focus again, it was empty. The clattering inside his head faded to the dull headache once more, and he felt cold. *And bone dry?* Not drenched in the clammy perspiration that should follow an adrenalin rush of emotion. So palpitations was no longer a likely explanation. *And I have never found Nurse Ramsey fetching, in any event.* Although, for the first time, it hit him that she harbored feelings for him. *How do I know that?* The air around her had hummed with a magnetic charge that tingled through his fibers. *But it was* my *heart, I felt. It had to be.*

Worry cast a shadow of intensity over his face. Raising a hand to the upright starched collar embracing his own throat, he pressed a cold thumb pad to his carotid artery and found a sluggish and disturbingly slow pulse. *Very slow, no wonder I passed out.*

He relived this morning's rude awakening, and Sir John's face, wearing an expression of glowering censure, filled his mind. *Being late is not an option.* Connor wondered how much time he had already wasted.

The ticking of his pocket watch invaded his consciousness. It most likely had *always* been there, but once he noticed, it became a strident plinking noise he couldn't tune out again. Connor palmed the watch, glanced at the pale ivory face, and felt the spring twanging inside it like the buzzing of a trapped hornet resting in his hand.

He hurriedly tucked the watch inside his pocket, and he could still feel it oscillating against his chest, even through the tightly woven fabric of his jacket. Connor dragged both hands down over his tight face and prayed that this was a nightmare. *Its fatigue, I guess. Or a brain tumor.*

Laughing bitterly at his own joke, standing still became the torture of unfamiliar sensations which he needed to escape, and so, he started walking along the corridor, fast.

His agitated footfall echoed off the white, porcelain-tiled walls and bounced around inside his skull. But, more disconcerting, the impact juddered up each leg, vibrating his tendons and tingling along muscle fibers that pumped like pistons and whisked him along at an exhilarating pace. But, still his heart rate slumbered.

Barreling forward, without pausing, he marched the half mile of the hospital's hallways and arrived outside Sir John's office. His mentor was a force of nature. After six months under his tutelage, Connor knew everything about the anatomy of the human eye. And, he also knew the one thing that would not be countenanced by Sir John. *Being late is a crime rarely forgiven.*

As always, Connor stopped outside the door and gathered his wits. He drew himself up to his impressive height, filled his lungs with a steadying breath, and held on to it. His routine was to pause for ten seconds or so, and, when his lungs ached as they hunted for more oxygen, release it in a slow forceful puff through tight lips... *and my nervousness along with it.*

The ten seconds ticked away to thirty. Still holding his breath, he slipped his angry waspish watch from his pocket and watched the minutes tick by. The rustling noise of Sir John shuffling papers on the other side of the thick oak door brushed over his eardrums and clawed at his concentration. Connor gently released the breath in a whistle of disbelief. *Seven minutes. Impossible.* There was no suggestion of lactic acid being burned inside his tissue. *Impossible.*

He rapped a distracted staccato on the door as his expression tightened to stony confusion.

"Come," said a baritone voice, thick with disapproval.

Connor folded his fingers around the brass doorknob, turned it silently and braced his muscles to push on the door. With the slightest bump of his shoulder, it flew open. The heavy oak did not offer its customary resistance, but moved effortlessly as though skimming over ice. He released the handle quickly as though it were hot coals when the polished-brass ball began to buckle in his hand. Perplexed, Connor entered the room, and the atmosphere rushed into his lungs, chest, and throat as though he had breathed in syrup.

A nauseating cocktail of odors settled in the pit of his stomach. The oak paneling tainted the air with a greasy, linseed aroma. The musk of furniture polish wafted from the desk; its decoratively tooled leather top smelled of tanning chemicals. The gas mantle lamp casting a yellow glow over the sheets of parchment-colored paper smelled of carbon, and Connor could taste the motes of dust which danced like fireflies in the eddying current of the moist atmosphere.

Even as he tried to make sense of the thickened air, he turned and carefully closed the door behind him, and stood still when Sir John appeared content to ignore his arrival. He thought about coughing, but taking in more of the toxin-flavored atmosphere did not seem like a good idea. He slowly took the nine strides needed to arrive in front of the aromatic desk, and gazed at his mentor's lowered head with its carefully combed gray hair. Connor's lip curled, and he ran his tongue over teeth that were on edge. *He smells of blood.*

"Sanderson, you are-" Sir John flinched as though startled by a pistol shot. "-late." He darted a glance towards the closed door before finding Connor's face once more.

Connor's apology died on his lips while he struggled to decipher the unfolding scene. He absorbed Sir John's open-mouthed, shocked expression, and as the static hum of the older man's alarm ionized the atmosphere, tingling through his nerve endings, he registered the truth. *He didn't see me move.*

Sir John's puzzled air persisted. A bouquet of iron and sugar swelled to fill the spaces left inside Connor's brain which were not yet cramped with his own fear, and this time, he realized the pounding, accelerated heart rate vibrating through his ribcage like a bass drum, was not his. *It is Sir John's.*

"Oh, I didn't see you standing there, Sanderson." Sir John's brows were undecided as his face fought to smother a shocked reaction and rediscover his usual quiet authority. Clearing his throat, Sir John injected disapproval in to his tone and started again. "What happened last night?"

I wish I knew. Connor stiffened. "In what regard, Sir John?"

"I charged you with tagging Mr. Donahue and arranging for his delivery to the teaching hall in readiness for my lecture first thing this morning. And, you were to choose a specimen of your own for dissection. It would appear that you managed to achieve neither one." Sir John rose to his feet, meeting Connor's carefully neutral regard with a spark of disappointment in his brown eyes. "My teaching hall is still empty. So, what happened?"

"My apologies-" Connor ran through his own recollection. Descending the stone stairwell down into the morgue was a clear image, now that Sir John's words had stirred the mire of his thoughts. "I'll go now, and remedy the situation."

Ten minutes later, Connor was re-enacting the lost hours of last night. He walked, with a determined stride, down the stone steps into the bowels of the hospital. An incantation seeped into his brain like a dim recollection of a childhood playground chant. "Mr. Donahue, and one for you." He remembered it now. It was all that had kept him awake. *I was literally dead on my feet, and longing to fall into my cot and sleep as soon as it was done.*

Connor arrived at the basement level and the dusting of quartz-fragments in the stone floor distracted him with a scattering of sparks. He hastily averted his gaze from the needle-sharp pinpricks of light which stabbed at his eyeballs, imprinting bright dots onto his retina. Staring straight ahead this time, he drove forward and shouldered open the rubber-sealed door to the morgue, recoiling when, instead of the sucker-like resistance he was accustomed to, it whipped back, cracked into the tiled wall, and a shower of annihilated porcelain hit the floor.

His palm rested on the cold tiles as he leaned around the door to inspect the crater of crumbling ceramic fragments, and he snatched it away as if an electric shock jerked through him. The cold tiles were warm. *I'm going crazy.* He expelled a deliberate breath, and, when there was no reassuring plume of warm vapor fogging the air and warming his cheek, the muscle in his jaw ticked as fear gripped the back of his neck.

His foot tapped out an agitated rhythm as his muscle fibers locked tight, and he resisted the urge that shrieked through his brain. *RUN AWAY.*

"Don't be ridiculous," he muttered.

Using his eyes as a scouting party, he scanned the room. Running slowly down one wall, his glance touched briefly on each cadaver chamber door, and finally took in the snowy landscapes of the white linen-draped corpses. His silent footfall followed the path as he steeled himself to walk slowly across the ceramic-tiled floor, avoiding the slippery trough of the terracotta gullies along which a copper-colored stain meandered, like the shed skin of a bizarre boa constrictor.

He flipped back the hem of the sheet on the eighth body in the row. "Bingo," he whispered as he read the toe tag. "Mr. Donahue." *So, I found him, then what?*

Connor's tight features blanched his cheekbones to chalk-white as he concentrated on chasing down the elusive memory. He idly plucked at the toe tag, the back of his fingers brushing Mr. Donahue's foot, and then he froze. He pressed his hand more firmly against the hard, cold flesh. *Not cold?* His harsh gasp hung in the air as Connor whipped his hand away and folded it into a fist. *No, I can't be colder!*

The snatched breath remained trapped inside his chest as panic slammed his vocal chords shut, and the lump in his aching throat swelled like cotton gauze dipped in water. He waited for his brainstem to recognize oxygen starvation, turn out the lights, and bring him the blissful release of a blackout. *But, no such luck.*

Ten minutes passed before he forced his eyes open and faced facts. *I'm not sure what the hell is going on, but, this is not a dream.* He inspected his milk-white palms, turning them over to focus on the blue-tinged rims of his nail beds. *Cyanosis, that can't be good. Anemia, maybe?* The straws of hope he grasped at were hard to wrestle from his grip. 'I don't need to breathe', was a realization he ran away from.

His gaze wandered past his outstretched hands to settle on the brown-colored residue sitting in the bottom of the curved terracotta gutter. A frown etched into his smooth white skin as he studied the network of channels in the floor, and focused on the darker, thicker puddle clustered around the square iron-grated drain.

Tracing its path back up the line, his eyes followed a trail that reached beyond Mr. Donahue. The irregular-shaped bulk of three other covered bodies loomed as outcrops of quarry chalk, obscuring his view.

The morgue attendant should have sluiced the gullies with buckets of water. So, why is that one branch of the conduit dirty? The fluid must be blood. The candy-sweet smell which clung to his nose and suddenly punched a hole into his mind told him that. The alarm bell humming through his cerebral cortex, strangely, filled his mouth with a wash of citrus-tainted emulsion again and unleashed hunger to gnaw through his stomach lining.

His insides knotted with fear, and he took a side-step that gave him a better view. His roving vision settled on an empty stainless-steel trolley where a soiled sheet lay like a tumbled avalanche of ice, punctuated by dark shadows of reddish-brown stains.

Dread-filled curiosity moved him slowly past the foot of each of the three corpses, until he arrived at the scene of what looked like a murder. *Of a dead person?*

Nervous laughter grated through his vocal chords as reaching out to twitch the rust-blotched sheet aside plumed the cloying smell of congealed blood into the air. A flood of saliva soaked his lips as he tried to breathe, and his pupils dilated to polished beads of jet framed by rims of steel-blue. His touch skimmed the tacky surface, collecting the brownish red paste on trembling fingertips that moved inexorably to brush across his lips, as though compelled by an invisible grip on his wrist.

Death of Connor Sanderson

When the smear of blood touched his tongue, an electric shock yanked every tendon in his body tight, snapping his head back. A guttural breath stirred gravel in the back of his throat as the taste coated his mouth. Connor fought for control as muscles spasms crushed his ribcage, clenching his sluggish heart in a relentless fist which emptied the chambers until it collapsed.

The acid bile of thirst rushed up from his stomach, and corded sinews in his neck tightened like vines around a tree trunk. As unbearable heat trailed over his skin, his spine arched into a taut bow, pulling him up on to his toes, and he hung there for an endless moment, like a macabre puppet with invisible wires twisting his limbs into a grotesque pose. The death rattle in his throat was the only sound that broke the silence.

The sip of blood which had fired the synapses in his brain, like a hit of cocaine, dissipated. His body suddenly snapped forward, his cold fingers, grappling for support, folded around the edge of the metal trolley and crushed ingots of steel into his palms.

His muscles relaxed and he gasped for breath, dry heaves racking his chest as he hung his head, and, as he squeezed his eyes tightly shut, a vision darted across his retina like a faded slideshow. He saw his own body lying there on the trolley with his vacant eyes staring up at the white ceiling, his muzzle and upper torso covered in blood. *The dried blood on my chest? No.*

A sudden breeze feathered over his cheek and a whisper stroked through his brain. "You are feeding too soon, your heart has not yet stopped."

His eyes snapped open, and a gray shadow snatched at his peripheral vision, jerking his head swiftly around. *Who said that?*

Finding nothing there, he twisted quickly in the other direction. *No one. I* am *going crazy.*

"You will see, I will show you."

Fear, riding a turbulent tide of frustrated anger, rushed up through his tensed thighs and gripped the girdle of his pelvis in a cramped embrace. It fizzed up along his spine like the flare of a lit fuse wire, and forced a bellow of pain from his throat. Rearing up and raising an arm, he accelerated one fist downward in the driving arc of a hammer blow and punched a hole in the metal trolley.

Shock stole every thought and movement as he stared at the torn metal; the fractured pieces folded back in an inverted parody of flower petals in bloom.

The clinician fought with the superstitious fool, and self-preservation found comfort in explanations he could believe in. *Hearing voices, the smells, hallucinations and violent behavior, even the incredible strength.* Delusion clung firmly to his shoulders, and his mind embraced the tunnel of vision that would save his reason. "Hebephrenia, of course. Voices, smells. Classic presentation. That's it." It was sanity of a kind, dressed in insanity, but it helped. "I'll find, Reggie," he muttered, "his uncle knows about this stuff."

He wheeled around and headed blindly towards the door, ignoring the rumble of laughter which filled the air, billowing like a rolling cloud of acidic poisonous gas that singed his nostrils. His long forceful strides were the blur of a comet trail, had the dead eyes of corpses been able to see them. Connor yanked the door open and another shower of dislodged porcelain fragments hit the floor in a thundering avalanche. Shouldering his way up the stone steps, he ricocheted from the walls as, despite his fear, he fought a magnetic compulsion to turn around and go back.

Chapter 3

As Connor emerged through the door, and back into the hospital corridor, he paused and tidied his appearance. Performing the actions by rote, his splayed fingers combed his hair back into place, he checked his black neck tie still fitted snugly beneath his starched collar tips, and adjusted his cuffs to ensure the correct margin – three eighths of an inch – of white shirt showed below his jacket sleeves.

For the first time, he did not run his palm over his pocket watch. He knew it was there, he could feel the vibration of the spring rocking inside its silver shell. He straightened his jacket, smoothing his palms over the soft fabric which now felt like wire wool to his sensitive fingertips.

He set off at a determined pace, although, his brisk walk soon dwindled to a frustratingly slow stroll as anything faster drew surprised looks from nurses and fellow medical students. It took him less than a second to register that the nursing staff were bustling as industriously as ever, with the crackling of their starched aprons a symphonic accompaniment to their movements. *It is me, that is faster.*

A frown settled on his pale features and he gathered the threads of the morning's experiences – *Was it only two hours?* – and tried to weave the events into a picture he could understand. Normality seemed the best place to start, so he headed for the lecture auditorium where he would find Reggie. *I hope he slept better than I did.* His lips crimped in an ironic smile. *Is there a subtle way to ask him about his Uncle Edgar's study on insanity, and this new-fangled electro-shock therapy?*

Connor was lost in the aromatic world of becoming a vampire. Suddenly fascinated that every nurse he passed along the corridors smelled differently. Not their perfume, they were not allowed that in any case, and certainly not their brand of soap, it was so much more. It was the pH balance of their skin, and the food they had eaten during their day, and finally, the amount of iron and vitamins in the bloodstream. All Connor knew was that some nurses made his mouth water, but he had no idea why.

He registered heavier male footfalls following on behind, and he recognized the smell of his adversary before he saw him. His hair pomade had an oily odor that Connor always found irritating, but now, it thickened the air around its wearer like the dense pea-soup smog which was the scourge of London. *Apple pulp and lard are a truly nauseating combination.* Connor preferred a sparing application of beeswax ointment.

"Well, if it isn't, Sanderson. The blue-eyed boy."

Stopping in his tracks, Connor turned on his heel to look into the mud brown eyes of Rufus Clare.

The sarcastic tone marred the young man's face with a spiteful sneer. "You've been licking Sir John's boots again, Sanderson, if your sour expression is anything to go by." His slick hair glistened like polished, beaten copper, and his face was devastatingly attractive.

Connor's frosted regard was hard with barely veiled disgust, but he savored the wash of confidence rolling like an electric storm through his mind. It short circuited his confusion and fear for a moment, and he embraced the prospect of sparring with an opponent of whom he had the measure.

Rufus' blonde companion, Lester Cartwright, instinctively hung back a step. Connor absorbed *his* aroma also, as a sheen of nervous perspiration broke out on the young man's skin. *Wise man, perceptive it seems.*

Throwing up his hands in a parody of startled surrender, Connor said, "Clare, I didn't see you there, been hiding in any linen closets, lately?" He grinned, enjoying his new-found sensitivity for a moment, when his senses were assaulted with delicious odors. Rufus' salty, dopamine-soaked sweat as he started and rocked back on his heels was enticing, as was the hot rushing tide shunting up his carotid artery as a ruddy flush stained his tight cheeks dull red.

Connor stared Rufus down, watching his barb hit home and angry annoyance clench his opponent's fists. The faint purple line of a broken nose cut across the perfection of the mask as Rufus hung onto the remnants of a malicious smile.

Taking a step closer, Connor looked down at the six-foot tall Rufus, who suddenly seemed much shorter recoiling under the weight of Connor's glare. "Do you want me to break your nose again? I'm sure Mary would thank me."

Connor's words spawned a subconscious gesture as Rufus' index finger dragged down the side of his healing nose and swept along the fading bruise on his cheekbone. The malicious smile became fixed and brittle as he said, "I'm sure she would. Was she suitably thankful last time? Spread her thighs for you, did she? Was she-?"

Scorn stiffened Connor's smile. He closed a fist around Rufus' shirt front, effectively strangling his words. He froze as his cold knuckles dug into the young man's throat, and his own chest echoed with the cadence of the pumping current of blood massaging his clenched hand.

An unsettling feeling of panic rattled at the cell door inside Connor's head at yet another sign that every sensation in his body was alien to him. He heard the capillaries creaking in Rufus' neck as if they threatened to burst. Before the young man registered it too, Connor eased back to human pressure. *I don't want others to question what I have become.* He absorbed the shiver rolling through Rufus' body as the chill of his iron grip bit into his victim's skin like freezer burn.

His gaze darkened to steel-gray flint in a face sculpted in ice, and Rufus' arrogant expression splintered, a flash of alarm stirring in the depths of the narrowed brown eyes.

Connor's own vision clouded as he played out the crystal-clear recollection of a night, three weeks before. It was the last time he had laid a hand on Rufus Clare.

It was the night when Connor checked on a patient on ward B, and, determining that the young man's delirium was pain induced, he decided a dose of laudanum was in order. He cast a glance around, looking for the attending nurse. The squeak of rubber-soled shoes scudding over waxed linoleum drew his attention.

The matron was pushing the medication cart along the foot of the beds at the far end of the ward. She had her nose firmly buried in the notes on her clipboard, and he paused, taking in the dark blue crescents framing her eye sockets which dressed her face in a state of exhaustion. Even the crisply starched fabric of her navy-blue uniform could not disguise the slump of her shoulders.

Recognizing a fellow sufferer of that dog-tired feeling, Connor took pity on her. *She must be going off duty soon. There will be a night nurse along in a minute.* His searching gaze took in the empty nurses' station, a glazed partitioned area which housed a utilitarian wooden desk with a lamp sitting upon it. The glowing gas mantle cast a yellow glow upwards over the ceiling with more enthusiasm than down onto the shadowy surface of cream-colored blotting paper and an abandoned ink pen.

Following logic, Connor walked slowly from the ward and searched the empty corridor. *Maybe the night shift has yet to arrive.* He tugged on the chain and glanced at his pocket watch. *It looks as though I have no choice.* Reluctant to add to her burden because he admired Matron Hartnell, he turned slowly, rehearsing an apologetic tone inside his head.

The sudden swell of a muffled groan stopped him in his tracks as he cocked his head and listened, rotating on his heel to face the direction from which it came. Silence had descended once more, but he knew he had heard it.

Someone is hurt. Without hesitation, he was moving with a stealthy long stride, straining his ears for the groan that he knew would follow. He was not disappointed. A dull thud accompanied by a panicked whimper fractured the stillness, and Connor rushed forward faster now. He broke into a short sprint and skidded to an untidy halt outside the door to the linen storage.

Cold nervous sweat dampened his brow as he gripped the brass door handle. He yanked the door open, and for a moment the tangle of limbs wrestling on the floor froze every muscle in his body.

It took a second for his brain to catch up with his eyes as the musk of male sweat filled his nose. The back of the man's neck flushed dark red, and the grating groan rasping through his anger-tightened lips scraped over Connor's eardrums.

The young nurse pinned beneath his bulk was terrified. The stillness of her body filled Connor's mouth with bile; he recognized it as immobilizing fear. Her glazed eyes stared at the ceiling, and a helpless keening noise escaped between the fingers of the large hand clamped over her white face.

The man's body rocked with jerking urgency while he scrabbled on his knees, fumbling with the buttons of his pants. His fingers dug into the girl's thigh as he shoved it roughly aside and the sound of cotton fabric tearing cut through the air.

The renting sound galvanized Connor into action and he roared as every sinew tightened in rage. Surging forward, he grabbed the man by the scruff of his neck and the seat of his loosened pants. Adrenaline fed Connor's anger as he yanked the man up into the air, lifting and pulling him back sharply.

The man's features reddened and a yelp of protesting rage exploded from him. He staggered awkwardly, his heels scrabbling for purchase on the slick waxed floor and his hand flailing for the steadying support of a wall. He bellowed in surprise when Connor spun him around and glared into his face.

Connor registered Rufus Clare's lust smothered expression in the fraction of a second before his fist landed a blow dead center of the tense features, and Rufus' nose collapsed with a satisfying crunch.

"You sick bastard." The words burst from Connor as he yanked Rufus sideways and rammed him up against the wall. Closing his grip to frame Rufus' jaw and lift his chin, Connor pushed his own face in close as he spat, "You slimy, little toad."

Satisfaction spiked inside Connor, as he buried a vicious uppercut into Rufus' abdomen, driving the air from his lungs in an anguished grunt. He stepped back and watched his victim double over clutching his stomach as, coughing and gasping, he dropped to his knees. Connor's cold glance took in the gaping button fly of his pants and the wet stain on the fabric. Disgust curled his lip, acid-bile scouring a fiery trail up into his throat as he growled quietly, "Get out of here, Clare. Before I kill you!"

Ignoring the staggering footsteps as Rufus launched his crouched body from the wall and ran, Connor stepped past the swinging door of the linen closet and paused on the threshold. His shadow sliced across the nurse's shocked features, and, turning her face away, she snatched in a petrifying breath. The silence inside the confined space was chilling.

The fight with Rufus had happened so quickly that now, suddenly faced with being gentle, Connor felt as though his limbs were made of lead, and his concern forced him into moving only in slow motion.

He carefully pulled a linen sheet from a nearby shelf and wrapped it around the young nurse's trembling shoulders to cover her torn bodice. He eased her skirts down over her thighs, trying not to notice the red welts decorated with oozing beaded droplets of blood. *Rufus' nails must have dug in.*

"Mary. It's okay. It's Doctor Sanderson," he said gently as he lifted her and folded her slight frame into his chest.

Her stiff body, locked tight with shock, was cold. Her hip grated over his muscled torso and, as her elbow dug into his ribcage with every forceful stride he took, he welcomed the jabbing pain as a distraction that prevented him tracking Rufus down and beating him to a pulp.

Anger burned a hole in his chest as he took off down the hallway to the infirmary. He collected the matron in charge of the pastoral care of the younger, more vulnerable student nurses, along the way.

That had been three weeks ago, and the cap on the well of Connor's anger was threatening to blow like an oil geyser as he stared into Rufus' face once more.

Connor's knuckles were healed, but glaring at Rufus, the memory still swilled revulsion in his stomach. Connor happily focused again on the ruptured purple vein which ran across the bridge of his nose, following the fracture line perfectly. "Not so pretty now."

Rufus Clare bared his teeth in a smile, and almost lost his life.

Connor froze as he battled with the surging desire to rip Rufus' head off and taste his blood. A storm of electrical impulses scattered through Connor's cerebral cortex, clenching his gut with a gnawing hunger that he instinctively knew was not for food.

"Just say when and where, Sanderson. I'd be ready for you this time." Rufus chin jutted in aggression, but his sweat stank of fear.

Glancing at Lester, Rufus' perennial side-kick, Connor asked, "You'd want to be this maggot's second? Defend this scum?" His gaze darted back to bore contempt into Rufus' brain. "My guess is, Marquis of Queensberry rules are not really your style. You're more of an ambush kind of guy." Connor smiled as the pulse in Rufus' throat stroking over his knuckles pounded harder. "If you think you can take me, Rufus, feel free to try. But I promise you, things will never be the same again. For either of us."

Connor watched closely, primed on a hair-trigger of control, waiting for Rufus to decide their fate.

Rufus shrunk in Connor's grasp, lowered his eyes, and admitted defeat.

With a fixed smile, Connor slowly released his grip. He tidied Rufus's collar and brushed imaginary dust off his cowering shoulders with a measured stroke of ivory clad fingers. Connor took a deep steadying breath, and embraced a feeling of relief as the sharp blade of hunger dulled to an ache which he could wrestle with, and win.

"I don't think you will be here much longer, Sanderson." Rufus swallowed hard as his words grated through compressed vocal chords. "The hospital board of governors have convened, and your days are numbered. I don't have to fight you to finish you."

"The board? And, how is *Uncle* Cecil?" Connor's tone dripped with sarcasm.

Rufus patted his breast pocket. "I have a letter to deliver to Sir John. You are out of favor, Sanderson."

Connor waited for the weight of frustration to press down on him. Losing his hard-earned ground with Sir John should matter. But he found, at this moment, with the ethereal laughter which had seemingly oozed from the walls inside the morgue still ringing in his ears, he did not care. *I have more pressing concerns.*

He smiled sweetly as he said, "Sir John is not a fool. Do your worst, Clare."

Connor turned on his heel and whisked away along the corridor, resuming his journey to the lecture hall. His preternatural acceleration chilled the sudden sweat of fear which blossomed on the handsome faces of Lester and Rufus as they stared into a blank space. The hair on their napes prickled as though someone walked over their graves.

Before Connor turned the corner and set his sights on the signage directing him to his mentor's teaching wing, he had already dismissed the pair, his mind racing on ahead.

Chapter 4

Connor passed through the double doors at the end of the featureless, antiseptic-odor tainted, white tiled corridor, and into the warm embrace of wood paneled walls and thickly carpeted floors. Gas flames in the wall-brackets were set to low, supplementing the daylight which struggled through the small panes in the leaded-light windows. They dissipated the gloom in the tastefully decorated hallway.

Hanging portraits of eminent physicians punctuated the row of large, brass-framed mirrors which made the most of every shaft of light slicing through the air. Connor became momentarily distracted by motes of dust dancing like a snowfall of fire-flies in the bright funnel ahead as the sun rejoiced in a moment of triumph.

Putting his palm to his watch, Connor considered checking the hour, but, as though an electromagnet inside his head had been activated, his hand fell away as he instinctively knew exactly where he was on the continuum of time.

I am late.

After the morning he'd had, finding Reggie and entering the lecture hall without attracting Sir John's disapproval would be the easy part.

He strode carelessly forward until the sun's rays glinted across his hair, picking out filaments of cobalt blue in the raven black sweep, casting a penetrating blaze over his concentrated expression and burning his flesh. He gasped and shielded his face as a tingling sensation crawled beneath his skin. *It burns like acid. What on earth?* Connor blocked the sunlight with a bent arm and a twisted shoulder, and moved quickly into the shade.

He froze in the awkwardly folded posture of a Machiavellian villain, imagining a blistering epidermis as fiery heat sizzled over his cheekbone and his lips tightened in a grimace of pain.

He had to know. Carefully tilting sideways, his reflection slid into view in the mirror on the wall opposite. A network of angry, red capillaries glistened like a patch of red lace draped over his cheek. He leaned closer and rubbed a curious fingertip over the mark. *Not sore, just hard.* Using his thumb, he compressed the tissue over his cheekbones in a masochistic massage and the red cotton-like threads felt like wire buried beneath his skin.

It's barely a first-degree burn, so why did it feel like Dante's inferno? And sunburn in three seconds? For a moment, his brain hit a brick wall as he shuffled through myths and legends, and did not like the one that was trying to tear the wool from his eyes.

His stubborn nature came to his rescue. *I shall rule out the probable, and only then will I entertain the impossible.* Deep down, he preferred the prospect of madness to being a monster.

He continued on, his left shoulder scuffing the wall as he gave the puddles of light spilling over onto the carpet a wide berth. Still twenty yards away from the double doors which opened into the amphitheater, the colorful tone of Sir John delivering a lecture played across his eardrums; each word rang crisp and clear. Connor acknowledged another truth. *Hypersensitive hearing.*

Like a Christian preparing to enter the Coliseum, he laid his cold palm on the warm wood of the door and inhaled deeply, dragging the air over his palette and tasting his surroundings. He battled with the cacophony of the human flavors of eighty-plus students seated just the other side of those doors. A clawed grip closed over his skull, and the veins pulsing at his temples throbbed inside his eyeballs, tinting his vision with a blood-red filter. *What now?*

Agitated. That was the only word to describe how he felt.

He remembered to ease the door of the lecture hall open with painful care and, imitating his usual fluid gait, he descended three steps, crossed the aisle, and slipped quietly into a vacant space on a wooden bench. *If I treat every object as though it is made of spun glass, I should be safe.*

He closed his eyes, and breathing in a calming meditative rhythm eased the knots in his stomach. When he opened them again, the redness clouding his vision had faded. He watched the myriad of human gestures playing out before him as an orchestration of distraction, and he felt serene.

An insidious infusion of tranquility weighted his sluggish bloodstream with lead, making his arms feel heavy. His movements met the resistance of wading through water as he reached up to rub his hand over his strong jaw.

Anxiety melted away and he was in control as he unwittingly discovered the semi-conscious state of vampire sleep. Just as horses in the wild sleep standing up, ready to flee from predators, vampires had their own instinctive survival technique, sleeping only one part of their brain at a time.

The trance-like state clung for a moment longer and then a laser sharp jolt of awareness jerked through him, waking up the temporal area of his brain... and he felt refreshed.

Skulking in the back row of the amphitheater was not usual for Connor, but he had some serious thinking to do.

Down below, Sir John stood in the pit of the teaching arena. The concentric circles of seating rose higher, the further away from the epicenter of learning a student chose to sit. Although, Sir John appeared smaller to those hiding at the back, the thirty degree gradient gave each student a clear view over the heads of his fellows.

Final year students chose the front row seats, close to the action. Today, Connor's seat was empty, and Sir John's keen eye landed there with pointed frequency. He usually addressed most of his remarks to those he considered talented, and Connor was the epitome of that: dedicated, talented, and destined to be an innovator.

Mr. Donahue was lying on a trolley in the repose of a sleeping sun worshiper, although the blue tinge to his skin gave a lie to that perception. For Connor, the congealed blood congested in the man's arteries was the biggest give away. He could detect the stagnant consistency from a distance of thirty feet. His attention wandered to the room full of warmly percolating students.

Interesting how each one smells different.

The smell of the English oak paneling on the walls created a mellow fragrant marinade for all the other scents assaulting Connor's nasal lining. He started with the students seated closest and worked his way along each row of the eighty or so young, floppy-haired, young men.

The scribbling of their pencil leads were akin to a herd of cats scratching at the bark of a tree. *Some pencil leads are harder than others, so some of the cats have sharper claws than others.* Connor smiled at the absurdity of his own analogy.

His eyes rested on the back of each head as he tuned into the vibration of the heart cantering inside each chest, collating the information. His learning focus today was to make sense of this hypersensitivity. *Will it pass? Like a viral infection?*

Connor already knew the answer to that, but in case he needed confirmation, his hackles rose and burning embers crawled under his skin as though he were again bathed in sunshine. He glanced across the amphitheater, and into a pair of dead, fish scale-reflective eyes, the color of mother of pearl.

The figure leaned forward until the face was undressed of its shadow, and a handful of bony digits waved slowly in a gesture of acknowledgement.

Connor expected fear. He did not expect relief. The prospect of answers was a heady infusion which brought a smile to his lips. *Ah, Malachi.* Confusion creased his brow. *Where did that name come from?*

The pale skin glowed with an eerily waxy sheen as Malachi grinned and nodded slowly, and Connor knew. *He put it there, inside my head.* Connor lifted his chin and met the probing regard head on. Pain pounded in his temples, and then darted around the back of his skull as the slide show of his own body lying in the morgue, smeared in blood, marched across his retina.

As the images melted away, Connor eased his tight shoulders. "Okay," he whispered, "Midnight."

"First sign of madness, you know?" said Reginald as he slipped onto the wooden bench seat next to Connor.

"What?" said Connor, losing his focus on Malachi for merely a second, but when his keen gaze combed the shadows again, as Connor knew he would be, he was gone.

"Talking to yourself... it's the first sign of madness."

"I thought you were in the front row?" Connor looked at his best friend, Reginald Cranham, with new eyes, tilting his head as the vein in Reggie's forehead throbbed with a mesmerizing rhythm. Connor inhaled deeply, and the scent of red-berries fermenting in sugar wafted into his brain and played havoc with his concentration.

"Thank you, gentlemen. That will be all for today, and if you have any questions, I'll be in my office for the next hour." Sir John's clipped words ricocheted off the walls in the domed space as he gathered his notes.

A smattering of applause accompanied his departure, followed by a moment of breathless silence.

The spell was broken by a sudden surge of movement punctuated by the clattering of tens of dozens of notebooks and pencils being hastily gathered, and soles of shoes hurriedly scraping over the wooden decking of the amphitheater platforms.

Connor got to his feet and glued his intent gaze on a spot between Reggie's shoulder blades as he followed him out through the doorway and back out into the corridor.

As the jostling students, impatient to escape, wove their scurrying bodies between the two friends, Connor whistled gently and stepped out of the tide. Setting his shoulder against the wall, he waited while Reggie swam against the flow and finally stood beside him.

Idly watching the frowning, earnest young men moving purposefully past, Connor felt Reginald's speculative gaze boring into him, and he took a casual step backwards, seeking out the shadows that clustered in the corners.

"Well, *I* was down the front, Cornelius Sanderson," teased Reginald. "And where, pray, were you hiding? Sir John's disapproval was burning a hole into your empty seat."

Even though Connor's features wore a mask of shadow, his derisive snort made Reginald grin in response.

"May I call you Cornelius?"

"Not if you expect me to answer," said Connor darkly.

Reggie laughed gently as their ritual unfolded. "I consider myself reprimanded, Connor it is."

Connor heard the muffled thud which signified that Sir John had left the teaching wing by the rear door, probably seething with disappointment, and he switched gear.

"How is your Uncle Edgar?" Connor asked nonchalantly, his avid gaze still tracking the enthralling flow of human bodies as they trickled along the hallway and disappeared around the corner.

"He's well." A raised eyebrow accompanied Reggie's answer.

"And his psychiatric research?"

"His theories on electro-shock therapy will be published in the Lancet in January." Reggie's chest puffed out with pride. "His trip to America was worth every hour of seasickness, so he said." Reggie chuckled lightly. "Sadly, he saw little of the dining room during his six days onboard the Lusitania. Its domed engraved ceiling was not conducive to his sea legs at all. He could not tell which way was up, I believe, were his exact words."

"I hear the White Star Line is launching sister ocean liners that will dwarf Cunard's fleet. Perhaps he will find the Olympic, or Titanic, kinder to his constitution," Connor said, distractedly.

"And I hear they will sail from Southampton. Much more civilized than trekking hundreds of miles north to Liverpool."

"Just so." Connor smiled tightly. "Is he attending the family's dinner tonight? I'd like to pick his brains on his findings."

Connor no longer believed he was insane. But Malachi's presence hinted at a far worse explanation, and maybe a lobotomy, or the blissful oblivion derived from electrodes set upon his head, would still be something he would welcome. *I'd just as well be prepared.*

"He is, yes."

"And Lavinia?" said Connor, laying a smoke screen that he knew would distract Reggie.

Reginald smiled widely this time. "If I didn't know you better, Connor, I'd suspect you had designs on my sister. Unfortunately, I do... and unrequited love is a painful place, so, be kind to her, hmmm?"

"It's an adolescent crush, nothing more. She'll be horribly embarrassed a few years down the line."

Reggie's face was serious. "Lavinia is no longer an adolescent." He shook his head ruefully. "I don't blame you, Connor, you barely notice she exists. You are much too busy making your mark as Sir John's houseman to consider courting. Needless to say, that matters little to a young woman and her tender heart."

For a moment, the thought of a tender heart enchanted him and set his taste buds tingling.

Swallowing resolutely, he said, "I'm sure you exaggerate, Reggie."

These past five years, he always thought of Lavinia as a child, but doing the calculation, he now realized that the fourteen year old girl was now a woman, and he had certainly overlooked that fact. The chasm of an almost six year difference in their ages seemed suddenly to have shrunk.

Reggie landed his hand on Connor's shoulder blade in a resounding slap. "You're probably right. There are many better catches than you out there."

Connor remembered to stagger obligingly under a blow that twelve hours ago would have sent him reeling, and grinned. "There are a dozen or so at dinner tonight? And eligible men to dance attendance on her, I'm sure she won't even notice me."

Reggie grunted dubiously and said, "What time shall I have the carriage waiting?"

"We'll set off at six, if that suits?"

Reggie glanced at his watch. "I'd better get moving, then. And you had better go and make your apologies to Sir John."

"I think I may be better waiting until tomorrow." Connor eased away from the wall and matched his pace to Reggie's with painful care. He sighed heavily as the electrical storm of activity in Reggie's preoccupied brain and the sudden acceleration of his heart rate filled Connor's mouth with saliva and dragged aching thirst through him.

The meeting with Malachi at midnight loomed as a far more pressing concern than Sir John's annoyance.

Chapter 5

Night had fallen, and Connor sat in the darkest corner of the interior of Reggie's Clarence carriage, waiting outside the hospital for his friend to make an appearance.

The carriage had room for four passengers, and he would surrender his forward facing place to Reggie when he arrived. The rear facing seats would put the glazed panels of the carriage and its mounted brass coach lamps at his back. Connor calculated that, sitting in that position, once they were moving, and until they headed out onto the country lanes, only Reggie would be bathed in the glare of the passing street lamps. His own features would be cast in shadow.

Every line of Connor's body spoke of relaxation, and if the footman, William, wondered at Doctor Sanderson's unusually silent demeanor, he made no comment.

"Why not take a seat, William?" Connor suggested as the young footman standing out on the sidewalk shifted his weight uncomfortably from one foot to the other. "I'm certain Lord Cranham will not object."

Smiling widely, William touched a hand to the peak of his cap and nodded before climbing nimbly up onto the pillion seat in front, and settling himself beside Harker, the coachman.

The young man was easy to please. After all, it was a fine autumn evening, even if the air was a trifle crisp, and waiting in attendance, ready to open the carriage door, was the easy part for William. Soon he would be running alongside the horses warning Harker of potholes in the road.

They had been waiting for the best part of half an hour, and Connor's usual wit melted away to serious contemplation. He had deception on his mind. Dining at Reggie's family seat of Cranham Hall, which was outside of London, nestled in the Kent countryside, was usually a pleasure. However, acting naturally at a dinner party of sixteen, many of whom knew him well, was suddenly a field littered with landmines.

Faking a spasm of coughing, Connor lay the foundations of his plan, paving the way for his unexpectedly early departure from tonight's family gathering.

William's concerned face appeared in the upper section of the window as the young man hung precariously from his seat.

With his face contorting convincingly, Connor breathed through tightened vocal chords, "I'm fine, William. Just a little stuffy in here."

William disappeared, and Connor smiled. *Step one.*

His fingertips played over the smooth leather that now felt like splintered glass, and he was enthralled by the cacophony of sound which accompanied a couple walking along the side street, still some two hundred yards away, and yet he felt their presence as though they had laid a hand on his shoulder.

He could almost taste the pheromone cloud that wafted on the breeze. He heard the whisper of skin brushing over skin as their hands clung together, and the shortness of breath that starved their hearts of oxygen and caused them to thunder inside their chests. He stared out of the window at the spot at which he knew they would appear, and catching a mere glimpse of their rapt expressions as they moved past the carriage confirmed what he already knew. *They are in love.*

As the percussive beat of their footsteps faded from his acute hearing, he curiously pressed his fingertips to his own wrist and was not surprised to find that rather than racing, his own pulse was impossibly sluggish. *About 15 beats a minute.*

He had a grasp on a handful of puzzle pieces but, as yet, apart from the certainty that he was forever changed, he had no clue how many more surprises his rioting senses had in store. He felt as though he was hanging on by his fingernails, until he met with the compelling and terrifying Malachi. Connor heaved a sigh, and knew instinctively that it would not matter if he did not take in another breath, ever. *I will be there in the morgue at midnight.*

As Connor rested back against the olive-green leather seat, and willed Reginald to put in an appearance, a motorcar rumbled its way along the street, metal and rubber grinding together as the bumps in the road threw the car chassis into disarray. The carriage lurched violently as the two chestnut geldings shuffled nervously sideways, their hooves clattering on the stones in the pitted surface.

Harker whistled a familiar calming descant as he murmured, "Whoa, boys, it's just one of them newfangled motorized vehicles."

Inside the carriage, Connor grinned. Harker was convinced that the horse and carriage was the only mode of transport befitting a gentleman. With the highways of London becoming a melting pot of trolley omnibuses, bicycles, and, the fastest growing trend, the motorcar, Connor was fairly sure that Harker was doomed to disappointment.

Putting step two of his plan into action, Connor twisted the brass T-bar handle, swung the half-glazed carriage door open and stepped out. "William, when Master Cranham arrives, beg him to wait in the carriage. I am taking a stroll around the block, I need some air."

William frowned as he peered down from his high perch on the carriage pillion seat. "Are you sure you are feeling alright, sir?"

Connor stared off into the mid-distance, the brim of his hat casting his carefully composed features in deliberate shadow. "It would be bad manners to cry off from dinner, now, William. I am sure I will feel much improved after a walk to blow away the cobwebs."

Tapping the rim of his hat with his gloved finger, Connor set off at a purposeful pace until he turned the corner and disappeared from view. A few yards further along the sidewalk, he stopped and sank back into shadow, leaning against the wall and embodying the eerie stillness of an indolent statue.

He listened to the jingling of the horses' bridles, and the snorting of breath from their velvet nostrils as they whinnied softly. He picked out the swishing sound of Harker running well-worn leather reins through his suede clad palms, and listened for Reggie's footsteps to ring out through the night air.

He did not have to wait long, before the ten feet tall wooden front doors to the hospital swung open and released a waft of antiseptic which sharpened his senses like a dose of smelling salts. As they bounced closed again with a satisfying thump, Reggie descended the flight of stone stairs, coming to rest at the bottom.

"Good evening, Master Reginald. Master Sanderson begged you wait in the carriage. He has taken a turn around the block." With the lowered whisper of a servant who enjoys gossip more than fearing its impropriety, William added, "Just between you and me, sir, I think the master is feeling a bit under the weather."

As Reggie drew in a concerned breath, Connor appeared beside him, startling William into a flush of ruddy embarrassment.

Darting a look of pretended indignation at the young footman, Connor opened the carriage door and ushered Reggie inside, saying lightly, "About time, Reginald. I was about to give up on you."

Connor bore Reggie's scrutiny, tilting his chin and allowing the moonlight to bleach his features.

"You do look very pale, are you sure you are feeling up to dining with the family?"

Settling a ramrod straight back squarely against the leather seat, Connor squeezed the handle of his walking cane until the metal creaked in his cold palm. "I could not disappoint your parents. I'm certain it will pass."

"If you're sure," said Reggie as he smartly tapped his own cane twice on the glass partition.

Harker clucked his tongue, the horses jerked into movement, and they headed out of the city.

The carriage careened steadily along the country lanes, and, under Harker's sure guidance, the horses remained poised at a fast trot which could not be allowed to erupt into a canter without overturning them into a roadside ditch. The miles were covered quickly. The companionable silence inside the carriage was broken only by the hypnotic rhythm of horses' hooves pounding on the carpet of damp autumn leaves covering the road.

Out of the corner of his eye, Connor caught the flash of charcoal-gray high in the night sky; where the graceful sweeping wings of an owl rode the evening thermal currents. Its orange eyes were beacons in the dark to Connor, who instinctively followed the line of sight, heard the rabbit rustling in the undergrowth and tuned into the fast beating heart inside the fragile chest. He frowned as the sound filled his mouth with a citrus-sharp flood of saliva and he anticipated the inevitable.

The owl dropped from the sky like a feather-clad stone, and as the rabbit died in the grip of needle sharp talons, the smell of blood hit Connor like a tidal wave of insatiable thirst.

He swallowed carefully as hunger dragged a blade through his stomach, and the pulse in Reggie's neck became a pumping tide of thick nectar. He could almost hear the blood cells jostling as they raced each other through the arteries.

Every sinew in his body tightened at the electric current zinging along his nerve endings, and his teeth were on edge when the memory of biting into flesh flashed into his head. *No, not a memory. A craving.* A desire that took his mind into dark places saturated with the copper-tainted taste of blood. Holding his muscles locked tight and clenching his fists, Connor battled for control, knowing that if he lost it he would plunge into a living hell.

The carriage lurched abruptly, and Reggie cursed as his shoulder collided heavily with the tooled-leather paneling at his side. "Steady on, Harker," hollered Reggie as pain shot down to his fingers.

Connor pretended that his own rock-steady body was struggling for balance, and, like a dropped pebble disturbing a tranquil pool, his macabre fascination was broken.

"Sorry, sir, hole in the road," yelled Harker above the jangling of the bridles and the beating of hooves.

As the carriage left the road, the vibration as the wheels crunched over the gravel driveway traveled up Connor's spine and sang like a tuning fork note inside his ears. He gratefully grabbed at the distraction with both hands, filing away the sensations, akin to a coma victim rediscovering the world for the first time.

"Five minutes, sir," yelled Harker as he steadied the horses and the rolling gait of the carriage became a gentle sway.

Twisting around in his seat and searching for his first glimpse of the house, Connor wondered if he was still capable of feeling the joy that usually went with it.

Death of Connor Sanderson

The dark silhouette of the dwelling loomed large, punctuated by a cheerful patchwork of amber squares where lamplight spilled out through the hand-blown glass window panes. Billowing clouds hung over the angular rooftop, staining the navy sky with a shroud of charcoal gray, and bright specks of ash danced above the many chimney stacks like swarming fireflies.

Connor speculated on how many of the fifty-one coal fires inside the Hall had been lit to warm the guests. He was about to make a joke of it when he clamped his jaw shut with a snap, knowing instinctively that Reggie could not see the dazzling display. *Yet another inhuman preternatural change.*

Reggie heard the clatter of Connor's clenched teeth and darted a glance across the carriage.

"Are you sure you're feeling up to this, Connor? Harker can take you back."

It was tempting, but then, he had no idea when he would cross paths with Reggie's Uncle Edgar, again. "I'm feeling much better, I assure you. So, your father has invited 'beaus' he hopes will meet with Lady Lavinia's approval," said Connor, changing tack swiftly, with a skeptical smile.

Easily redirected, Reggie frowned as he said soberly, "Oh, he is aware she has a mind of her own, but marriage is expected and her dowry is considerable. She is lucky father puts such stock in her happiness. Though, he fears her heart is already bruised."

It was the second time today, Reggie had made reference to Lavinia being smitten, and Connor did not like it. "Perhaps, if the opportunity presents, I should make it clear to Lavinia that I think of her only as a sister?"

"Oh, she knows that, Connor. But, hope is hard to suppress." The moonlight sliced through the trees and illuminated Reggie's grimace. "Is it such a crime to wish for the ideal world?" His warm regard sought Connor's face. "To wish my best friend and my sister were a match?"

"No, Reggie. But the ideal world is thousands of miles away." Connor's voice swelled to fill every space in the carriage with regret. *More than thousands.*

The carriage swung in a graceful arc, following the curving horseshoe path of the driveway, and drew up outside the Hall, beneath an impressive pillared portico. It was an Edwardian enhancement to the cream-colored facade. After all, it would never do for the ladies' finery to suffer in a downpour of rain.

Lavinia stood framed in the door way, the skirt of her long emerald dress shimmering like the breeze over soft grass in the meadow as it flowed over her curves.

Reginald tutted loudly. "I see Lavinia has forgotten her manners. Mama will not be best pleased, and Mr. Phelps will be muttering under his breath, I am sure."

Connor smiled. "Opening the front door to family is hardly a crime, although, I concede, Mr. Phelps may not agree. And you forget, *Lord* Reginald. You are hardly conventional. Lords do not usually work. I am surprised His Lordship did not have a heart attack when you insisted on becoming a doctor."

"Father has Jonathan as his heir to the estate." Reggie met Connor's amused regard. "You could join me in doing nothing, after all, you are family in father's eyes."

"Touché, Reggie. But, I could not abide sitting in a drawing room drinking tea all day."

The carriage rocked as William jumped down onto the ground and pulled open the door.

Connor waited for Reggie to alight first, and, as he stepped out to stand beside him, he dipped his icy-cold hands into his pockets and closed his fingers around two pieces of warm coal, each wrapped in white linen handkerchiefs. He took a moment to smooth his elegant black dinner jacket and tug on the tails of his ivory brocade waistcoat before gracefully ascending the wide stone steps and entering the house.

"Reggie. Connor. So wonderful that you could come." Lavinia's enthusiasm was brittle and awkward, and both men played along, smiling down at her. She linked her arms through theirs and self-consciously drew them across the thick gold and cream-colored carpet of the spacious entrance hall. "Mama and Papa are in the drawing room."

As they headed through the doorway, Reggie shot an apologetic smile at Mr. Phelps, the butler, which helped smooth his ruffled feathers.

"I have announced your arrival, Your Lordship," said Mr. Phelps stiffly, making the point that he was still performing those duties Lavinia had not interfered with.

Connor entered the drawing room and smoothly extricated himself from Lavinia's hold, shooting a fleeting glance down into her face. Her hopes were etched across her features, and Connor decided it was kinder to be cruel. Gazing out across the busy room, he said dismissively, "I hear you have young men vying for your attentions this evening. I shall release you to dazzle them, my dear."

As he turned away, feeling like a callous heel, Connor could not miss the rush of blood which stained her cheeks with embarrassment, and the delicate aroma of her sudden perspiration. Pinning a careless smile on his face, he took a deep breath, presented his broad back, and left her standing in the doorway.

The large salon was tastefully decorated with deep, leather-covered couches arranged in intimate pairings. The dozen standing lamps scattered throughout the room cast pools of light over the polished wood of the occasional tables, and picked out the golden threads in the richly patterned carpet.

However, Connor barely noticed as his senses were assaulted by the cocktail of human emotions which drenched the space. He could pinpoint the placement of every person in the room even had he closed his eyes. *And, three of those assembled here are incredibly nervous.*

Curiously scanning the room, he sought them out.

Lady Tilly Cranham, Reggie's seventeen-year-old sister sat with a fixed smile on a face which still had the plump contours of childhood. It was her first dinner party with single men in attendance, so Connor understood why her mouth was dry and her fingers plucked nervously at her skirts.

Reggie's eldest sister, Lady Victoria Fountain, was alone this evening. Connor had heard about the crisis at Birkbeck Bank, and her husband, Larry Fountain, was up to his neck in securing a way out. The delicate pucker carved between her brows showed that she was worried. *That too, I understand.*

Connor honed in on his final victim, and the unexpected air of irritated anxiety which clung to the smartly attired Captain Matthew Rice. Connor flicked a glance over his upright figure, resplendent in a scarlet uniform with his empty sword scabbard at his belt. As the captain's fingers played over the scabbard as though, in his head at least, he prepared to face an opponent in battle, Connor wondered why.

The puzzle can wait. Good manners, first.

Drifting smoothly across the room, Connor sought out Reginald's mama, Lady Isobel Cranham. He took the hand she offered and brushed his lips over the back of her lace glove.

"Lady Isobel," Connor said, "you look magnificent this evening."

"Cornelius Sanderson." Lady Isobel frowned fleetingly, her mature beauty still eye catching as her hazel eyes danced with indulgent amusement. "It has been too long. You know you are always welcome."

Connor nodded and said on a smile, "Of course, My Ladyship, and my mother would be grateful that you did not allow the truculence of a seventeen-year-old boy to drive you away."

Chapter 6

Lord and Lady Cranham, George and Isobel, were like an aunt and uncle to Connor, whose own family came from more humble middle-class beginnings. When his mother, Clarissa, a distant cousin of Lady Isobel, died of consumption, his father, Victor, unable to cope, had chosen to spend all his time at his gentlemen's club, immersing himself in the wining and dining of peers and clients, and hiding behind his duties as a lawyer in the City of London.

Within weeks of Clarissa's death, Victor Sanderson, dependent on port and whiskey, descended into a drunken stupor by the end of most evenings. Being in no fit state to travel the dozen or so miles home to the Sanderson country estate, he would sleep at the club, leaving the seventeen-year-old Cornelius to fend for himself.

Anger at the loss of his mother boiled inside the young Connor until he could no longer stand it. He had taken to hiding out in the attic, avoiding the constant assault of the well-meant kindness of strangers, and the servants. The encrusted grime on the leaded panes in the window blocked out most of the natural light. The dank gloom suited his mood, and when his candle guttered and died before he could light another, Connor swore softly.

He spat on the white lawn handkerchief he always carried in his pocket, and scrubbed at the dirt in determined sweeping strokes until a funnel of sunlight forced a path across the black, aged floorboards. It was then that the glint of gold caught his eye. Stepping forward, he closed in on a box with metal-capped corners which protected its floral design from damage. He remembered it instantly. It had stood on the bureau in his mother's sewing room for years.

"When did it disappear?" He could not remember.

The hinges creaked as he prized them open, and as he expected, it held bundles of letters tied together with frayed red ribbon, from the days when his parents were courting. He weighed them in his palm, thinking, this was all that remained of his mother's heart and soul. As he reverently laid them back inside, unread, he discovered a loose envelope with the address written in a different hand.

A weight nestling in one corner piqued his interest and, turning the envelope in careful expectation, he caught his breath when a heavy gold signet ring fell into his palm.

"The Cranham crest." Connor knew the coat of arms well. His governess had taught him the importance of English aristocracy, making sure he knew the correct term of address, and how to carry himself in their company.

"Why would mother have this?"

Connor turned the ring over in his palm; his thoughts tumbled at the same time as his fingers toyed with the edges or the letter which had fallen into his lap.

Integrity lost out to curiosity, and he unfolded the notepaper and read it. The note was from a distant cousin who begged Clarissa to get in touch. They shared a great-great-grandfather, and Lady Isobel Cranham had just learned the Sandersons were living relatives.

I beg you, Clarissa, if ever you have need of us, present this crest at Cranham Hall, and your welcome will be warm, your cousin, Isobel.

Connor would never know why the letter went unanswered, but what he did know was that he could use the facts to his advantage. He was tired of marking time, and waiting for his father to surface from the depths of a grief he refused to share.

His father had abandoned the pretense that he could bear to be in the house without Clarissa, and had rented a townhouse in London, promising Connor that he would send for him when he was more settled. Connor, who was the image of his mother, sharing her dramatic coloring of raven black hair with sapphire-tinted highlights, striking ocean blue eyes, and pale skin, knew his father was avoiding looking at his face.

He had no reason to stay at the Sanderson family home. He, too, wanted to escape. The groundsmen and gamekeepers were more than able to run the estate, and his father's butler received his orders via telegram. *I am still a callow youth in their eyes.*

One night, lying in bed staring at the ruby-red, curtain swags framing his four-poster, claustrophobia pressed down upon his chest. Turning his head, he stared at the heavy gold ring which had sat upon his bedside chest since he had found it, and as it winked in the flickering candle light, he decided. *I will go.*

He packed his belongings in his father's largest leather trunk, and handed his governess, who he considered had no more to teach him, a forged note from his father. Drawing his tall seventeen-year-old frame to its impressive six feet height, and squaring shoulders which were broader than they had been six months ago, Connor exuded mature determination.

"At her invitation, I am spending the summer with my mother's cousin, Lady Isobel Cranham. Father bids you visit your family and return in the autumn, on full pay, of course." *Staying close to the truth when fabricating a lie is always the best way to go.*

Miss Smythe, the governess, no doubt seeing her own chance of escape, nodded sagely. But the glint in her keen eye filled Connor with momentary panic.

But then she folded her hands demurely at her waist and said quietly, "Enjoy your summer, Master Cornelius."

Unspoken words of final farewell hung in the air as Connor stood for longer than was necessary before bursting into movement. Picking up the heavy case, he left the house and climbed into a hackney carriage.

He made the journey to Cranham Hall, and may have been brave enough to knock on the door, but as he took in the impressive edifice in all its splendor, the dozen chimneys reaching proudly into the ice blue sky and the ornately carved buttresses standing as sentinels on each corner, he felt he would be leaving one prison behind only to enter another.

Instead, he followed his gut instinct. Watching his mother's death, as consumption had filled her lungs with fluid, ignited an appetite to understand the weakness of the human body beyond the reach of the governess' schoolroom.

For Connor, the human brain held the same degree of fascination. So, when he reached London, hoping to learn more about his father's increasingly fragile mental state, Connor landed himself a position as a porter inside the East Kent Lunatic Asylum, using his height and bulk as a smoke screen and lying about his age.

He could not become a medical student until he was twenty-one, but that did not prevent him studying alone in his rented rooms by the light of a guttering candle.

Connor would have gone undetected, except that he dared to challenge a young intern whom he knew had misdiagnosed a patient. The man was suffering mental delusions, that much was true, but he was also displaying the signs of consumption. *I will not stay silent, and allow the man to die.*

Major John Hall-Edwards from Birmingham had delivered his lecture on how to use an x-ray machine, something Harker, the coachman, would doubtless have called newfangled, but reading the results was not so easy. Connor noticed the deformed club-like fingers on the hands of the patient, and his head was screaming lung disease.

Like a terrier, he nipped at the heels of the young intern until he had listened, and taken the x-ray slides to his consulting physician. Connor was proven correct, and that was the start of a deep-seated resentment as he recognized Connor as a threat.

Foreboding gathered in the corners of Connor's mind as the weeks of summer drew to a close. Deep inside, he was still a child waiting to be caught out breaking the rules.

He carried Isobel Cranham's ring in his pocket, rubbing his fingers over it as a talisman, expecting his father to walk through the door at every turn and order him back to the schoolroom.

Working, getting one's hands dirty, was not the done thing.

The middle classes hung determinedly onto the coat-tails of aspiration. The Sandersons had climbed to a rung on the ladder where running their country estate fed the family and a modest number of household staff. *Father would be livid if he knew my situation.*

His pretense was shattered one evening when he returned to the porters' station to make a mug of tea, and to wait for one of the bells mounted in a row along the wall to clang and summon a porter to wheel a patient back to his bed on a ward.

He walked into the small bare room, and six sets of eyes turned to graze over him and scuttle away again.

Connor frowned as he said, "What's happened?"

The words had barely left his mouth when a policeman entered the room. Quietly closing the door, he turned in Connor's direction.

"I take it that you are-" Flicking a glance down at the notepad he expertly flipped open, he looked back at Connor and said, "Mister Cornelius Packham."

Connor's youthful complexion flushed as he said firmly, "Yes."

The policemen's narrow-eyed stare settled on the mutinous chin, taking in the gritty determination embedded in Connor's flint-gray gaze as he mused, "Now, where would a young, working class lad get an eighteen carat gold signet ring? Bearing the Earl of Cranham's seal, no less?"

Sweat broke out on Connor's brow. He drove his hand into his pocket, and finding it empty, suddenly, borrowing the surname of his father's under-footman at the estate yawned as a chasm of ill judgement.

Constable Cavendish's tone dripped sarcastic triumph as he said, "It wouldn't be this you'd be looking for, hmm?"

Cavendish held out a hand containing the ring. His lip curled as he looked Connor up and down, seemingly irritated by the young man's well-groomed appearance, despite the frayed cuffs and badly sewn-on buttons.

Connor instinctively made a grab for the ring, and Constable Cavendish slammed his fist shut.

A grim smile failed to light up his eyes as he said, "Cornelius Packham, you are under arrest. You do not have to say anything, but it may harm your defense if you do not mention, when questioned, something which you later rely on in court. Anything you do say may be given in evidence."

The police officer grabbed a handful of the coarse serge fabric of Connor's cheap uniform, yanked him around, and twisted his arm back. He snapped a metal cuff on one wrist in a deft practiced maneuver.

"You've got this wrong," Connor ground the words through gritted teeth. "I can explain. My name is Sanderson... the ring belonged to my mother."

"You'll explain down at the police station."

The other cuff clicked in to place.

Connor's anger simmered inside his tight frame as the copper jabbed him in the back, and he lurched his way out of the hospital loading bay doors.

Surreal crossed the boundary into stark reality, when Connor saw the black Mariah parked in the street outside. The policeman behind the steering wheel leapt out when the hospital door burst open. Stepping smartly around to the rear, he twisted a handle and revealed the dark cavernous space in the back of the wagon. Connor's blood boiled as Cavendish's hard grip spanned the top of his head, ducked him forward, and shoved him headfirst into the holding area of a cage of wire mesh walls, lined with wooden bench seats.

It was difficult to hang on to dignity with his hands cuffed behind his back. The metal links rattled as he lost his balance, smashing into the wall with one shoulder, before sliding down until he hit the seat with a bruising crash.

Connor's eyes watered at the smell of urine stinging his nasal lining, his ears reverberating as the metallic thump of the door plunged him into darkness.

He braced his feet on the slatted wooden floor, distaste stirring in his stomach as the soles of his boots slipped over the greasy surface. Connor bellowed loudly, and the echo of his anger was drowned out by the gunning of the engine as the car lurched into motion.

"Shut up, laddie. You'll get your chance," a muffled voice shouted and a fist banged on the partition beside him.

"Damn it," he muttered. Picturing his father's apoplectic face when he discovered his son had been arrested, Connor decided the anger of strangers would be easier to handle. Calmness descended as he surrendered control. He thought of his mother's gentile features and knew that this Lady Isobel, even if she shunned him, would not see him rotting in jail.

A half hour later, sitting in the stuffy police cell, listening to the descant of voices, ranging from angry through to drunk, seeping through the cracks in the crazed plaster of the walls, Connor hoped he was right.

"But will she even remember her cousin, Clarissa?" The letter had been in that box in the attic for a long time, after all. Sitting on a narrow bunk, Connor rested his head back on the pillow of his folded jacket, rolled up his shirt sleeves, and settled in for a long wait.

Cavendish had taken his watch, but the shadows creeping across the floor, and the chill settling into his bones marked the passing of hours, rather than minutes. Finally, his chin fell onto his chest, his eyes closed, and sleep brought down the shutters on his exhausted brain.

The shake on his shoulder rattled his teeth, and as his head jerked up, a boot scraping down his shin laid a trail of fire which shot him to his feet. His fists clenched and ready to punch out, he focused on the midnight-blue uniformed figure grinning at him and took a deep breath.

"Go on, laddie," said the smug officer, lifting his chin to catch the dim light. "You know you want to."

Staring the copper in the eye, Connor studiously unrolled his sleeves, buttoned his cuffs, and beat the creases out of his jacket. "Do I take it I am free to go?" he said brazenly, even though he could not hope it would be that simple.

The constable laughed harshly and said, "Not so fast. You're wanted in the interview room."

Laying a rough hand on Connor's shoulder, he pushed him towards the door and escorted him down the bare corridor. Connor knew the officer was looking for a fight, a reason to charge him, and he delighted in the small victory.

Shaking off the restraining hand, Connor walked over the threshold into a room where a solid wooden table dominated. Seated beyond it were a gentleman and a lady Connor knew instinctively to be Lord and Lady Cranham.

Constable Cavendish stood resting against the wall with a sour expression on his face. The Cranham's gold ring sat on the table top, still inside a plastic bag until Lady Cranham picked it up and turned it out into her palm. Looking Connor in the eye, she said quietly, "I believe this belongs to you? Cornelius Packham?" She smiled, and Connor's heart felt lighter than it had in many years as a semblance of his mother's expressions flitted across her features. "Or would that be Sanderson?"

"Forgive me, Your Lordship, but surely you need more proof than that?" Cavendish could not contain his irritation.

Cranham shot him a crushing glance. "I thank you, Cavendish, for bringing the situation to our attention. We will deal with it. There is no question of theft, and there is an end to it. Now, if you can leave us."

Seconds later, as the door closed and they were left alone, Connor said, "I apologize, Your Lordship, Your Ladyship."

"Why did you not come to us?" A small frown settled over Lady Isobel's features. "We would have helped you. Sponsored you. The chief consultant at the hospital tells us you saved a man's life." Indicating Connor's porter's garb, she added, "You are better than this. Clarissa would be turning in her grave... you must let us help you."

"I thank you for clearing my name, but no."

As Lord Cranham barked his disapproval, Connor stared him down.

"You are very generous, but this is enough. I shall not be a porter forever. But I shall do it my own way."

Approaching the table, Connor softened his words with an apologetic smile, and accepted the ring Lady Isobel offered. "If I may keep this, that really is all I need right now. If you'll excuse me?"

As Connor left the room, pulling the door closed behind him, regret settled in his gut. He did not feel good about snubbing Her Ladyship, and her muffled words of entreaty drifting through the air brought him no relief.

"But George, surely there is something we can do?"

"He is a fine young man. Clarissa would be proud. Don't worry, my dear, I shall keep an eye on his progress, and when, as I am sure that he will, he applies for an internship, he shall have my sponsorship."

Connor walked away down the corridor, shaking his head, but the glow inside him was undeniable. He had felt an instant connection to the Cranhams. *Maybe getting to know them would not be so bad.*

True to his word, His Lordship kept his distance, and if Connor suspected his hand in transferring out the incompetent intern who had taken the ring from his pocket and hoped to see Connor go to jail, there was certainly never any proof of it.

One day, just before Connor's twenty-second birthday, George Cranham arrived at the sanatorium bearing the bad news that Victor Sanderson had drowned in a ditch of dirty water when he had wandered from the road on his way home. The axle broke on his carriage, and Victor, having an appointment with a client, rashly set off on foot, leaving the coachman to wave down the next carriage that came along the road, and ask for help. Connor's father had been drunk. Lord Cranham did not refer to it, but Connor knew.

It took Lady Isobel another six months to persuade Connor to let the Cranhams help him, but finally, he enrolled at the Royal Eye Hospital at St George's circus, along with his distant cousin, Reggie, and the two became firm friends. *Has it really been seven years since a stolen ring decided my fate?*

Chapter 7

Inevitably, Connor being merely middle class was like a red rag to a bull to the likes of Rufus Clare. He was less happy to have the dynamic, driven young Connor join the team... and threaten his place. And now Connor had beaten Rufus to a pulp, things were set to get a lot worse.

In a world where connections and sponsorship were crucial, Rufus' uncle Cedric holding the position of chairman on the hospital's board of Governors had a lot to do with their mentor, Sir John Creedy's tolerance of Rufus' mediocrity. *Lord Clare has a lot of clout. Are my days under Sir John's tutelage numbered?* Of course, Connor admitted, being dead, or undead, or whatever the hell he was, was going to cramp his style.

Connor had wondered if Lord Cedric Clare would be at Cranham Hall this evening, and he was relieved that was not the case, and he would not have to suffer the older man's scrutiny.

"Not just a truculent *seventeen*-year-old, you were somewhat pig-headed and stubborn right up to your twenty second year... as I recall," Lady Isobel rejoined lightly to Connor's quip.

When he did not respond, Lady Isobel suddenly frowned and Connor knew instinctively he had been standing too still. He quickly plunged his hands through the raven sweep of his hair, as was his habit, and transferred his weight from one foot to another. *I must be careful of that.* Standing unblinking and not breathing were becoming a natural state, discomfort and cramping muscles was a thing of the past.

The dinner gong sounded with a mellow note, and the drawing room erupted into concerted movement. Lady Isobel rose gracefully to her feet, and whispered, "Lady Victoria is alone this evening, with Larry working away. I'm sure your company will cheer her up."

Connor was relieved to be partnering Reggie's eldest sister at dinner. At twenty-five years of age, and married to Sir Larry Fountain, she was an earnest young woman and had always been easy to talk to.

As Lady Isobel left him, and before he sought out Victoria to offer his arm, Connor scanned the assembled company until he found Uncle Edgar. Inclining his head, Connor smiled and raised a hand in greeting. Disguising his urgency, he smoothly closed the distance, arriving at Edgar's side as the ladies, scattered around the room like a meadow of flowers in full bloom, stood and shook out their colorful skirts.

Connor carefully shook hands with the gray-haired, stout figure.

"Good evening, young man. I hear you are interested in hearing about my trip to America."

"I am, indeed, sir. I understand that electro-shock therapy is proving very effective in managing hallucinations and delusions?"

"Ah, yes. The advances are remarkable." Edgar's enthusiasm for his subject lifted his clouded gray eyes to clear blue as they twinkled in the lamplight.

Connor stared into the florid jovial features, clenching his fists tightly as excitement made Sir Edgar's heart beat faster. And, as his mouth watered, Connor suddenly wondered what adrenalin tasted like.

Glancing briefly at his wife, Lady Stella, and collecting her mew of disapproval, Edgar smiled regretfully as she said with gentle reproach, "Now, Edgar..."

Connor smothered his own smile as the enthusiasm of Edgar's sharp scientific mind transformed to the meek indulgence of a man still smitten by his wife of thirty years.

Tidying his mustache with a thoughtful hand, he said, "Why don't you come by my offices tomorrow, Cornelius? I'm sure the ladies would find our conversation very tiresome. Let's say, midday, tomorrow?"

Remembering the burning sensation of the errant beams of sunlight on his skin, Connor arranged an expression of regret on his face. "Sadly, it is a busy day for me. I wonder, would five o'clock be too late?"

Sir Edgar nodded obligingly as he tucked Lady Stella's hand into the crook of his arm. "Of course," he said as they drifted towards the dining room.

Following suit, Connor found Victoria, bowed, and lifting a mocking brow, he said, "May I escort you to dinner? I think Lady Isobel is hoping you will keep my manners in check."

Victoria laughed. They both knew that he ran the risk of being the most proper young man in the room.

The low murmur of conversation accompanied the procession through to the dining room as Connor concentrated on his timing. Walking slowly presented an interesting challenge. A flash of red serge caught his eye, he noticed that Lavinia had chosen to favor Captain Rice this evening, and aversion swilled an oil-slick of distaste in his gut. *I don't trust the man.*

During dinner, Connor's keen sight tormented him. He watched as Lavinia laughed delicately at Rice's amusing quips, and, taking a deep breath, he drowned in the delicate scent of perspiration as her cheeks flushed at his compliments. He felt like a Peeping Tom. Even their lowered tones were clear as a bell to him as he discovered he could tune into the pitch of each human voice at will.

Connor frowned. Lavinia's heightened pheromones were easy to understand, but, Captain Rice sweating and his jittering nerves were a mystery. *He is scared? Well anxious at least. Why?*

After dinner, the ladies departed in a gliding procession of silk draped swans, drifting by to enter the salon. Connor chivalrously bent over Lady Victoria's hand and touched it to his lips. "It was a pleasure, My Lady. It has been an age since I have had such an enchanting dinner companion."

Victoria laughed. "You are very kind, cousin."

Her levity melted when Lavinia passed by. With a heavy sigh, her restless fingers rustling the fabric of her skirts, Victoria said, "Captain Rice is very..."

"Pompous?" supplied Connor, smiling tightly.

Meeting Connor's direct gaze, she held her tongue. 'He's not you', was the thought clearly written in her wistful glance before she moved away.

It was the first time that he realized awareness of Lavinia's crush had rippled throughout the Cranham family. *No, he is not me. And I do not trust the skunk.*

As he followed Reggie into the library, joining the other men for cigars and cognac, his thoughts turned to his plan of escape. His meeting with the mysterious Malachi loomed as a specter, floating in and out of Connor's consciousness. But, seeing Captain Rice's guarded look sweeping the room, intrigue held him still. *The man is up to something.*

He did not have long to wait. Captain Rice clicked his heels, bowed smartly to Lord Cranham and left the library. *He's visiting the restroom...* or so the discreetly murmured apology to His Lordship had revealed.

Connor doubted that very much, as the heady aroma of adrenalin oozed enticingly from Rice's pores. His heartbeat thundered beneath the gold buttons on his chest, despite the calm, half-smile on his handsome face.

Cocking his head, Connor listened to the receding sound of the captain's footfalls as the gleaming boots brushed rapidly over the thick wool-pile carpet that ran the length of the hallways of the house.

My, he is in a hurry.

"If you'll excuse me one moment, Reggie, I seem to have mislaid my handkerchief." Connor smiled absently as he placed his brandy bowl on an occasional table, rose to his feet, and left the room.

Tracking Captain Rice through the rambling corridors of the house, Connor battled the urge to close the distance too quickly. *It is good practice, moving in deathly silence.*

The dopamine-rich trail thickened to a mouth-watering aromatic cloud, and Connor knew Captain Rice had stopped walking. He darted a glance around the corner, and fifteen yards away his quarry was tapping his foot, impatiently waiting for someone to arrive.

Six inches from the toe of Rice's gleaming boots the rich burgundy shade of the carpet stopped, marking the end of the upstairs territory. On the other side of the line was a thinner oatmeal-colored carpet. The grubby stripe along its length marked the path of the constant coming and going of the upstairs servants.

The ones that wore starched uniforms, served the Cranham family, and were all but invisible.

Connor heard the shallow breathless sighs at the same time as he registered the swish of cotton fabric brushing against her thighs. *So, he is meeting a maid.*

He slipped smoothly across the hall and stepped inside the morning room. Closing the door all but a half an inch, he watched as the slight girl came into view. A grimy cap covered her hair, and sweat stained the collar of her pale-gray dress to charcoal.

Ivy, the tweeny! Connor was not a snob, Lord knows he had had his tough times, but he considered a ladies' maid to be far more Rice's style. The tweeny was not good enough to be seen above stairs. The thin girl's red raw hands, with coal dust ingrained in the cracks in her fingertips, told the tale. She was up at four a.m. cleaning out the grates of each one of the fifty-one coal fires required to heat the three floors of Cranham Hall. Emptying the chamber pots and stripping the beds when the family were safely downstairs was about as glamorous as her life got.

Connor bunched his hands into fists. He instinctively knew he was not going to like what happened next.

The tweeny maid was still a yard away when Captain Rice reached out a hand, grabbed her arm and yanked her sharply forward.

"Ow, Mattie, that 'urts," she hissed.

The captain shoved his jutting chin down into her upturned face, his stubble grating across her cheek as she shrank away. "Don't call me that. And how do I know it's mine... that Doctor Sanderson is always sniffing around below stairs."

"'E's a gent," Ivy breathed raggedly through the pain as Rice's fingers dug in harder.

"So, you say." His other hand caught hold of her starched cotton skirts and jerked them up viciously. He shoved her back, his knee pushing between her thighs as her shoulder blades collided painfully with the wooden rail that ran the length of the wall. "But, I bet he's sampled the goods, so don't tell me the brat is mine."

Connor clenched his jaws shut and reined in his anger.

"I swear. It's yours, Matti..." Her face drained of color and she flinched when Rice spoke again.

His fingers framed her jaw and he squeezed. "You listen to me. I have my sights set on better things than some scrawny, filthy servant. You'll drink a bottle of gin and keep your mouth shut if you know what's good for you."

"But, I'll be put out in the gutter. You said you loved me."

Her eyes flashed defiantly, and, sensing the tension sweeping through Captain Rice as his blood flushed his face plum with anger, Connor took action.

Taking a lump of still warm coal from his pocket, he unwrapped it and bowled it accurately along the hallway, bouncing it from the wall where it left a black smudge, before it clattered down the strip of carpet and landed at Ivy's feet.

She gasped, and the captain stepped back as though he had been burned.

"Willie's coming with the coal scuttle."

Shooting a glance up the empty passageway, Captain Rice hissed, "Just remember what I said. Keep your mouth shut." Turning briskly on his heel, he swept away, and as his footsteps faded, Ivy buried her face in her hands.

Connor wanted to comfort her but she must not know he was there. He wiped his hands clean on the lawn handkerchief, and stuffed it back into his pocket as he retraced his path to the library and slipped silently back inside the room. His step faltered when he realized the ladies had joined the party.

The captain was already there, standing at the hearth, warming his hands at the burning coals poor Ivy had most likely struggled to pile high in the fire grate. The smile on Rice's face was fixed, and spite glistened in his eyes as he stared across the room at Lavinia.

So, thought Connor, this would be his better thing?

Connor scanned Lavinia's gently radiant features as she laughed aloud at Reggie's joke, and his gut ached. The wide scoop of the neckline of her green silk dress accentuated the graceful line of her shoulders. The feminine sweep of silken black strands of hair piled on top of her head drew Connor's eye to the entrancing arc of her throat, and he was certain the pulse beating there stuttered as Lavinia glanced over at him.

Her eyes were darkest-brown with flecks of smelted copper dancing in their depths. And her skin, dressed with an ethereal glow to Connor's new vampire-acute vision, was dusted in pearl-tinted glitter.

Captain Rice abruptly obscured his view when he appeared beside Lavinia and offered his arm.

Connor's mind turned urgently to escape as his muscles tingled with anger, and suddenly the darker-red shade of blood, spilling over the scarlet fabric of Rice's uniform became an enticing prospect. He swallowed the wash of citrus tainted saliva, and tamped down the desire to feel hot blood pumping into his mouth. His cold, firm skin hardened to a harsh mask and without words, he caught Reggie's eye.

The laughter on his friend's face melted as he excused himself from his father's conversation and quickly crossed the room.

"You look like hell, Connor. Do you want the carriage brought around?"

"No, it's fine. I'll borrow Sabre, if I may. I can leave him at the farriers."

"Certainly."

Connor laid a gentle grip on Reggie's hand as he reached for the bell to summon Mr. Phelps, the butler.

"I know the way." He cast his eye around the room. "I'd rather just slip out, if you can offer my apologies to your mama?"

Leaving the library, and closing the door silently, Connor headed towards the servants' quarters. Crossing from the burgundy carpet to the oatmeal, he glided down the stairs and out of the entrance which led to the stables.

He pushed open the wooden slatted door. Collecting Sabre's bridle from its hook, he edged forward to lay a calming hand on the horse's nervously twitching glossy coat. In a lowered tone, he whispered to the stallion. The flared equine nostrils, blowing anxious gusts of air which plumed with condensation, told Connor the horse *knew* he had changed. His sure deft strokes over the gelding's solid shoulder calmed the nervous shuffling of hooves, and stroking his hand over the brushed velvet of Sabre's muzzle had the hypnotic pull of a rattlesnake.

"There you go, boy," Connor said as the horse's lips snatched at his coat sleeve. "I'm still your old friend, hmm?"

As he eased a cold breath of relief and gathered the reins in his hands, he heard voices in the garden. Beyond the scope of human ears, a couple were talking as they strolled some two hundred yards away along the path through the rose garden. Connor immediately recognized Lavinia's scent, and that of Captain Rice. In the next moment, he abandoned Sabre, leaving the horse in his stall, and jogged quietly around the perimeter of the Hall until he had them in his sights.

His body sank into stillness as Connor tuned into the words of the engrossed couple.

"Lady Lavinia," said Rice, "may I say, you are a very beautiful woman."

Lavinia was young enough for the compliment to make her blush.

Connor's eyes narrowed as her suddenly pounding heart rattled through his own chest, and the pain of hunger pierced him to the core.

Captain Rice stopped walking, and, catching hold of Lavinia's wrist, he smoothly turned her back towards him. "You must know, My Lady, that I am attracted to you."

Lavinia tilted her chin and looked up into his earnest face. "Captain Rice-" she began.

"Matthew, please. And before you speak let me just say, I don't expect your love, not yet. But if you will let me, I would like the chance to earn it."

Connor had heard enough. Ivy's tear stained face came to mind and he burst into movement. The gravel of the pathway crunched loudly as he left the wet dew-soaked grass, and closed the distance towards the couple who were both now looking in his direction.

Connor absorbed the expressions on their faces with satisfaction. Captain Matthew Rice's features tightened with anger. And Lavinia looked radiantly happy to see him. It was enough. He had left everything too late. He had nothing he could offer Lavinia, now, but he could save her from this snake.

Being dead sucks, he thought, because even before he finally got the chance to meet this Malachi, Connor had come to that conclusion. *Somehow, I am dead.*

"Connor." Lavinia dimmed her smile, realizing that her heart was on her sleeve. "Reggie said you had already left?"

His gray eyes warmed. Finding out she loved him was a bittersweet moment of revelation as he inhaled the heady aroma of her skin, where the flush of attraction laid a fragrant scent.

Not taking his eyes from her face, Connor said, "How could I leave without saying goodbye? And in any case-" His focus snapped around to enjoy the annoyance twitching the tendon in Captain Rice's tight jaw. "I wanted a brief word with the Captain."

Connor smoothly captured Lavinia's hand in his and dropped a kiss into her palm, enjoying the sound of her breath catching in her throat. "If you'll excuse us for a moment?"

He turned to face Rice, cutting off his escape and driving him back a pace. Rice had the sense to look nervous, and Connor's eyes were drawn to the pulse thudding in the captain's neck as his immaculately shaved chin tilted in defiance.

His expression hard, Connor dropped his voice and said conversationally, "You know, Rice, it is very bad form to make advances when you have another young lady... waiting for you."

"I have no idea what you mean," Rice said, darkly.

"Oh, I think you do. Lady Lavinia may well be the better thing that you have your eye on."

Rice's eyes flashed when he heard his own words quoted back at him. "Maybe, it is you who has been slumming it. It is more your style, going back to your lower class roots." Rice sneered as he imagined the barb had hit home. "I know your game."

Connor chuckled. "Trust me, you have no idea what you are dealing with."

"Lavinia is above your station that much I *do* know."

"Lady Lavinia, to you." A growl rattled in Connor's throat and in a blur of preternatural movement his hand closed on Matthew Rice's neck. The shocked white complexion of the captain's face rapidly turned purple as his wind pipe creaked beneath Connor's fingertips.

Connor was fascinated as he felt the blood capillaries bursting and bruises stained the Captain's neck. The heavy scent of blood coated his nasal lining, and Connor swallowed his hunger. Leaning forward, he could almost taste Rice's fear.

"If you come anywhere near *Lady* Lavinia again, I will hunt you down and kill you." Connor dug his thumbnail into the flesh of Rice's throat and froze. A plump pearl of blood swelled before, touching the white starched collar of his uniform, it blossomed into a ruby red stain. Mesmerized, Connor licked his lips and swallowed hard as he ached to sink his teeth into the thundering pulse throbbing beneath his touch.

The constricted expression on Connor's white face stuck fear into Rice's heart. The Captain stumbled backwards, sweat sprouting on his cold brow. Connor shoved him, and Rice collided roughly with a tree trunk, his teeth snapping smartly together as he hit his head, hard.

Connor did not speak. His icy glare sent shivers through Rice as he struggled to control his legs and lurched away.

Squaring his shoulders, and wiping the anger from his expression, Connor turned back to Lavinia.

She stood closer than he expected. *Did she hear? See the fear on his face?* But the moment he reached out a hand towards her, the crease of concern between her delicate brows dissolved.

"Walk with me, Connor." The affection in her half smile caught him unawares, and without thinking, he found himself at her side offering his arm.

Lavinia's fingertips trembled as they rested upon his sleeve, and as her warm palm branded his skin, a lava flow of longing flowed through him.

They walked the length of the rose garden in silence, moving into the dappled shadow of the arbor. Tree branches arched gracefully overhead, creating an intricate canopy where stray moonbeams scattered jewels of light along the shingle path.

Watching those same jewels play over Lavinia's carefully composed features, Connor frowned as the heat of anger directed towards Captain Rice evaporated, and yet, heat still burned in his chest.

Arriving beside a bench carved in stone, he paused and urged Lavinia to sit beside him. Glancing down into her face, he saw a different woman to the one he expected. He realized that he had not considered her appearance in earnest for many months, years even, and that Reggie was right. *She is no longer an adolescent.*

Even at nineteen years old, there was wisdom in the worried depths of her copper-flecked gaze. The glint of melancholy in her eyes burned a hole in his heart as he admitted that he had been lying to himself. *I love her, and now it's too late.*

"Lady Lavinia-" Connor's words stopped when she sighed delicately.

"So, serious," she murmured, "but really, there is no need. I love you, Connor. You know this, so there is little point pretending that Captain Rice, or any of the others, matter. But thank you for feeling the need to rescue me."

His protests died in the face of Lavinia's blunt certainty. Gazing back along the path, he laughed wryly. "If I am honest, for all my thoughts of protecting your virtue, I saw Rice off for my own sanity as much as anything."

"Connor-" She turned to look into his silver-gray eyes, and the glittering sparks buried in their depths made her catch her breath.

Her frozen surprise made him jump to his feet. Dread crushed him, the kind that feared the veil would be torn from her sight and reveal him as a monster. "I'll take you back," he said quickly, straightening his jacket and preparing to move.

Still sitting, Lavinia tugged on his hand until, slowly, he sat beside her once more. "Connor, I know there is something... different about you. I just want to say, you can tell me."

"My future is uncertain," he said heavily. Folding Lavinia's hand into his cold palm, he watched a trail of goosebumps chase up over her skin. "I can say only this; I wish I had come to my senses earlier." A rueful smile tugged at his lips. "Threatening Captain Rice is not exactly my style, but it is all I have at my disposal, because you are right, there is something different about me. I cannot make you a part of it. I'm sorry."

"I will wait." Her raised hand silenced his protest. "You cannot stop me. While there is hope, I will wait."

Connor did something he had ached to do since he saw her radiant smile of welcome, he leaned forward and very gently stroked his lips over hers, begging for her to let him in. He deepened his kiss until it stole her breath, and the blade of hunger in his throat cut deep. When the yearning to taste her accelerated pulse almost overwhelmed him, he withdrew.

His whispered word of 'goodbye' hung in the night air as he vanished.

Moments later, Lavinia heard the thundering of Sabre's hooves churning up the gravel. The stallion galloped away along the driveway as though demons clawed at his heels. She could only guess at the terrible things that were taking Connor away from her, and she sat in a storm of her own emotions.

"He will come back." Deep inside, she knew she was changed, too, and he would come back to her.

Chapter 8

The horseback ride from Cranham Hall to the hospital took Connor along treacherous, tree-lined country lanes in pitch-black, which forced him to concentrate – not to consider his own safety, but that of Sabre. *I may be dead already, but my old friend is not.* Even so, by the time he passed beneath the yellow glow of the London streetlights, exhilaration sang through every fiber in Connor's soul. He was an accomplished rider, but tonight, he became one with Sabre's powerful frame. He felt every muscle of the stallion rippling beneath the black-velvet coat as though they were his own. Connor had never felt more alive.

Back in his room in the students' quarters, Connor stripped mud-splattered clothes from his body. Pulling the solid oak wardrobe door open, he selected a shirt and pair of pants, avoiding looking in the mirror as he pulled them on. The merest flash of his reflection had been enough to tell him that his eyes glittered with gray ice, his skin, instead of being ruddy from exertion, was layered in frost, and his heart had at last stopped.

He could not resist testing for a pulse, and sure enough, there was none. *It is time to find this Malachi and learn the rest.* Leaving the chamber he had always thought of as his refuge, he headed out with the certainty of a heat-seeking missile.

The brick built surgical wing of the building was old, and cracked ceramic tiles lined the corridors. A horizontal stripe of glazed royal-blue tiles divided the iceberg-white expanse, perfectly placed at waist height, it disguised the marks where hasty porters scraped hospital trolleys along the walls.

Drafts haunted the ventilation shafts like ghostly whispers which chilled the air. And, the nurses on duty were grateful for the extra warmth of the shawls draped over their shoulders, provided as part of their uniform. In the eerie quiet of the hospital at the dead of night, Connor slipped along the antiseptic tainted corridors; his wraith-like shadow barely registered with the exhausted angels of mercy burning the midnight oil on ward duty.

His surroundings became the blur of a time-warp tunnel, but still Connor could not help but notice that everything looked as it always did, and yet, so very different. The crazed enamel surface of the tiled walls resembled a delicate filigree of exquisite lace, and they were not white, they were a lake of milk sprinkled with glitter.

Connor tamped down the pleasure at his heightened awareness, as he finally arrived at the top of the stairwell leading to the morgue. He slowed his pace. Making his feet touch down firmly on each tread of the cold quartz-dusted steps, he descended into the basement where the final door waited. Once he passed over the threshold, he would know his fate.

He pushed against the sheet of cold rubber-trimmed steel, stepped inside, and let the door thud gently closed behind him. He automatically lit the mantle of a gas lantern and held it above his head, scanning the room slowly.

The hairs on his nape prickled, and even though he could not see him, Connor knew Malachi was there.

Feeling foolish, Connor muttered, "Hello?"

In answer, a rhythmic tapping sound grew steadily louder, forcing Connor to set the lantern down on an empty instrument trolley and press his palms over his ears. He swung around, scanning the cold clinical space and combing the shadows dancing in the yellow glow of the flickering lamp. Imagining ghosts in every corner, he felt unfazed when Malachi materialized less than an arm's length away.

Connor's hands dropped to his sides, even though the scraping noise continued with a hypnotic rhythm.

Malachi's aged, gnarled fingers caressed a glass vial encased in an intricately woven gold shell, suspended on a heavy chain hanging around his scrawny neck.

"What's that?" The words were out before Connor could stop them.

Silence clung to the cold air as the tapping noise ceased abruptly.

"*This* is your salvation, or it will be, if you choose it." Malachi's colorless eyes raked over Connor's face. "You know you are dying?"

Connor's tumbling thoughts – crowded with questions – slipped like grains of sand through his mind. While he fought to gather them and string them into sentences, they were collected by Malachi, who already knew everything he wanted to ask.

"Yes, last night, you were bitten, fed upon, and you, in turn, were fed." Malachi cocked his head and waited. "Do you remember?"

Malachi's words unlocked a door inside Connor, and his lost hours of last night arrived in an avalanche of sensation. He recalled walking the row of bodies, and finding his first specimen, Mr. Donaghue. He saw himself peering into the dead eyes of the bodies laid out on the metal beds until, flipping back the cold-stiffened sheet on body number eight, he had felt the sharp gaze of Malachi's eyes dart through his brain like the stab of a red-hot needle.

He had jerked back, but a clawed grip had dug into his shoulders and whipped him through the air. He landed heavily on his back. The cold of the metal autopsy table had bitten through his cotton shirt in an instant, forcing a gurgling gasp from Connor as strong jaws closed over his throat. Fear had made his mind scream. His fingers tingled with hot ash as their blood supply was sucked away.

The screaming had continued on inside his head as a sharp cheekbone ground against his lifted jaw, and the whirlpool of his thoughts raced towards the black hole of unconsciousness. There was a moment of feeling nothing at all, and then thick paste oozed into his mouth and settled like a plug in his throat. He choked on the icy lava that trickled down inside his chest.

Connor's eyes locked on the vial again as the memory made him gag, a suffocating feeling welling up inside him.

Malachi nodded. "Yes, it is immortal blood that is keeping you alive, for now."

"Why? How?"

"Venom is spreading slowly throughout your system. It will penetrate each blood cell and attack the new cells your bone marrow makes, until your blood becomes so thick that your heart can no longer pump it around your body. At which point, your cells begin to die, and *you* die."

Anger pulled Connor's features tight as he spat. "So, what are you telling me? You have invited me here to gloat. Watch me die?"

"It is a test. I had not thought you would last this long. But, you are strong, and your mental powers are impressive." Malachi's long bony digit tapped his temple. "Suicide is an easy out when you think you are going crazy."

"Who *are* you? What the hell are you?"

Tilting his head to one side, Malachi arched thin eyebrows and etched deeper wrinkles into his forehead. "Some call me a 'demon', or a 'blood drinking spirit'. I prefer the term 'vampire'." His fingers played over the gold casket around his neck, swirling the contents as he slowly removed the cap and said, "You don't *have* to die, of course. But, time is running out."

Connor's mouth watered as the smell of blood drifted across the room.

"But only vampire blood, *my* blood, completes the transformation. Your heart has stopped, but your body will remain frozen in time, forever at the peak of the fitness you now enjoy, as long as you feed it and keep your tissue hydrated."

Connor's pupils swelled to black pools as the ruby-red vapors billowing through his cerebral cortex made thinking impossible.

Malachi lifted the vial to his own lips and downed the contents before facing Connor's confusion. "Choose, Doctor Connor." The blur of Malachi's face sharpened into focus bare inches away, his pearl-tinted gaze boring into Connor's brain. "But you can't just *drink*, you have to feed. *Only* feeding awakens the survival instinct trapped inside you, and releases the monster who can satisfy your thirst."

The curiosity gleaming in Malachi's eyes transformed them to diamond-white as he placed the blade of his nail on the marble white skin at his wrist and, with a vicious stab, cut it open.

The thick brown blood oozed, holding its form in a grotesquely growing teardrop until a snarl broke from Connor's throat and he jerked forward, gripped Malachi's arm, and grazed his teeth over the stone-hard skin until his mouth filled with the vampire's blood.

He drank, his teeth grinding away at the chalky flesh, scoring a set of grooves with each draft of blood he dragged out of the hard tissue. The growl in his throat thickened to a purr as his chest, lungs, and stomach began to tingle, and the synapses in his brain scattered a light show across his vision.

Malachi's powerful grip closed over Connor's shoulder, and, with irresistible force, Malachi pushed him back. The keening frustration of a feral animal tore from Connor's throat.

"Addictive, isn't it?" said Malachi.

A snarl cramped Connor's features, and congealed blood stained his bared teeth the color of rotting meat. Reining in the hunger, he straightened, and wiped the back of his hand across his mouth.

"I was right. You are strong."

Connor realized that Malachi's voice was inside his head, his words appearing as writing etched into his brain. He clawed his way back from the feeling of insanity. His stomach roiled and blood filled his mouth once more as he finally found the courage to look at his tormentor. The skin covering Malachi's face clung to his skull like crumpled tracing paper, and opaque, colorless strands of hair barely concealed the putty gray membrane stretching over his scalp.

"I don't understand, if I will always look like this, have my youth, then were you…?"

"Old?" Malachi laughed a paper-thin sigh of self-derision. "No, I said, 'if you feed your tissue, hydrate your brain, *then* you will remain young and strong'." Waving a hand to indicate Connor's bulk, Malachi's beaded eyes glittered as he took in the young doctor's physique, and grinned ruefully. "I, too, had good raw material, but I was untutored."

Connor was fascinated as Malachi's presence inside his head began to take on color and shape.

"Sadly, I was not instructed by my maker. But, perhaps he didn't know. After all, in the beginning, vampires were an abhorrent notion. We were cursed by nature, and more died out than learned how to survive."

"So, how old are you?" asked Connor.

"In vampire years? Many centuries, and, as for the rest, it no longer matters." Malachi shrugged. "I did not feed enough in those early undead decades, when rehydration transforms vampire tissue to thirst pockets. It is a little like charging battery cells which boosts your strength at your will's command."

"Decades? The change takes that long?"

"Yes, building your strength takes decades. But, you have only a day, two at most, to master the art of rehydration; the time it takes for the reproduction of cells in bone marrow to cease. But then, as a doctor, you know this. Every twenty-four hours, cells in your body die and are replenished. This will no longer happen for you, so you must nurture the ones you have right now."

"And there is an *art* to this rehydration?" Connor's features tightened, not believing the words which were about to come out of his mouth. "I just have to drink human blood. Where is the art in that?"

"Merely *drinking* human blood will feed your body, but not your brain. Gray matter is not the same as muscle and sinew." Malachi's chilling smile soaked his lips in saliva. "Think of the brainstem as the gatehouse of a fortress. Inside the fortress of the brain, you have three prisoners, each locked inside a cell. Unlocking a cell door, means we are no longer fully alert. You can only release one at a time, but each one must be fed or part of your brain will die. *That* is where the art lies."

"Why one at a time? Why not all at once?"

Annoyance jerked through Malachi's bony body. "You dare ask why. Ask yourself this, do sharks sleep?"

"They drown if they sleep... sharks," said Connor slowly.

"And so will you. Vampires do not sleep. Although humans wish that we did. If you feed all three centers of your brain at once, you lose control, permanently. You will not die, not until your brain rots away, but you will not 'wake-up'."

Stillness crept over Connor until it was complete. "And if one of these... prisoners inside my head starves?"

"Vampire dementia. Not a pretty sight." Malachi said, "From what I have heard, the vampire, literally, dies of thirst as his brain desiccates. The hardened tissue locks the jaw shut and immobilizes the neck.

"Heard? You've never seen it?"

Malachi's grin exposed rows of yellow pegs buried in white gums. "In Egypt, vampires walked out into the sun before they suffered the final strangulation."

Connor wiped his hands down over his tight face. "Is it too late for me, now?"

Running a cold fingertip over the tear in his arm which had closed to a thin silver-tinted trail, Malachi said, "Yes, you fed from me. It is too late."

Anger boiled up inside Connor. "You tell me this now? You did not let me choose." He struck out at Malachi's complacent features. But his fist accelerated through empty air and buried itself in the tiled wall. As the shattered tile fragments clattered to the floor, his mentor's ethereal laughter clawed its way up Connor's spine. Breathing heavily, Connor laid his forehead on the cold surface. It burned his skin, and he groaned, "There's more, isn't there?"

The silence lasted barely a second, before Connor straightened, turned back into the room, and demanded quietly, "I know you are still here. Tell me the rest. Do I have to hide from sunlight? Am I some boogieman who can only come out at night?"

Malachi's words arrived before his body. "For many years I believed that to be so. Because the sun burned my skin, I thought I could come out only at night. In the deserts, my only choice was to bury myself deep under the sand during the hours of scorching sunlight, but the sand was like a blast furnace." His bone-dry finger dragged over the cracked parchment coating his cheekbone like tanned leather. "Life became easier when I took refuge inside the pyramids. The royal tombs became my home for centuries."

Remembering the burning sensation on his face when the sunlight had caught him out, Connor ran his fingertips over the hardened skin on his brow to find it was as smooth as glass once more.

Malachi nodded. "You have fed. Minor sun damage repairs easily."

"But you... we can go out in daylight?"

"We can go out during the day time, yes, but we need cloud cover and shadow as protection." Malachi grinned. "England, with winter approaching, is a good place for you to practice."

Connor examined Malachi's face. "Your sun damage was not so minor then. Another lesson you learned the hard way," he said quietly, "what was it like for you, in Egypt?"

Chapter 9

"As a human boy, I was a member of the Pharaoh's household. I brought him his clothes and ceremonial jewels. I helped my father to dress him. I suppose, in English society, you would call me the valet's apprentice?" Malachi held out a bony hand and the oil lantern flame glinted on the band of gold, fashioned into a serpent, which wound around his fingers. It meandered between three of the bone-white digits. The serpent's head rested on the last knuckle, facing upward, as though it was about to slither up over the back of his hand. Its ruby-red eyes appeared to glitter with intent.

"If I remove it, I will die. Superstitious rubbish of course, but Egypt was built on that." The complacency faded from Malachi's stare.

Connor waited, without breathing, sensing a moment of candor.

"My brother and I heard stories of the scraping sounds echoing from inside the pyramids at Luxor. A Pharaoh was always buried with his chattels. My uncle told us all his servants were buried alive inside the tomb, and went with him to the afterlife to live in glory and splendor. But, it was said that three decades after the sealing of the tomb, in the dead of night, you could still hear their broken fingernails scraping over the stone slabs."

Staring at Connor, Malachi painted his memories inside Connor's head until the ceramic white-tiled walls of the morgue became streaked with copper-colored veins in rock, and the smooth surface ruptured into rough-hewn stone wall...

The day my master was buried, I was there.
Malachi's words whispered inside the cavern of Connor's skull. A band of tension gripped his head as, suddenly, he was walking along behind a boy who wore a gold-embroidered cloth band, tied tightly around his forehead, like a fabric, jewel-encrusted crown.

The biceps in the boy's wiry arms were braced, as if he carried something heavy in front of his body, which could not be seen. Connor judged him to be about twelve years old. The boy glanced back over his shoulder at Connor, a nervous sheen glistening like tears in the fish-scale opaque eyes.

Ah. Is this Malachi as a boy?

That was Connor's last detached thought as he became a conduit for every emotion rattling through the boy's reed thin frame, as though he was inside him.

The boy entered a chamber, and Connor caught sight of the burden he carried; a bowl fashioned from beaten gold. The dead pharaoh lay on a stone plinth.

When the boy set the bowl down, without thinking, Connor reached out and boosted him up onto the concrete platform. Connor frowned when he noticed his own arms were as thin as sticks. Hoisting himself up too, Connor sat beside the youngster and watched the boy's thin brown hands wringing out a leather cloth. Beginning at the pharaoh's forehead, his companion began to wash his skin.

Connor leaned forward to get a better view, and froze, as the reflection looking up at him from the bowl of water was not his *own* face, but another boy. A boy who looked just like Malachi. *So, they were twins?* In this surreal world of dreams, Connor tried to decipher the meaning, but the sudden noise of a man entering the chamber disrupted his train of thought.

The tall Egyptian wore a white headdress decorated with a gold cobra positioned at his forehead, its hood flared and ready to strike. "Faster boys. The high priest is waiting, and you must be gone before he arrives," said the Egyptian in a guttural tone.

"Yes, Ebanar, we will be gone." The boy sitting near Connor placed his palms together and touched his thumbs to his brow as he bowed his head. As the stern Egyptian stared at Connor, the simmering resentment inside the body Connor now realized was not his own, burned brighter as he reluctantly imitated the salute.

Grunting, the tall man left.

Alone together once more, the twin looked deep into Connor's eyes, the pearly sheen glistening with calculation as he said, "Hurry, brother. We must hurry."

Plunging his childlike hands into the water, the boy Connor now embodied helped his brother wash the pharaoh's body. They cleaned the soles of his feet last, and then, together, they unfolded a thin linen sheet and covered the corpse.

As agile as chimps, both boys hopped down, landing silently on the sandstone floor. The brother collected the bowl and emptied it onto the ground in a corner where the sandy residue devoured the liquid, becoming a dark brown stain.

Connor felt irritation tight in his chest as he hissed, "Fool, brother, they will see."

The other boy shrugged. "So, we are skinny boys. They will think we were too tired to carry a heavy bowl, so we emptied it first. Come, we have to hide."

As Connor tried to move quickly, breathing in the thick, damp air of the tomb exhausted him, the lack of oxygen draining him of energy.

Climbing up onto a marble dais, relieved to be resting at last, he and the other boy folded their bodies into crouched balls. Staying close to his brother, Connor burrowed into the irregular space of an alcove until both boys were concealed behind the carved skirt of a gold-colored statue of Isis.

The murmur of rhythmically chanting voices drifted into the chamber, and the soft sound of shuffling feet grew louder. Finally, the high priest walked into the room, dressed from head to toe in gold, the pleated fan of his gilded mantle trailing in his wake. He stopped at one end of the waist-high plinth, positioned at the feet of the resting corpse, and looked up towards the Pharaoh's head.

Connor had no hope of deciphering the musical stream of words which began as a whisper, and swelled into a lilting prayer. Two tall Egyptians held marble bowls from which wisps of smoke spiraled upwards, obscuring their striking faces behind shifting ribbons of mist.

The priest's attendants removed the cover from the body, and with the deft touch of practiced hands they wrapped it in strips of linen infused with a blend of aromatic oils.

"Why are they covering his face?" the other boy asked Connor.

Connor did not know the answer, but the quick mind he shared this body with, did.

"Do you not know anything, brother? The ceremony demands that his breath be locked inside his chest, it keeps his spirit whole," said Connor's host pompously, the voice sounding thin and reedy, as though it had not yet broken.

The pharaoh's retinue exuded proud reverence. Their impressive physiques, bared to the waist, created a fitting spectacle.

Four-inch deep golden fans fastened at the base of their throats accentuated broad shoulders, and the simplicity of milk-white cotton skirts was transformed by the drama of gold belts molded to the chiseled muscles at their waists. The candlelight picked out cobalt strands in the fall of poker-straight, jet-black hair.

Connor felt the thin boy he embodied tremble in awe at their presence.

After the incense bearers set the mortar-bowls of fragrant burning wood fibers down on to a ledge, four other warriors joined them, lining up three abreast on either side of the pharaoh's body.

The high priest stepped back, and the fierce expression on his face dared the cortege to ruin his ceremony. With the gliding control of finely honed muscles, the six men lifted their pharaoh up onto their shoulders.

Tapping into the mood of his host body, Connor absorbed the boy's uneasy fascination of the ceremony, and the feelings simmering inside the mind he shared. *We should not be here.*

The other boy failed to smother the giggle tugging at his lips as he said, "The pharaoh is stiff as a board, Malachi, do you see?"

Shock erupted inside Connor as he turned to look at the excited face only inches from his own. It still looked eerily similar to the *adult* Malachi he had met. *So, if I am Malachi, we are identical twins, then?* The closed fist of Connor's boyish hand aimed a hard blow at his brother's arm, and it wiped the smirk from his face.

"Shh, Numu," Malachi mimed with the barest sound.

The chanting reached a crescendo as the high priest turned around and led the solemn attendants from the chamber. The boys remained as still as the statue which shielded them, until the melodious baritone echoes faded and silence thickened the air.

Connor wondered where the procession would lead, and the answer appeared inside him as Malachi thought about it too.

Along an ornately decorated passageway beyond this chamber, lay the burial chamber. *Malachi has clearly been inside it.* Three sarcophagi were laid out in order like a series of Russian dolls. The wrapped, embalmed body would be placed inside the smallest, made of sandstone. The second was carved in granite, and the final sarcophagus, engraved with the pharaoh's likeness, was encased in a thick layer of gold leaf. The detail of the pharaoh's garb of office, painted in the most exquisite intricate design, transformed the gilded surface into a work of art.

"Come, we should follow," said Numu, his punishment at Malachi's hand forgotten.

Connor agreed with the other boy. He wanted to see, firsthand, the scene Malachi's memory had revealed.

Malachi gripped his brother's arm, his fingers digging in hard as he snapped, "Don't be a fool, brother."

The other boy winced, but still his feet scrabbled as though his legs would leave without him.

Malachi reached out, closed his fingers over his brother's chin and brought his face around until he could see his eyes. "Numu," said Malachi gently, "We will wait, look at me."

The boy's eyes ceased the skittering movement that Connor, as a doctor, recognized as a sign of a simple mind. The vacant gaze focused on Malachi's face. "We should not be here, so just stay quiet." Enclosing his brother's thin body in a restricting bear hug, Malachi hung on tight until Numu stopped struggling and his limbs went slack. "Hush, brother." The sensation of speaking, but the thoughts not coming from his own mind, was disorienting.

Through the eyes watching for movement which could mean they had been discovered, Connor saw elaborate pictures painted on the polished stone of the chamber. The garb of the warriors that had borne the pharaoh away were replicated on the walls. The images were laid with gold leaf and painted with the pictorial narrative of Egyptian fable. The depiction of curiously erect, awkwardly posed rows of figures, with their faces presented in profile, fascinated Connor. He had never seen anything like them before. *What kind of civilization is this?*

Inside the chamber, hushed whispers drifted through the cracks, and a shower of sand scurried down over the wall, to gather in a miniature dune on the floor. *Is that normal?* Connor wished he had control of a voice to ask. He knew now how coma victims felt, trapped inside a conscious, but unresponsive body.

Impotent frustration was a stranger to him. He scanned the sand dusted wall, knowing Malachi was doing the same, because he could only see what his host saw.

Malachi's head whipped around as the clattering noise of a heavy rainfall of sand gave way to a distant shout echoing down the corridors, accompanied by the slapping sound of bare feet running.

"Numu, quick." Malachi leapt to his feet, dragging his hapless brother by the arm until he fell to the floor of the chamber with the yelp of a startled pup.

The ground vibrated beneath them, and the distant shouts became punctuated with blood curdling screams. Grabbing Numu's hand, they were running. Scrawny legs pumping as hard as the thin muscles could manage, they raced up the slick stone slopes. Like rats running through a maze, Connor saw the walls whipping past him, and every one looked the same, but Malachi dived left at one intersection, and right at the next.

He knows where we are going then. His lungs were burning, and the air tasted of sand, laying an emulsion of grit onto his tongue as he gasped for oxygen. Rounding a final bend, his body hit a dead end, pain shot through his shoulder and he heard a snap. Slabs of sandstone filled the exit route, the fractured surfaces forming an absurdly beautiful gold-leaf draped avalanche which sealed them inside the tomb.

The boys fell to their knees, and the world went black as Malachi screwed his eyes tightly shut, and bellowed. His rage and pain was a potent cocktail of despair.

Connor felt the pain too, for a moment, before it eased, and he knew that the vision was over.

Chapter 10

Connor wanted to stay to see the rest, and his throat muscles worked as he tried to find the words, but it *was* over. He still could not breathe until the mid-brown, tumbled outcrops of rock faded. The glossy sheen of the white tiles of the morgue walls rose to the surface like a layer of frost, and he was once more standing on solid ground. Gripping onto the edge of an empty autopsy table, he stared into the aged, wizened face of the thousands of years old Malachi.

"So, you and your brother were buried inside the tomb?" croaked Connor, horrified.

"Yes."

"What caused the structure to cave in?"

Malachi's thin lips bowed in a resigned smile. "My master had enemies. And Numu and I were the lucky ones. They wanted my pharaoh to rot in hell, his soul un-cleansed. While the preparations were only half done, they severed the ropes that held the counter weights in place. I remember lying there on the floor, hearing the grinding noise as rock moved slowly over the stones, and the shuffling dunes made the air so thick that I could not breathe. I was choking, dying..." Malachi's smile became spiteful. "It turned out to be only the beginning."

"But in the vision, you were only a boy." Connor frowned. "Vampires do not grow."

"No, we were buried alive, along with eight others. The inner chambers of the pyramid did not collapse." Malachi's eyes glistened as he said, "I think you can guess the rest. Numu and I stayed in hiding. We dug out a hole behind that statue in the ceremonial chamber, and we stole some of the food the demon brought in for the group. He fed on the servants, but he kept them alive, at least, until their hearts gave out."

"He did not know you and Numu were there?"

"We did not think so. We became braver, and sat with the others around the altar candles, telling fables, and painting our own stories onto the walls. They accepted that the stranger who left the food demanded sacrifices in return. It didn't seem so bad after a while."

"So, you were being kept like cattle?"

"Exactly that. The warriors remained strong for the longest time. And then the wounds in their necks refused to heal, weeping. When the thin trickle of clear blood flowed down over their chests in a trail that glistened in the candle light, I started counting down their final days."

Malachi's long pale fingers scraped through his lackluster hair and his fingertips trailed over the sinews in his neck, to where, Connor imagined, the bites he suffered could still be felt.

"We *thought* he did not know about us, but, we were wrong, of course. When he ran out of food, he came for us." Malachi's expression became distant as he continued. "He found the stone behind which we were hiding, my brother and I. He kept us alive for many years, until we grew from children into men. When I, too, finally became weak, after years of waiting to die, I was *relieved*. And then, the pyramid slabs shifted, and another avalanche filled the tomb with a tide of rushing sand."

"So, the others, he killed. Why not you?"

Malachi focused on Connor's face. "I don't know for certain." Malachi's dry throat crackled as he laughed. "Perhaps if the tomb had not collapsed... I think in his way, he was saving me."

Rousing himself as though from a waking dream, Connor's words stuck in his thickened throat. "You? Only you survived?"

"Survival is an interesting notion. I existed. I think the demon regretted his act somehow, because, the very night it was done, he left. And, for decades, I never knew other vampires existed."

Connor, despite the terrifying agony of the last twenty-four hours, began to wonder what would have become of him if Malachi had run. He felt a wave of unexpected gratitude. "I guess, if I can't be glad you bit me, I can thank you for this, for helping me now."

An evasive look clouded the oyster shell sheen of Malachi's gaze, and Connor was touched by doubt.

"I felt I owed it to you. A debt to repay. But, if you are to survive, you must know there are *others* in London. You are not alone. There are rules and consequences to your existence."

"Consequences?"

Malachi nodded. "It's not just a case of avoiding direct sunlight. You have to become strong or other vampires will sense your vulnerability. We are good at sniffing out the weak."

"And I become strong by feeding?"

"Feeding, yes. But covering your tracks is critical. The Undead Council in London has no patience for vampires who threaten to expose us. They... Principal Julian, will order your internment if you threaten that."

'Council? What on earth?" Monsters roaming by chance was one thing, but the notion that there were enough of them to become 'an organization'? Connor swallowed noisily.

Malachi locked gazes with Connor. "It should not be so surprising. Hunger must be controlled. The deterrent must be compelling."

"Internment? So, he, this principal, won't kill me? How..." The question Connor wanted to ask evaded him. His human understanding did not extend to things worse than death.

"Death would be too easy."

Connor's mouth hung open, while he still tried to work out how death could be easy.

Malachi suddenly closed the gap between them and whispered, "Trust me."

Connor's collar pulled tight as a bony, vise-like grip closed around it. A rush of warm air preceded the feeling of hurtling through space. His preternatural vision allowed Connor to fully comprehend the speed Malachi moved at, the walls of the ice-colored hospital corridors becoming a surreal toboggan run.

Like obstacles in a ten-pin bowling alley, the hospital staff going about their duties hurtled towards him, frozen in mid stride or mid word. Malachi effortlessly avoided them. Although the wash of their vampire flight startled the humans, their ruffled hair and chilled human skin making them feel as though someone had walked over their graves.

Outside the hospital, Connor concentrated on the darkened deserted streets whipping past, but soon gave up on trying to work out where they were going. *I'll just have to trust him.* Connor knew he should be afraid, but when he met Malachi, gut instinct told him that the vampire was his savior.

When the ornate gates of Kensal Cemetery came into view, Malachi stopped before them and released Connor. "Follow me."

Shrugging to settle his shirt back into place, Connor nodded.

"This way." Malachi's hollow whisper echoed inside Connor's head as he watched the angular bony figure move forward.

Malachi scraped his fingernails over the stone blocks of the cemetery walls, easily finding near invisible seams to grip onto. Using the ornate carvings in the masonry as footholds, he quickly scaled the wall and disappeared over the top.

Connor arrived at the top of the wall in time to see Malachi drop and land silently on the lush grass on the other side.

Without hesitation, Connor followed him across the graveyard. He had a surreal moment of wondering why the grass in cemeteries always felt thick and lustrous.

They came to a halt outside the rusted gates of a mausoleum. Malachi effortlessly eased the seized rusted hinges open and went inside. Connor glanced back around at the deserted landscape of moss-covered tombstones and quickly followed.

The musty air inside the tomb felt like breathing in dirt, and without thinking Connor stopped breathing. He heard the sound of grating stone and a shiver trickled through him. It felt eerily creepy, and every human sense he still had screamed 'run', and he may have, if Malachi's heavy hand had not descended onto his shoulder and nudged him forward.

Even in the darkness, Connor found he could see more than he wished. Looking down at a shrunken figure lying in the sarcophagus, he was poised to ask Malachi what he was supposed to be looking for, when he heard, rather than saw the eyelids dragging back over dry eyeballs, and a pair of oil-black eyes stared up at him.

"He's alive!" Connor jerked back.

"Barely," said Malachi, "this is The Butcher. He is serving a sentence of eternal death, at the command of Principal Julian."

"Eternal death?" The words punched a hole in Connor's chest.

"Yes. This is your warning. The Butcher killed humans and almost revealed our existence to the living. We cannot have that. We are the thing of nightmares, the boogieman that rattles bones in the closet of human fancy. It is one thing to be a creature of myth or legend, but The Butcher crossed the line. He coined the term serial killer, leaving a trail of bodies littering his hunting ground, and was nearly our undoing."

"So, this is his punishment? To slowly shrivel and die?"

"Shrivel, yes. Die, no." Malachi eased the stone lid back in place. "He is regularly fed a small dose of human blood, enough to preserve his brain function, and to allow him to suffer. Principal Julian is not a vampire to be crossed, Doctor Connor. Make sure you learn the lessons I teach you, well."

A sense of fatality filtered into Connor's mind as he stared into Malachi's alert crystal clear eyes. "You don't save all your victims, do you? Why me?"

"I sense strength in you, power which would have been wasted in the shallow pools of being human. Call it sixth sense, every few hundred years I come across a soul too important to let die. You have a purpose, of that I am sure."

Connor tolerated the probing assessment of Malachi's opaque eyes. "Of course, you must learn how to hunt. Meet me here tomorrow at sunset."

"Hunt?" His questions rose to choke him, but Malachi disappeared, leaving only laughter rippling through the air and stroking over Connor's sensitized skin like a wave through water.

Emerging alone from the mausoleum into the still dark night, Connor had no reason to stay. He straightened his jacket and found himself at the bottom of the steps leading up to the students' quarters at the hospital before he had fully realized the thought. He did not need to sleep, but he did need somewhere to hide and to digest the maelstrom of thoughts rambling around inside his mind.

I have to be careful of that, he thought, as he pulled himself to a dead halt, pressing the indent of his thumb pad into the copper doorknob. As he stepped into the bleached-white glare of the corridor, his pupils closing down to a pinprick of glacier-blue awareness, he heard a scream.

It was the distant keening of breathless pain, and, his training stepping in, he took off. Remembering to travel the maze of corridors at vampire slow, he hugged curves and took sharp corners like a heat-seeking missile. He mapped out the terrain as a vista of thudding pulse rates, warm moisture-laden respiration, and fever hot skin.

Reducing his speed to the urgent walk of an attending physician, he burst into the medical ward and joined the cluster of two nurses and a burly porter, as they tried to restrain a patient who reared and writhed in pain. The sheet covering his body billowed and sagged on one side where his left leg had once been.

The honey-soaked sweet smell of blood swelled Connor's hungry nasal lining until air could not pass.

Connor's presence invaded their consciousness as he stepped forward and, with a well-placed shoulder, shunted the porter aside.

With his cold hands drawing a gasp from the patient's agonized mouth, his skin scalding to Connor's touch, he immobilized the man effortlessly and, locking eyes with the muddy delirium, Connor's stillness seeped into the tense body.

Both nurses launched into an explanation, blurting their thoughts at the same time. "He just started screaming, Doctor Sanderson. Fred did his best, but he is demented with the pain. Tore the gauze from his wound. He's so strong."

One nurse stopped talking, absorbing Connor's almost casual grip on the relaxed man's shoulders and a frown chased across her features.

Connor arranged his face into a smile, injecting warmth to melt the ice in his eyes as he said quietly, "Well done, Nurse Green. The patient has clearly exhausted himself, energy drains away so fast in the sick."

Not allowing her to analyze more than the reassuring tone, he began a quick examination. He flipped back the sheet where the ruby-red stain blossomed, the red leeching into the snowy fibers in an intricate pattern like fingers of frost. A spasm slammed his throat shut and he drove determinedly past the poker-hot stab of ravenous greed twisting inside his gut.

He examined the amputation stump, grateful when his cold fingers helped stem the bleeding, and, using that unexpected benefit, he molded his cold palm over the wound and barked instructions at the distracted nurses.

Their stuttering speech and clattering nerves suddenly made something crystal clear. He measured distended pupils and the layers of delicate perspiration on their brows. The pheromone drenched aroma of attraction was almost his undoing as he ground out through clenched teeth, "Morphine and gauze, now! Nurse Green, ice pack. Move!"

Packing and dressing the wound was accomplished at a frustratingly slow human speed, when all he really wanted to do was escape.

Are all the bloomin' nurses attracted to me? Why have I never noticed? Making a hastily retreat to his room in the students' quarters, he laid out on his bed. Closing his eyes, he wished for sleep, but knew he would never again experience the oblivion of conscious thought that human sleep embraced.

Chapter 11

The hospital corridors were deserted, although he could hear the labored breathing of the patients on the medical wards. They were diseased, consumptive, and death rattled in their chests.

Should I put them out of their misery? Choose a meal that will find relief in my attentions?

He considered it for barely a hair's breadth, and then with a hideous grin, he headed out of the hospital. Leaping the set of eighteen stone steps and landing as silently as a shadow, he flitted along the sidewalk, weaving tauntingly in and out of the glow cast by the gas-lamps, flirting with the human imagination of those that caught a glimpse if they glanced out of their windows. His white face floated like a magician's illusion, a pale-gray ethereal orb with the bowed gash of a sinister smile, and even moving at speed, his vampire senses collected the satisfying odor of dopamine drenched skin, as the flesh on human necks prickled with unease.

He unerringly retraced the route the carriage and four had traveled merely hours before and, as the dark silhouette of Cranham Hall fractured the blanket of stars in the sky, each tall chimney reaching hungrily for the sharp pin pricks of light, hunger of his own scythed through his windpipe and dragged a path into his gut.

"Nearly there."

The stones of the gravel driveway rattled nervously as he skimmed over their dew soaked faces. He swung left to the servants' entrance, still undecided on his victim. The scullery maids would rise at four a.m. and the dairy delivery would be soon after.

He stopped at the solid oak door and, pressing his hands to its warm surface, he closed his eyes and inhaled the moist warmth of the house full of slumbering humans. He scored a line around the small pane of glass with a diamond hard nail and dislodged it with a sharp tap.

Reaching through and unbolting the door, he shouldered the door with the clumsiness of a human intruder. To twist the handle and mangle the metal inside would cause the police to be suspicious. *And that will not do.*

Once inside, he passed into the bowels of the house. The brass pans hanging over the large wooden chopping bench swung in his wake. The stable boy was asleep in his cot. Stopping briefly in the door of his sleeping alcove, the intruder swung away and mounted the stone steps which gave way to carpet covered floor boards on the first floor level.

He crossed the line where grubby oatmeal carpet met the sumptuous burgundy twill of thick hand-woven wool, and ascended the impressive central staircase.

His hand folded carefully over the wooden balustrade, stroking it through his grip, its warm, smooth polished texture reminding him of the time, before his turning, when he had touched a copper hot-water pipe and burned his palm. The sweeping rail whipped through his fingers as he glided up the thick-carpeted treads of the stairs. *Even a human intruder would delight in effortless stealth. The rich were easy pickings.*

His reflection flitted across the glass plated silver-foiled mirrors, the imperfect distortions giving him pause as shadows cut across his features and his eyes glittered like ice-chips in blackened sockets. He anticipated the scream that would tear from human lungs if he allowed the victim sight of his face, and decided blood thickened with the adrenalin of heart stopping terror was a delicacy he could not resist.

The servants' quarters were in the attic of the house, and their access was via a much less impressive rear stairway. The vampire paused on the landing. On one side, the balustrade formed a barrier to the sheer drop to the parquet floor of the entrance hall, and on his other, was a row of richly carved oak doors. A heartbeat thrummed behind each one; the Cranham family slept.

Moving swiftly to the last chamber in the row of eight, the preternatural intruder entered the near black room, and, with a wet smile, he lit a candlestick on the mantel piece, watching with satisfaction as his shadow danced over the forest-green velvet drapes of the four-poster bed.

It will be no fun, if he does not see me.

The drapes formed a shield, keeping out the draughts which whistled through the gaps in the window frames, and preventing a chill penetrating the cotton of a gentleman's nightshirt.

Opening the drapes with a decisive sweep, the brass rings rattled and the slumbering man turned swiftly.

His eyes shot open, and he pushed his black hair back from his face. His assailant allowed him to shoot up to a sitting position, and even, not surprisingly, reach for the dagger he kept hidden under a cushion.

Of course, he would be watching his back. Much good it will do him.

The blade glinted in the candlelight as a harsh groan filled the air.

The young man felt his spine snap as his chin was whipped up and the ceiling above the bed filled his vision. A glitter of stars punctured his sight and pain sliced through his throat. His vocal chords snapped as blood rushed down his windpipe and dripped into his stomach.

The vampire clamped his jaws over the gushing jet, and let the blood wash down into his lungs and stomach, only starting to massage with his jaws when that first euphoric geyser faded to a pulsing ooze.

Hitting the jugular was the secret to a quick death, and created the exhilarating rush of bloodletting at its peak.

The empty body flopped back into the bed and the vampire was satisfied. He had not spilled one drop. He took a handkerchief from his pocket and wiped his lips before, lifting his victim's chin he filled the slack mouth with the linen square, and used the dagger hilt to push it down past the shredded gullet. Turning his victim's head to hide the torn throat, an ooze of blood marked the feather down pillow, but was easily covered by the linen sheet and thick tapestry comforter. He slid the blade back under the cushion, crossed to the window and lifted the lower frame up, hearing the sash chords grating, and he vaulted out over the edge.

Enjoying the second of free-falling, his dense body dropped like a stone. The gravel crumbled beneath his boots as he launched himself into a whipping pace which tore at his clothes. The vampire shed the confines of his dark coat, letting the howling wind take it as he embraced the adrenalin-charged rush of being fully fed.

Chapter 12

Connor lay in his cot staring at the intricate pattern of cracks on the ceiling, and wondering at the transformation preternatural sight made to his world. Now he knew what had happened to him, he felt in control. Malachi's words drifted through his brain like a hypnotist's mantra. *It is a matter of filtering out the background noise.* Connor would instinctively tune in to those sights, sounds, and smells his survival depended upon, provided his brain was fully fed of course.

"So, take every opportunity to feed. Learn how to open the sleep compartments in your brain at all costs. Becoming stronger than others, will elevate you up the hierarchy of vampire society," Malachi had said.

"How will they know?"

His piercing gaze had dragged over Connor's six-feet three-inch height, and the wall of muscle moving over his torso as Connor stabbed perplexed fingers through his jet-black hair. "Oh, they will know."

Connor had yet to master the rules of the game and he didn't like it.

Lying out on the cot last night, he wasn't sure *when* his 'thoughts' melted away to a meditative state, but he certainly stopped processing the world around him. The pearl-tinted haze of dawn filled the room now, and he didn't remember that happening.

Suddenly, the door of his chamber rattled loudly in its frame. "Open up, Mr. Sanderson." A shouting voice, accompanied the thundering noise. "Open up, sir. Police!"

Connor looked at the clock and was surprised to see four hours had passed. *It must be the brain cells charging, as Malachi said.* Once all the gray matter inside his head had been broken down and mutated by the vampire cells, he would never lose complete awareness again. *Clearly, I am not yet at that stage.*

He sprang to his feet, reached the door, and then remembered to wait the time it should have taken him to walk the distance before opening it.

Three policemen stared at Connor in expectation. The blue wall parted. A police inspector stepped forward and looked Connor in the eye. The jutting chin on the smug face had not changed much in five years.

"*Doctor* Connor." Inspector Cavendish's lip curled.

So, you remember me, too. Connor checked the embellishments on Cavendish's uniform and looked insultingly surprised. "*Inspector.*"

"You will accompany us to the station for questioning."

Connor deliberately eyed the other officers. "Surely, rounding up suspects is beneath your rank?" Connor smiled.

"Let's just say I am taking a 'special interest' in this enquiry," Cavendish replied.

A constable skirted round Connor into the room and waited for directions.

"Where are the clothes you wore yesterday, Doctor Connor?"

"Over there." He indicated the neatly folded pile set upon a chair.

At Cavendish's nod, the constable went to retrieve them.

"Don't you need a warrant?" Connor asked, quietly.

"I can get one, certainly. But if you have nothing to hide, then you should have no objection to my constable bagging them up for examination."

"Can you tell me what this is about? Am I under arrest?" Connor moved aside to let the policeman leave with his spoils.

"At this point in time, we merely wish to ask you some questions. If you object, then you will be detained." Everything in Cavendish's expression begged Connor to argue; arresting him would give the inspector pleasure.

Connor stared the man down. "You'll give me five minutes to dress for the occasion." It was not a request, and on a tight smile, he shut the door.

The missing four hours gave him pause as he leaned back against the wood and waited out four of his five minutes. He ran his tongue over his teeth. *They feel clean.* The face looking back from the mirror when he made his way to the basin and subjected it to a searching inspection, appeared clean too, and sane. *Would I remember if I had been hunting?* He somehow felt sure he would.

Once he was dressed, had combed back his black hair, and warmed his hands in boiling water, Connor walked out of the door and straight past the policemen on guard.

"Come along gentlemen, I'm sure Inspector Cavendish is a busy man."

The clink of hand cuffs swinging from the fingers of a stout officer drew laughter from Connor. "I don't think so. I'll come quietly, officer, after all, you have me at a disadvantage. I have no clue on what matter you are in need of my help."

His ride to the station was a more dignified affair than the last time. The stout policeman took one look at Connor's uncompromising expression and directed him to a police car rather than the wagon.

Half an hour later, Connor was seated in a small interview room, very similar to the one he remembered, face to face with Inspector Cavendish.

"Do you know a Captain Matthew Rice?"

What now? "I met him last night. He was a fellow guest at Cranham Hall when I joined the family for dinner."

"I understand you did not get along with the Captain."

"He is not a man I would choose as a friend, certainly."

Cavendish laughed, and then stopped abruptly. "And you left alone?"

"I was feeling a little under the weather. I rode Sabre, Reggie-Reginald Cranham's horse back to London. The fresh air blew away the cobwebs."

"And what time would that have been, Doctor?"

"About eleven o'clock."

"You came straight back to the hospital?"

Connor inclined his head.

"And yet, two hours later, you had not retired for the night."

Connor raised a brow and waited.

"You attended an emergency on the ward. The nurse said you were dressed and alert."

Ah. His outing to the mausoleum would be harder to explain. "Has Captain Rice lodged a complaint, Inspector?"

"We will get to that." Cavendish flipped a page on his note book. "The under-housemaid at Cranham Hall, Ivy Tindel. Do you know her at all?"

"Of course, I know Ivy, she has been at the Hall for years. She was fourteen, I think Reggie said, when the nuns suggested her to Lady Isobel."

"You seem to have got your feet under the table at Cranham Hall. If you don't mind my saying so."

"I do mind, Inspector."

"How well do you know Ivy?"

Careful. Her pregnancy was not something he should know about. "I share a cup of tea with the under-stairs staff on occasion. It is a shortcut through to the house from the stables. Mrs. Burnham, the housekeeper, is always very welcoming."

"I see. Doctor Connor, we have it on good authority that you had an argument with Captain Rice last evening. Would that be accurate?"

"It is true I found his behavior unbefitting a gentleman. I told him what I thought of him. I would not say we argued. Ask him. I am sure he will agree." *Lavinia would not have backed up Rice, so who?*

"Would you say you have a temper?"

"Not particularly, no."

Cavendish nodded sagely. "And yet, Mr. Rufus Clare is sporting a broken nose. He says you have been behaving oddly of late."

"Mr. Clare earned his injuries."

"And, Captain Rice?"

"What about Rice? His pride took a dent, but that is all."

"Captain Rice was found dead an hour ago."

"Dead! How?" Connor's four missing hours rattled around inside his chest. "He was alive and well when I left the Hall. How did he die?"

Cavendish sat motionless, although he couldn't mask the zealous gleam in his eye.

Connor leaned back in his seat and folded his arms. "If you had evidence, then you would have arrested me, already. I take it this is a fishing expedition," he said, quietly.

Footsteps in the corridor outside grew louder and someone knocked on the door.

"Come in," Cavendish said in a clipped tone, still staring at Connor.

An officer entered the room with pants and a shirt folded over his arm, a pair of shoes clamped in the other.

"You have friends in high places, Doctor Connor. I hope they don't come to regret leaping to your defence." Cavendish confirmed Connor's suspicions. "The clothes you are wearing will also be examined for blood, if you'll kindly change into these. I apologize they are not of the quality you are accustomed to." However, Cavendish didn't appear 'sorry' at all. His chair scraped across the floor as he got to his feet. "Shoes, too, if you don't mind'

It was on the tip of his tongue to say, 'and if I do?', but he knew this was more about power and making Connor jump through hoops.

"The constable will wait outside the door until you are done. That will be all for now. Have a good day."

Seconds later, Connor was left alone, with the clothes sitting on the desk in front of him. He knew Rice's blood would not be found, or did he? Those missing hours gnawed away at him. *Surely, I'd know if I murdered someone?*

Stripping off and folding his clothes neatly, he found himself scouring the fabric for stains. He smiled grimly. *I don't suppose even vampire sight is as thorough as the Kastle-Meyer Test.* In the seven years since its invention, it had gained popularity in murder enquiries. *Let's hope Rice and I don't share the same blood group. I'd hate to go down because I cut myself shaving.*

The pants he put on were three inches too short and too loose in the waistband, and the shirt, too tight and a loud yellow and red woven check. The creased, well worn, tan leather shoes were uncomfortable. Connor felt certain it was a deliberate act to humiliate him further.

He opened the interview room door and greeted the policeman outside.

With a smile, Connor said, "Thank you, constable. Inform Inspector Cavendish, I'll return these clothes to Mr. Barnum next time the circus visits London."

The constable chuckled as he went in to collect the 'suspect's' belongings.

Connor wondered if he would bump into Cavendish on the way out, but the inspector appeared to have resisted the urge to gloat. Outside the police station, he hailed a Hansom Cab and settled back in the cool gloomy interior. The coach rocked as the driver turned the horse around and headed back towards the hospital. Connor closed his eyes and tried to make sense of what he knew. *Rice was a cockroach, but who would want him dead? How did they get into Cranham Hall? And how did he die?* He guessed Cavendish must have an ace up his sleeve. *How far will he go to see me hang for murder? It seems extreme, but who knows?* Would Cavendish fabricate evidence? Connor didn't think he would go that far.

He sighed deeply and realized he'd stopped breathing for a while. Something else to watch out for, he thought. The minefield he walked through seemed to be getting bigger. Reggie had stayed the night at the Hall. *He must know something.*

Back at the hospital, Connor stopped at the front reception desk and wrote a brief note. Carrying on to the porters' staff room, he gave the envelope to a porter he knew well, asking that he deliver it to Master Cranham as soon as he saw him.

"Very well, Doctor Connor." The porter's gaze flicked down over Connor's garb, but to his credit, he kept a straight face.

"I know," Connor said, "the new tailor is not working out."

His next task was to go to his room and change, and then drop the clothes over at the homeless shelter. *That's if they don't throw them back at me.*

Chapter 13

Reggie and Connor sat side by side on a bench on the embankment, looking over the gunmetal gray waters of the River Thames. The dullness of the afternoon eased one concern for Connor, who had chosen a time late in the day to meet him at their old stamping ground.

"Where the hell have you been all day?" Reggie's annoyance was tinged with concern. "I was so relieved to get your note. I've been worried sick."

"I'm sorry, Reggie. I decided a meeting at the hospital was unwise. And, I didn't want you running out on Sir John's lecture, either. It would arouse suspicion." He carefully patted Reginald on the shoulder. "I knew you'd get word in time."

Reggie looked up and down the deserted pathway. "We're not med students hiding from lecturers any longer."

Connor grinned. "I wish my life was still that simple."

"No, I guess it's not. I thought Inspector Cavendish had taken you into custody." He darted a glance at Connor's profile. "You know who he is, of course?"

"I recognized him," said Connor, "he has risen rapidly through the ranks. Does that make him a good detective?" Connor hoped not. "Or a lucky one?"

"He's a bulldog that much I know. If he has you in the frame, he will make your life a misery until someone calls him off."

"He gave nothing away. What happened at the Hall, Reggie?" Connor felt bad asking because Reggie would be breaking the law talking to the chief suspect.

"I don't know what you said to Captain Rice, but he came back into the library and made it clear he did not enjoy meeting you." Reggie's voice dropped to a whisper but Connor's preternatural hearing caught every word like a stone thudding against a wall.

"He told father you were not the gentlemen he thought you were. He said he had seen you talking to Ivy, and you were clearly taking advantage of the poor girl."

"But that is garbage, surely your father knows that?"

The wind whipped along the embankment tossing Connor's hair into his face and for a moment, without wanting to see, he waited for Reggie's words to release him. *Sir Roger can't have believed Rice?*

Reginald's heart rate shuddered through his ribcage and the pumping blood flooding into his face could be either anger or embarrassment. Finally, he said, "Mrs. Burnham says Ivy is pregnant, but the girl won't say who the father is."

"Surely, you don't think-?" Connor's ice-white complexion, for once, reflected how he felt.

Reggie shook his head. "Of course, I don't. But, Inspector Cavendish has asked Mrs. Burnham to bring Ivy down to the station tomorrow. I think it would suit him if you were implicated."

Ivy's words to Captain Rice rang inside Connor's head. "E's a gent." *Will Cavendish twist Ivy's defense of him into something else? A girl covering for a man she has feelings for. Shit, this does not look good.*

He wondered if Malachi had any suggestions. He could just leave London. But he would be a wanted man, and the Cranham family would be left looking like fools, or worse, conspirators. *No, I have to clear my name.*

Reggie shuffled uncomfortably.

"What?" asked Connor, quietly.

Gazing out over the gray expanse of choppy water, tracking the ribbons of froth the gusting wind drove over its surface, Reggie swallowed loudly. "I'm not supposed to say, but they found your handkerchief."

Connor frowned. "Where?"

Reggie closed his eyes. "Inside Rice."

"Inside!"

"Shoved down his throat, almost into his stomach. They've taken the poker from the grate. And Rice's dagger. They think they will find the weapon."

"Shit," breathed Connor.

"You must not let it slip that I told you. I overheard Papa and Cavendish in the library. No one is supposed to know."

"Thank you, Reggie. Why didn't Cavendish arrest me? He must think he has grounds."

"My father," said Reggie. "He pointed out a monogrammed kerchief is hardly conclusive. It doesn't place you at the scene of the crime. You could have lost it, or had it taken. *And,* it was covered in coal dust. Cavendish isn't happy, but he accepts he needs more. Rice's blood was on it too, so he hopes to find blood on your clothes."

Connor remembered tossing the warm coal he had wrapped in his handkerchief along the under-stairs corridor last night, interrupting the ugly scene with Rice and Ivy. He got slowly to his feet. Suddenly, it was not so hard to move at human speed.

"I don't think we should see each other alone again. Not until this is over. I don't want you getting into trouble over this, over me."

"Rubbish, man," said Reggie briskly.

"For me. I don't want you drawn into this."

Reggie stared hard at Connor's closed expression. "Very well, if that's what you want."

"For now, yes. But, thank you, Reggie."

Connor left his friend contemplating the roiling waters of the river, and *he* felt just as much turmoil inside.

Could I have done this, murdered Rice in my 'sleep'? I don't want Reggie anywhere near. Pulling his watch from his pocket, Connor found he had an hour before his meeting with Malachi.

Chapter 14

Connor walked with a measured stride, aware of every noise occurring within the houses he passed. He stopped for a moment, when he heard children laughing, acknowledging that he could never have that: a home, a wife, children. At this moment, his path seemed all rocks and no flowers. *But, only time will tell.* As a youth, he had been told hard work was its own reward, but once he made it to London, he learned hard work needed a friend called 'good fortune'. The worst of it was, being born with a silver spoon in your mouth meant a free pass for the 'Rufus Clares' of this world.

Turning the corner, he saw yellow funnels of lamplight draped over the paving stones. Saturday evening, shops stayed open late. Shop keepers knew that men worked five and a half days a week; Saturday was payday.

From the glass frontage of a general provisions store a lava flow of light bled onto the sidewalk. Connor had the sudden urge to be among people who didn't know him and would not judge him.

Peering through the window, he saw many wares on display, packing the shelves. They ranged from cherries through to flour, and every foodstuff in between. The pendulous gas lantern overhead, suspended from a graceful arc of brass, called to shoppers like a flame to moths.

Connor changed direction and entered the shop. The bell overhead chimed and several customers automatically glanced his way and the hubbub of chatter stuttered before revving up again. The counter running the length of the shop was lined with assistants weighing, measuring, and cutting a variety of foodstuffs.

Precision was key. A measure of butter came up short on the scales. The assistant slapped another dollop on and used wooden paddles to reshape the rectangle before wrapping it. The smells were overpowering for Connor. He closed his eyes and drowned in the scent of tea, cabbage, sugar, bacon, and many more odors.

Someone jolted his arm, and Connor's eyes shot open.

"Sorry, sir, I didn't see you there." A lad peered up from beneath the peak of a too large cap. He clutched two paper parcels to his

104

chest – one smelled of bacon, the other bread, and his reddening cheeks smelled of blood.

As Connor's mouth filled with saliva, he realized he'd made a mistake. Spinning on his heel, he used every ounce of self-control to open the door slowly and step out into the street. Grinding his teeth together as he began walking once more, he glanced overhead at the darkening sky. *What was it Malachi said he had yet to learn? Hunting?* Connor decided the next hour could turn him into a murderer if he did not take care.

Up ahead several shoppers spilled out of another store, and Connor darted down a side road away from the high street. What he needed now was isolation. His footsteps echoed as he crossed to the other sidewalk on a long diagonal. He turned another corner and stopped dead in his tracks.

Was there a God? Someone trying to test him? The gleaming cap of copper hair of the man who paused beneath a street lamp to light a cigarette was unmistakable. In case Connor doubted it, the match flare died and the man lifted his face, expelling a gossamer thin plume of smoke. Even though the golden glow above bleached out the man's features, Connor's suspicions were confirmed. Rufus Clare.

Cavendish's words floated into focus in Connor's mind – 'Rufus Clare is sporting a broken nose. He says you have been behaving oddly of late.'

"Ah, if it isn't Doctor Death."

Rufus' shoes scuffed the paving stones as he sauntered forward. Connor smelled the whiskey before the man staggered sideways and gripped a metal railing to steady himself.

"Let's not do this, Clare. You are inebriated."

His brown eyes glittered as he waved the lit cigarette in the air. "I thought you'd be in a cell by now."

To add to Connor's irritation, Lester emerged from a nearby house, skipped down the steps to the street, and then froze for a moment. He quickly recovered and rushed over to join his friend.

"Doctor Connor." Lester nodded, glancing nervously at Rufus' bullish expression.

"Look at him. Doctor 'Lord All Mighty'. Strutting around as if butter wouldn't melt." Rufus weaved forward, his lack of height making it impossible to get into Connor's face. "Let's finish what you started." Tossing the cigarette aside, he unconsciously touched the ridged scar on his nose before balling his hands into fist. "C'mon. Queensbury Rules. Lester, you can call it."

The stink of whiskey helped Connor to kill his appetite. He imagined Rufus' blood tainted by it and the muscle in his jaw twitched as he clamped his mouth shut.

Rufus swung a fist and Connor dodged. He could do this all day, or rather, all night. It was like watching his opponent move through water; each movement sluggish.

"Take him home, Cartwright."

Rufus bellowed and delivered a left jab, a right cross, and then weaved until he staggered.

Lester grabbed Rufus by the arm and saved him from falling to the ground. "Ru, let's call it a night."

Connor stepped back, turned, and started walking away. He heard the scuffing of dragging feet fade into the distance. Glancing back over his shoulder, he saw both men shuffling along, Lester's arm around Rufus. In the gloom, their bodies fused into a four-legged mass. With a sigh, Connor turned away. He'd had enough of pretending, enough of human slow. His muscles burned with the effort. It was time to be alone.

Connor was three streets away within four seconds, but he still heard agonized retching, and a sharp breath hissing through Lester's teeth. He stopped and listened. A dull thud joined the cocktail of sounds, and Connor's heart felt like a stone as he resigned himself to going back.

"Help. Someone help."

Connor appeared beside Lester as he struggled with Rufus' convulsing body where it lay on the ground, vomit gurgling in his throat.

"Get out of the way, Lester. He's choking."

The young man jolted back, landed on his backside, and scrabbled further away.

Dropping to his knees, Connor rolled Rufus onto his side, as if he was no heavier than a toddler, and scooped the detritus from his mouth.

"I should have seen it coming. I should've seen it coming." Lester's muttered mantra continued, his eyes glued to his friend's face which was bleached gray by the moonlight.

"Yes, you should have. Why was he so drunk? Celebrating?" *Celebrating my downfall.* Connor kept the thought to himself.

"It's his birthday," Lester said quietly. "He's jealous of you. That's why he acts like a raging bull when you are around. We all are, envious, at least."

Connor rested back on his haunches and watched Rufus' still face, listening to his breathing whistling through a raw throat.

"You shouldn't envy me. My life is not a bed of roses, trust me."

"You always get it right, Sanderson." Lester waved a hand towards where Rufus' lay, passed out, but out of danger. "I couldn't even roll him over. Couldn't even save my friend."

Connor looked at the young man's anxious face. "You've heard the term 'dead weight'? Don't be too hard on yourself. An unconscious body feels two times as heavy." Panicking didn't help, but Connor didn't lay that at Lester's door. The youth had enough guilt to deal with.

"Call me, Connor. And I know it will be difficult, but *try* and get Rufus off my back."

Groaning as he surfaced, Rufus spat foul smelling dribble onto the sidewalk and rolled slowly over onto his back, keeping his eyes closed.

"Get him home, Lester. You can break the news that I saved his life in the morning." Rising to his feet, Connor grinned. This time, he set off at a brisk walk until he was out of sight, then moved up to a fast run that made him invisible to the human eye.

Chapter 15

Connor stood on the parapet on the roof of the hospital, wondering if the gathering fog was thinner than usual, or if his eyes just cut through it easier. He knew the moment Malachi arrived, although he couldn't say how. The breeze? The smell? The drop in temperature, even though it was chilly on the roof top? No matter.

"Why are you standing here? The plan was to meet in the park and go hunting, as I recall."

Without turning around, Connor said, "Malachi, did I kill Rice?"

"You need to ask, Connor?" Malachi's paper-thin laughter crackled in the night.

"Damn right, I need to ask. I can't remember." Dragging a hand down over his tight face, Connor said, "I'm not safe out there."

"Hunting might be the last thing on your mind, but I am here to make sure you don't do anything stupid." Malachi stood beside Connor and admired the view. "You still need to hunt, and *then* you can find the killer and hand him over to the police."

It was Connor's turn to laugh. "My need to master hunting is very much at the front of my mind. I've had an eventful evening. I also learned something very disturbing."

What did you learn? Malachi's voice filled Connor's head much like the haze Rufus had expelled when smoking. *Thoughts can't be overheard.*

My handkerchief.

What about it?

It was inside Rice. Connor looked at Malachi's profile, his skin appeared almost translucent. Aloud, Connor said, "If it wasn't me, then it was you."

"That would be too easy, don't you think? There are more vampires in London than you can imagine."

Connor nodded. "But it's a huge coincidence that Rice is connected to me. To Lavinia. And now he's dead."

"Let's hunt. Talking can wait, you won't find a killer with a shriveled brain." Malachi thumped Connor on the shoulder and leapt over the parapet. He dropped like a stone until the fog swallowed him. Connor sighed and launched himself into the void. *Using stairs is clearly not an option.*

Landing on the sidewalk, Connor automatically scanned the streets for movement. Malachi was a speck in the distance and Connor felt irritated. The feeling of eyes watching made him slow to follow. *What did Malachi say? There are more vampires in London than I know about?*

At the corner, he found Malachi leaning against the railings.

"You waited? Feeling sorry for me?" Connor grinned.

"That would be a waste of time. Learning to hunt is crucial, but remaining undetected, even more so. You can hunt foxes and badgers, even rabbits. Hunting is hunting. But the best place to get the human blood you need will be the hospice, or perhaps the emergency room. There are a few there who will welcome our attention."

"So, what's first?"

"First, we learn how to *feel*. Come." Malachi dropped to the ground.

Connor realized they were standing by a manhole cover.

With long bony fingers, Malachi easily dislodged and lifted the iron lid. "After you."

Barely pausing to look into the hole at the glimmer of draining water, Connor stepped out over the edge. The air in the sewer was thick with moisture and rancid odors. Automatically, Connor stopped breathing. It became pitch-black when Malachi pulled the manhole cover back into place, and scum-filmed water splashed up over his pants when Malachi landed two feet away, at his shoulder.

At first, he thought he couldn't see anything, but after a moment, he picked out texture in the darkness. Water glistened on the walls of the sewer. *Light must be getting in from somewhere.*

Looking up ahead, Connor made out a storm drain framed by light, defused like a cloud of frost. He tuned into the whisper of trickling water, the thin rivulets of condensation running down the walls and into the pooled water in which they stood. High-pitched scratching caught his attention next, overlaid by a snuffling sound.

"Rats," said Malachi, in answer to Connor's thought. "Sewer rats."

Connor wrinkled his nose. The scratchy scampering sounds thickened as more rodents began to move. The arrival of the intruders had made the rat population freeze, but, with darkness restored, and no movement detected, the creatures resumed their scurrying back and forth, doing whatever it was that rats do.

Please tell me we're not here to drink rat blood. Connor looked at the vague smudge of Malachi's face.

The challenge is to catch a rat without crushing it. A test of speed and control. Whenever you are ready.

Connor flexed his fingers and tuned into the noises. Dropping slowly down into a crouch, he lowered his hands until his fingertips skimmed the film of scum coating the water. He felt the ripples rushing over the surface. He waited until water splashed onto his hand and he detected the radiating heat of flesh, and then his hand darted out and he felt wet waxy fur in his grasp. The popping sound of tiny bones cracking surprised him, the minute explosion vibrated through his palm. The heartbeat stopped suddenly.

He didn't need Malachi's short sharp thought bolt of *'again'*, to tell him he had failed. Releasing the body to drift away in the sluicing current, Connor lay in wait, again. Twice more, the ribcage of his catch imploded with a wet pop.

Take a breath, Connor.

He didn't really want to obey Malachi, already anticipating the stench. *Why?*

You'll see why.

Breathing out first, emptying his body of stored stale air, Connor inhaled carefully through his nose. Dozens of threads of different odors filtered through him and he understood why. He sensed that the rats had different smells, so it was a matter of working out what that meant.

Three more carcasses later: one snapped spine, one crumbled pelvis, and one with burst lungs, Connor understood. The fourth rat he chose, wriggled in his hand and gnawed at his hard flesh, but was unhurt. Its accelerated heartbeat pulsed the blood in a drumbeat which made Connor's mouth water. However, he thought of the slick matted coat of his prey and found it easy to resist.

Like dogs can smell cancer in humans, Connor detected the calcium deposits denoting skeletal strength in the rats.

Now the catching part was over, Malachi spoke aloud. "Each species has its own 'tell'. The strongest are also the most nutritious. Except in humans, where we, through necessity, pick off the weak. Allowing humans to believe monsters are only in their dreams works better for us."

"So we aren't here to dine on rats?"

"There may come a time when you will do precisely that. But, for tonight, no. This is purely the first part in your survival training."

Wiping his hands down the side of his pants, Connor wondered where he'd be if Cavendish wanted this set of clothes. Silvery moonlight suddenly streaming in overhead nudged Connor into action. Malachi was on the move, and waiting for him.

As Malachi dropped the manhole cover back into place, Connor asked, "What now? Slugs?"

Malachi clucked his tongue in disapproval and took off along the deserted street. Connor knew they were headed east, but other than that, he felt like a child being dragged along by a hurrying parent. *Time is short.* The words bled into his mind. He was becoming expert at distinguishing his own thoughts from Malachi's. But what did that mean? He repeated the thought over again, hoping for an answer. The wind felt exhilarating as the buildings became a blurred wall of the reds, oranges, and cream colors of their facades.

The gas lights thinned and finally disappeared as they headed out into the countryside. Malachi passed through a gap in the tall hedgerows and eventually, when he came to a halt, they were in a forest. It was not Richmond or Greenwich, they were Royal Parks and a drop in deer numbers would be noticed.

"Where-" Connor stopped at Malachi's penetrating look, although the sharp 'shhhh' echoing inside his brain felt like it would crack his skull. Connor's irritation grew.

It is early, so time is not short. Why the hell are we here?

Laughter rang inside his head and Malachi bared yellow teeth to show his amusement was real. It struck Connor, for the first time, how used to Malachi's hideous appearance he had become. Once seen, never forgotten would fit him well. He would inhabit a human's nightmares for years. Monsters existed, *they* just didn't know it.

It is not the hour that is late. Time is running out for you. You need to feed.

As soon as Connor heard those thoughts, his mind shifted into overdrive. He noticed the muscles in his thighs were cramping after their run. *Is that usual?* Were his hands stiffer than before? He flexed his fingers and regretted passing on the rat he caught earlier. Paranoia began crawling through his mind, until Malachi placed a hand on his shoulder.

You're wasting time. What creatures can you see, hear, smell?

Closing his eyes, Connor tuned into the undergrowth. Snuffling sounds became amplified, and he picked out a rhythmic noise of chewing. He could smell grass as teeth tore it from the ground, releasing the odor. Then he detected the thick scent of blood pumping behind flesh and the creak of muscle fibers.

Track down the sound. Malachi nodded as Connor opened his eyes and scanned the trees.

Like hotspots in his sensory map, the clusters of warm blood inside five nearby mammals clamored for his attention. Connor had to choose. Did he try for the biggest target, or the closest? Venom scented saliva flooded into his mouth as he emptied his mind and reflexes took over. Speed was the weapon which his prey could not escape. Connor plunged through the forest, bumping his shoulder into a tree and unleashing a distracting cascade of autumn leaves. Connor used that distraction to chase down a fallow deer. The splashes of white fur on its pelt glowed like beacons for Connor, as he closed the distance, blind siding the young buck before it could run.

The deer swung its head like a club, and its horns, crested by blades of flattened bone, tore into Connor's shirt at his shoulder. He ducked his head and buried his face into the buck's neck, his arms wrapped around the animal's ribcage as the impact knocked the deer over onto its side. Without letting his human side take stock, Connor was unerringly drawn to the thundering pulse of the carotid artery below the smooth pelt of fur, and he bit down hard.

Blood pumped in a geyser, hitting the back of his throat in a suffocating tide, but he didn't need to breathe, just swallow in time with the pulsing flow until the heart stopped beating and the river of blood dried up.

The exhilaration Connor felt was like the flare of a lit fuse rushing through his veins. He felt his flesh become plumper, the cells in his body welcoming the saturation. Getting to his feet, he smiled.

"You had better throw that shirt in the hospital incinerator when you return," Malachi said, as he appeared beside his student. "Your police inspector will think you have become a mass murderer, in a heartbeat."

Connor laughed drily. In the gloom, the front of his pale shirt appeared black. The sweet smell of blood filled the air. He should feel revulsion, but he did not. Examining the deer carcass with its ruptured throat, he asked, "What now?"

"A shallow grave. Return to the earth that which nature provided. Scavengers will dine well tonight, and the earth will take the rest, in time."

Connor nodded before scuffing around in the banks of autumn leaves, looking for a damp soft area before dropping to his knees and scooping out a deer sized hollow in the earth. Handling the dead animal with gentle reverence was an unexpected instinct. Somewhere deep inside, he felt sorrow at ending the life of another creature. He understood acutely what survival of the fittest meant, and he could show his gratitude in a small way. He found some broadleaved bracken to place over the buck's face before covering it with a shallow layer of earth and mulch.

Malachi stood quietly watching, and Connor thought the hunting lesson was over.

Brushing the earth and dust from his pants, he joined his mentor.

"That is the body attended too, but you must feed your brain. Do you remember what I told you? Only human blood can hydrate it, and travel up past the brain stem. Come."

Connor's body crawled with distaste, but he knew he did not have the luxury of choice. *Perhaps, I'll choose death once my name is cleared, but until then, I'll do whatever it takes.*

He recognized the large functional building which loomed up ahead. St Thomas' hospital was near the River Thames. Connor felt a moment's relief. We aren't attacking a random stranger, then. It will be someone whose time has come.

Vampire speed meant Connor and Malachi entered the hospital and searched the critical care unit and the men's surgical wards without being noticed. If a night nurse registered them at all, it was just the chill as though someone had opened a window.

Sitting beside the bed of his chosen prey, Connor held the bony hand, and knew the smell of decay and the paper-thin crackle of skin would forever haunt him. *Do you ever forget your first victim?*

Malachi slowly shook his head.

The man's breathing rattled quietly in his throat, the shallow movement barely moving his chest beneath the white linen sheet.

"How do you know it's his time?" Connor asked Malachi.

Although, Malachi had the same skeletal gaunt features, his eyes were alive with sharp intellect. Connor assessed the peaceful grin on his mentor's face. "You are a doctor. You *know* it is time."

Cannulas used to administer intravenous drugs had left pinprick holes along the old man's thin arms. They had all been removed – no longer making any difference. Healing was slow and some of the sites remained inflamed.

"How do I do this without leaving a mark? Causing suspicion?"

"You'll be surprised. He is not expected to last the night. No postmortem or real time will be spent examining his body, but, luckily for us, we have everything on hand to make *certain* no one knows. With a wry grin, Malachi's form stuttered in a strobing effect, as he crossed the room and returned before the dim light could track the movement. "Here."

He held out a syringe.

Lifting the old man's arm gently, Connor placed a thumb where he expected to find the brachial artery in the patient's stick-thin limb. Trying not to think too closely about why he was doing it, he slid the needle beneath the fragile skin and watched the ruby nectar pour eagerly into the syringe barrel. Even though Connor knew the science – blood, just like air under pressure, poured out if a puncture was made – it still seemed odd how blood appeared so keen to rush out of a body. Thirst scratched at Connor's throat as the thick sweet scent filled the air.

Instinctively knowing that one would not be enough, he deftly removed the full chamber and inserted another needle in its place and filled that syringe, too. He very gently extracted the final needle, leaned back, and prepared to step away.

"You still need to feed. Until your transformation is complete, you have to *feed* to unlock the gate. Just take a little."

Connor had remembered drinking was not feeding, so he felt prepared. He sealed his mouth over the seeping hole left by the needle. The blood needed encouragement, but trapping flesh between his teeth, he managed to create a flow that warmed his throat and dropped into his chest. The buzz in his skull gave him the sign he needed. It allowed him to stop.

Without looking at Malachi, Connor took the syringes his mentor held out, and drank the blood from them both, pushing the plungers down fast and discharging the contents into the back of his throat.

Returning the patient's arm to his side, Connor felt the sluggish pulse still throbbing. He felt better that the old man still hung onto life.

Following Malachi, Connor dropped both the syringes into the incinerator bin as he walked out of the door. The porter wheeling supplies along the slick, waxed floors appeared to freeze in place as Connor and Malachi moved so much faster than him, and their wake fluttered the papers on the clipboard which sat on top of his load.

The chalk-white walls of the hospital corridor began to glimmer with silver fragments. The odor of starch told Connor a nurse was sitting just inside the ward door they were walking past, even though it was closed; listening to the whispered breathing of sleeping patients, he knew without thinking that there were seven occupied beds. Human blood sharpened his senses and lit up areas of his brain in ways the deer had not. Connor enjoyed the feeling and could see how intoxicating and addictive it could be.

Outside on the sidewalk both vampires paused, taking stock of the cloudy night and damp atmosphere. Connor felt condensation forming on his cold skin.

The journey back to St George's Circus was completed in silence. Malachi kept even his *thoughts* to himself.

When they arrived outside the side entrance to Connor's domain, waving a bony hand in Connor's direction, Malachi said, "Don't forget, burn your clothes."

Connor glanced down at the shirt front stiffened by dried deer blood. When he looked up again, Malachi had disappeared.

Checking his watch, he was shocked to realize barely an hour had passed since the confrontation with Rufus and Lester. Time no longer had meaning.

In the last two days, for him, so much had changed, and he felt rattled by the uncertainty of the future. Connor knew Reggie's version of what had happened at the Hall last night, but, left alone with his thoughts, he found himself worrying about Lavinia. *Does she hate me now?* He admitted that, although there was no future for them, he cared what Lavinia thought of him.

Chapter 16

Drinking animal blood merely blunts the edge of hunger. Running his tongue over sharp teeth, he could still taste his last meal. The streets of London offered the ultimate high; human blood. Standing in the shadows, he watched the rolling stride of men leaving the public house. The laughter inside escaped into the chilly night every time a patron left to make their drunken way home. The door swinging shut behind them snuffed out the revelry like wind dousing a flame.

But where is the fun in that? Inebriation contaminated the flavor and left an unpleasant after taste for vampires. Having heightened senses had its draw backs.

A couple poured out through the doors, letting it close behind them, the golden glow through the glass framed their silhouette as they stopped to steal a kiss. This was more interesting. Snatching happiness away from feeble humans, those who thought life was good and they had control, now that was more exciting.

He smiled, watching their stuttering gaits as they walked along the sidewalk opposite to his hiding place, trying to match their strides and still embrace at the same time.

They could have been entertaining. But, in the hunt for human blood to refresh his brain, he focused on a more enjoyable prospect.

Kicking up a gusting breeze which caused the young couple to stop giggling and check the street around them, he left his cloak of shadow, and launched himself down the sidewalk and headed for Vauxhall Bridge as the closest route over the river.

His coat flared behind as he hit his top speed and he skimmed along the country lanes until the familiar outline of Cranham Hall rose into the night sky and carved its angular shape into the lilac tinted horizon.

Dawn was on its way and time was short. *But, there is enough.*

Slowing to a walk, he enjoyed the crunch of the gravel driveway beneath his solid weight. Like all alpha males, knowing that he was at the top of the food chain made discovery more dangerous for any unfortunate creature who came across him. He feared no one.

Leaping lightly over the gate into the stable yard, he was greeted by the clatter of hooves and nervous whinny of the Cranhams' horses. Pausing to look inside one stable, he recognized Sabre. The black coat gleamed, accentuating the bellowing of the stallion's lungs as panic set in. The whites of his eyes flashed as the horse strained to detect from where danger may strike.

Not tonight Sabre. Tonight, you are safe.

Moving silently on, he ducked into the tack room and took a horseshoe nail from the box on a shelf, and then headed to the rear entrance. One gloved hand gripped the handle, holding the door still as he used the nail to grind open the lock. He did not want his forced entry to be obvious.

Now, at best, the lock has worn and the barrels are harder to turn. The butler will get the handyman to grease it. When that made no difference, then a locksmith would be called in. *Things wear out, after all.*

Stepping inside, he closed the door and took a deep breath. Smells from the kitchen filled the air. Bread had been baked. The evening meal had been pheasant and venison and desert was something with apples. The fire grates had been brushed clean ready for the morning. The servants would be stirring soon. Ivy would come down the stone stairs at four a.m. and fill the coal buckets to set the fires in the upstairs rooms ready for the family.

He sat in the rocking chair and waited. He could see the door, but he would hear her first in any case. She slept in the attic in a room which was hot and stuffy in summer and so cold her breath came in plumes in winter. The tweeny was on the bottom rung of the ladder and had the worst of everything, including pay and rations, but a roof over her head and food in her belly were a luxury to the Ivy's of the world.

The family should evict the girl now. Becoming pregnant was disgraceful. But who is the father? He grinned. That is the only thing that is staying the hand of Lord Cranham. The girl should be paid off and sent back to the workhouse, but he heard the Cranhams were decent people.

Still, they won't need to worry for much longer.

His smile became broader as he heard the whisper of feet on the stone stairs. The girl tried to be quiet. Mrs. Burnham was asleep in the house-keeper's rooms at the end of the corridor leading off the kitchen. It wouldn't do to wake her.

Shall I surprise Ivy here, or wait until she's making up the fire in the upstairs parlour. Motes of dust danced in the air where a funnel of light cut through the kitchen. Her lantern held out in front of her, Ivy didn't notice the figure sitting quietly in cook's chair.

Clutching her pinafore in one hand, Ivy hung the lantern on the cast iron hook set into the wall beside the open fireplace, and then dipped her chin to put the apron over her head. Suddenly, the apron strings were pulled tight, and before Ivy could cry out, a gloved hand gripped her face. Pulling her soft body hard against his chest, savoring the surge of heat in her cheeks as waves of terror stiffened every muscle in her body, he enjoyed the moment of anticipation. With a sharp wrench on her jaw, he whipped her head round and her spine gave way with an ear popping crack. He held her up as her legs sagged, her arms swung down by her sides and she hung there like a puppet with cut strings.

He stepped backward taking her with him, and then eased her back into the rocking chair. After tilting her head to one side, he closed her eyelids.

Taking a knife from the butchers' block, he pierced the pad of Ivy's thumb. The blood oozed slowly. He lowered her hand allowing gravity to work until a perfect red pearl glistened. With no heart to pump it out, it swelled slowly. He pulled a scrap of torn fabric from his pocket and blotted the cut, watching the stain grow into a snowflake of crimson, the size of a copper penny.

Folding the cloth and pushing it back into his pocket, he arranged her hands in her lap and left her there. He wished he could stay to see Mrs. Burnham's indignation at Ivy neglecting her duties and sleeping on the job, only to discover she was dead.

That would be so sweet, but he had to return to London before sunrise. *Perhaps next time.*

Chapter 17

Connor splashed his face with water and wiped it dry. Looking in the mirror, he made sure the white flecks of his shaving foam were gone. It was the same face which had stared back at him, every morning, for twenty-four years, but somehow, it was very different.

He had taken Malachi's advice and tossed the blood-stained shirt and pants down the incinerator chute in the early hours before dawn.

He tried to relax on his bed, but ended up pacing the floor. *Who killed Rice?* Last night, Malachi had changed the subject and used misdirection. It wasn't until afterwards, that Connor realized he had not given up any information about these 'other vampires'. *Maybe there aren't any. Perhaps the truth is closer to home.*

Attending Sir John's lectures usually featured as a high point for Connor. He knew he still had a lot to learn. But, today, the schedule weighed him down, like carrying a millstone on his back. He'd lose his place on the surgical team if Sir John noticed his absence, but then, being suspected of murder would do that, too.

I'm sure Reggie will cover for me, if he can. Pulling on a tailored jacket and checking his pocket watch, Connor left the students' quarters and, projecting calm he did not feel, made his way to the main entrance. He turned up his collar against the blustery rain and headed towards the front door.

"Doctor Connor, sir."

From behind the reception desk, a young receptionist flushed when he turned his head.

The girl had brown curls and a tentative smile. "I have a letter for you, Doctor. The young lady who delivered it said it was urgent."

Frowning as he took the envelope from her unsteady hand, Connor softened his appearance with a smile. "Thank you-?"

"Grace," she murmured. "Grace Watkin. I'm new here." Her eyes matched the brown hair and she played with a chain around her throat.

"Thank you, Grace."

She flushed pink, and the rush of blood was distracting, but Connor held onto his smile, lifted a hand in thanks, and walked away.

Pausing inside the doorway, he tore open the lemon-colored envelope he knew must be from Lavinia.

'Connor, meet me at Lyons Tea Room. The Strand Palace Hotel near Covent Garden. I must talk to you urgently. L.'

Connor frowned. The Tea Room was a newly opened establishment. He had never been there and he doubted that Lavinia had either. The choice of venue exuded secrecy. *That can't be good.* The abrupt note gave nothing away. *Something is wrong.*

Outside on the sidewalk, he hailed a Hackney Carriage. Once inside, he sat drumming his fingers on his thigh and watching, but not really seeing, the scattering of pedestrians hurrying along, jostling beneath a sea of umbrellas. Unrelenting rain ran from the paving stones and filled the gutters with rushing water. The soot stained clouds promised many hours of wet misery – and Connor rejoiced. It was one less hazard on his radar.

Alighting from the carriage, Connor paid the driver and ran up the steps into the tea room. Within seconds, he spotted Lavinia seated at a square table against the wall. The room bustled with diners, many of them accompanied by children – girls dressed in bows and boys with slicked back hair. Lyons Tea Room was clearly becoming a place for treats to be shared between grandparents and precious offspring.

Connor, not wanting to move too quickly, waited for a sign that he had registered with those in the room. Whipping across the space like a tornado would be hard to explain. His emotions were running high – he wasn't sweating, but he wasn't blinking either.

Despite his preoccupation, Connor appreciated the splendor of the establishment. The ceiling was impossibly high. Marble pillars supported by ornate square plinths ran in two rows across the room. Georgian panels gave the walls texture and above the grand fireplace sat a gilt enamelled coat of arms.

He turned his fixed smile up a notch when Lavinia saw him, at last.

She stood and raised a hand.

Connor slowly released a sigh, which eased the tension inside his chest, and concentrated on planning his movements and weaving a fluid path between the tables.

Taking Lavinia's gloved hand in his, he dipped his head in a bow of greeting. He waited until she subsided into her seat before sitting down opposite her and pulling his chair in closer to the table. Finally, he took a deep breath and noticed how pale she looked. Foundation cake could not mask the dark smudges beneath her brown eyes.

The tension he felt humming inside her eased a little as she removed her hat, concentrated on replacing the hat pin securely in the dark rose fabric, and then arranged it on the cushion of an empty seat at the table.

"This is not your usual dining establishment," said Connor, scanning the sea of tables. The crisp array of rectangular covers were so white, they seemed to glow beneath the crystal chandeliers. Even the driving rain outside could not dim the elated mood of the diners.

Lavinia appeared absorbed in arranging her silverware, but a small frown flitted across her features before good breeding covered her emotions beneath a placid air.

"When you see Reggie, tell him I had a run in with Rufus last night." Connor chuckled drily. "I saved him from choking. He'll hate me even more, now."

Lavinia smiled, but Connor knew he had failed to lighten her mood.

Touching the bone china teapot and finding it cold, with a raised eyebrow, Connor asked, "How long have you been waiting?"

"About an hour, but it's perfectly fine. I just needed to speak to you."

"What has happened?"

"It's Ivy."

"I know, she's pregnant. Reggie told me," Connor said quietly. "I also know Rice said the baby is mine, before he died." He reached across the table and took Lavinia's cold hand. "You know that is untrue. But, you must look out for her. I believe *Rice* treated her very badly. You must see the girl is looked after and not sent to the work house."

Lavinia stiffened and withdrew her hand. "You seem very concerned."

Connor sat back and scanned her tight face. She was no longer a carefree girl. He easily sensed the turmoil she battled with. "I apologize. I have no right to tell your father how he should handle the family affairs," he said, gently.

Tears glistened in Lavinia's eyes, and Connor reached for her hand again. He stroked her fingers as though each one was made of spun glass, and for him, that was not so far from the truth.

"Linny, please, you can't believe I would use Ivy. You know me better than that."

The last time he had called her Linny, she had been thirteen and in her playroom. Connor used to tease her, but once he detected her 'crush', he took refuge behind formality to save her heartbreak.

"No, I don't believe that of you." She gripped his hand and her knuckles blanched white.

"What do you need to tell me? You're scaring me." Connor forced a reassuring smile, but he realized his words were true. Dread sat like a stone inside his chest. He concentrated harder on replicating human breathing and not breaking the bones in her fragile hand.

A tear ran down her cheek. "Ivy. She's dead."

For what seemed an eternity, Connor stared at her face. The tear left a pale mark in its path and, without thinking, he reached out and ran his thumb over it. "How? What happened?" he said, gently.

She should her head. "No, you don't understand. She was *killed*."

"What?" Shock jolted through him. Connor imagined a fall. An accident. But then a small voice inside him said, 'liar'. He just wanted it to be so. He slumped in his seat. "How did she die?"

"I don't know for sure. The police are up at the Hall. I wanted to warn you." Her eyes darted to his face. "And no, I don't think you did it. I swear. But after you being questioned about Matthew, Captain Rice, I just thought I should warn you."

One word hurt him more than it should. *She thought of him as 'Matthew'.* That was a shock. He tuned back in as she spoke again.

"The servants are saying her neck was broken." Lavinia gulped down a mouthful of cold tea to ease her dry throat.

"She couldn't have fallen?"

Lavinia shook her head. "No, Mr. Phelps told Papa she was sitting in Mrs. Burnham's chair." A bubble of hysterical laughter erupted before she swallowed it down. "It was Mrs. Burnham shouting at Ivy that woke Mr. Phelps. She woke the whole house, I think."

Her cup rattled in its saucer when she carefully placed it down. Connor gathered both her hands on the crisp white table cloth and covered them with his own. "I'm so sorry."

Lavinia, because she had grown up at the Hall, had eaten cakes in the servants' hall and played below stairs. Ivy was invisible to the family, her low station made that usual. But not to Connor, who used the tradesman's entrance often as a youth. And not to Lavinia, either. Ivy was a friend.

"Thank you for telling me."

"I knew you would want to know. You liked Ivy. And I know she liked you, too." At his sudden probing look, she hurried on, "I know she was smitten, Connor. But I also know you are above reproach."

'Thank you, for that," Connor's grateful smile lit his eyes. What Lavinia thought, really mattered.

Glancing at the ornate clock on the wall, she sighed and slowly picked up her hat. "I better return home before they miss me."

"Of course. If Inspector Cavendish is involved, I know he bears a grudge. He will find a way to use Ivy's crush as a motive against me. Reggie said she was due to be interviewed today. It doesn't look good. But Linny-"

He waited until she pushed the pin into her hat, pulled on her gloves, and looked at him.

"Don't worry about me. Promise? I'll be alright."

"Just be careful, Connor."

"I will. I promise you that." Tugging on her fingers, Connor said, "I'll put you in a carriage."

With a weak smile, Lavinia nodded and got to her feet.

Resting his hand at the small of her back, he guided her through the sea of diners and out onto the sidewalk. The rain still fell, and they stopped inside the porch-front of the Tea Room.

Turning to look down at her, Connor lifted her chin. Strands of glossy black hair framed her anxious face. He missed the impish flirtatious girl of the last few years and suddenly realized he was a blind fool. He cared much more than he should. He couldn't let the word 'love' pass his lips, but even though his heart was dead, he still felt it.

"Take care, Linny. You are very special to me."

He knew she would kiss him, and he should move away, but he stayed. Her lips were warm and sweet as she ran her hand into the hair at his nape, and pressed her mouth to his. It was a stolen second for her, but he drowned in it for an eternity.

She glanced up through dark lashes, daring him to be grumpy.

With a smile, he darted out into the rain and hailed a cab. Handing her up into the carriage, Connor kissed the palm of her hand, in an intimate gesture he couldn't resist, and said, "Stay safe." He shut the door, stepped back, and stood in the downpour watching the departing carriage jostle for a place in the stream of traffic and disappear around the corner.

Chapter 18

Connor walked back to the hospital, lost in thought. Rain from his hair ran down over his face and beneath his collar, and passersby changed direction when they saw him striding towards them.

How long have I got before Cavendish comes for me? It was not until he turned the last corner, that he noticed the downpour. Sluicing the water from his face and scraping back his hair, he tried to look at least halfway human once more. Changing his mind about using the front entrance, he headed down the side of the building, tracking along railings which resembled a row of stout black spears. Checking around and finding the street quiet, he vaulted smoothly over the top and swung up onto the concrete ledge of the first-floor window. Repeating the maneuver, he worked his way up three levels and forced the latch on the window of his room.

Dropping inside, he grabbed a towel and dried his hair, stripped off his clothes and dropped them into the enamel bath. The clean shirt clung to his cold damp flesh as he hurriedly dressed. With a quick check in the mirror, he pulled his white coat from the tallboy wardrobe and left the room.

Moments later, he swung through the door into the nurses' station and stopped at the counter.

"Good morning, sister."

With a smile, she handed Connor the clipboard holding the list of patients. Scanning the pages, Connor said, "Mr. Hodge. Is he still complaining of sharp pain?"

"Yes, Doctor. He says the pain is still the same."

Connor frowned. Mr. Hodge was a surgical patient admitted when metal filings became embedded in the cornea of his left eye. Sir John operated, but could not save his sight.

"I'll look in on him, now," Connor said, walking away slowly until the sister caught up.

The side ward had eight beds in total. Connor stopped beside the fourth one on the left, and the sister drew the curtain along the rail until the illusion of privacy was complete.

The man in the bed had other problems, too. Ulcers wept on both legs, not helped by poor circulation, and he would be discharged from The Royal Eye Hospital, only to be admitted to a general hospital. Mr. Hodge had both eyes closed, although he opened them a crack when Connor arrived.

"Hey, Doc," he muttered.

"Mr. Hodge," Connor glanced at the clipboard. "How are you feeling today?"

"Just hurts like blazes. You said it would be better by now."

"It should be. Let's take a look. Eye-drops please, sister."

Taking a light-pen from his pocket, Connor eased the eyelid open and passed the light over the opaque orb. He could not see any redness on the rim of the eye or post-operative inflammation of the eyelid. "It should feel more comfortable by now, Mr. Hodge. There is no discharge." Connor pressed gently around the eye socket. "Any tenderness?"

"No," the patient admitted, almost grudgingly. "But it hurts. At night, mostly."

Connor pulled up a chair and put the clipboard down. "Are you going to tell me what's going on?"

Although Hodge blinked both eyes rapidly, tears still escaped onto his cheeks.

Connor scanned the wooden bedside table where a photo of a smiling, happier Mr. Hodge had an arm around a slight woman. Three small children used her skirts for balance, or as a hiding place, Connor couldn't be sure which.

"You can tell me," Connor said, gently.

The man sniffed. "It's the hospital."

"Sorry? What do you mean?"

"My Lucy. She can't pay the bus-fare to the General. I'll never see 'er, or the kids, if I goes there."

Connor sighed. "Sadly, Mr. Hodge, staying here isn't going to help Lucy or yourself, in the long run." He patted the man on the shoulder. "I have a better idea. You provide the sister with your home address, and I'll see to it that Lucy can afford the bus-fare."

"I can't do that."

"Yes, you can." Connor stood up. "You'll be doing me a favor. I haven't done a good deed for a while. Let me do this one for you." He left the ward wishing everything in life was so simple.

His next stop was Sir John's office. Mr. Donaghue's post mortem results would be ready by now, and Sir John would expect Connor to show an interest in the patient. Usually, he would be eager, but it had dropped down the list of his priorities of late.

Knocking on Sir John's door, Connor detected two sets of lungs breathing.

"Come in." Sir John's clipped tone seemed softened by distraction.

Entering the room – the door presenting no problem now Connor was accustomed to his own strength – he stopped in mid stride as Inspector Cavendish rose from the seat facing Sir John's desk.

"Sanderson, I was about to send for you," Sir John said, heavily. "Inspector Cavendish wants to talk to you."

Cavendish smiled. If malice had an odor, then Connor was certain it smelled like the mix of hormones radiating from the inspector.

"Doctor Sanderson." Cavendish did not look away as he said, "Thank you, Sir John."

His mentor bristled. "This man is my student. Surely you can divulge why you are looking for him. I might be able to help."

"I'm sorry, sir. It is police business. There's nothing more I can say."

Connor returned Cavendish's even glare.

"If you wouldn't mind, Sanderson, I'd like you to come down to the station."

"Of course." Connor turned to leave before turning back briefly. "Sir John, can I ask you to inform Reginald Cranham that I am helping the police with their enquiries. He is expecting me to dine with him later."

Cavendish reached out to lay a hand on Connor's shoulder, but changed his mind at Connor's ice-cold stare.

◇◇◇

Half an hour later, Connor faced Cavendish across the table in an interview room. Dark rings left by tea and coffee cups stained its surface, as well as deep scratches, where, he guessed, anxious detainees left to stew needed something to distract them.

Cavendish made a show of shuffling papers and making notes, and Connor adopted a relaxed, 'I've got all day' pose. When a constable entered the room and silently took a seat in the corner, Connor got the feeling things were becoming more serious.

"Firstly, Doctor Sanderson, I must read you your Miranda rights." Clearly enjoying himself, Cavendish said, "...You do not have to say anything, but it may harm your defense if you do not mention, when questioned…"

Connor knew the drill and tuned it out, running through the possibilities of what could lay in store. *If he's detaining me, he must have something. But what?*

"You understand we have twenty-four hours to charge you?"

Connor nodded.

"We have a search warrant for your room at the hospital. My officers are there, now."

Connor raised an eyebrow.

"Do you have anything to say?" Cavendish seemed disappointed when Connor remained calm.

"I'll answer any questions you put to me, Inspector. I can't really contribute to this little chat without knowing why I am here."

Leaning back in his chair, Cavendish clasped his hands behind his head and stared at Connor. "It's an interesting world, don't you think?"

"Very much so. I enjoy it when people surprise me." Connor reluctantly said, "Thank you for not arresting me in front of Sir John."

"If you'd resisted, I would have. Talking of Sir John. Doctors hold a position of trust. I'm sure you'd agree."

"All human beings should be trustworthy, in my view," Connor replied.

"But with authority comes power," Cavendish mused aloud. "Have you heard of Doctor Crippen? He was an eye and ear specialist, I believe."

"I've heard of him, yes."

"Now, he killed his wife. Once the appeal process runs its course, he faces being hung in Pentonville." Cavendish unlinked his hands and sat forward once more. "Now, where were we? Ah yes, do you know Ivy Tindel?"

"Of course, she works at Cranham Hall."

"Just so." Cavendish placed a photograph face down on the desk. "When did you last see Ivy?"

No one knows I saw her with Rice two nights ago. Connor decided to bend the truth. About a week ago. The last time I saw her, I was having a cup of tea with the housekeeper, Mrs. Burnham."

"Where were you last night, Doctor Sanderson?"

"I saw Reginald Cranham for a short while, then walked back to the hospital."

"Did anyone see you return to the hospital?"

"No."

Cavendish flipped the photograph over. In it, Ivy was lying back in Mrs. Burnham's chair sleeping. "Ivy is dead, Doctor Sanderson. But I'm sure you know that already."

Does he know about Lavinia's visit? Connor didn't think so. Another lie hatched. "No, I didn't know." Connor turned the photo and took a closer look. "How? What happened?"

"A broken neck. The assailant knew what he was doing. Very strong. Wore gloves and inflicted localized damage to the third and fourth vertebrae. Medical man, it seems."

"I wish I knew something, anything. But I can't help you, Inspector. I'm sorry."

Cavendish silently retrieved the photograph.

"If you remember anything that can help find her killer, then let us know." Cavendish glanced at his watch. "Suspending the interview at sixteen hundred hours. You'll spend a night in the cells. We're holding you until the search warrant has been executed."

Connor was sure the choice of words was deliberate. "Very well," he said, "oh, Inspector?"

Cavendish paused in the act of gathering his paperwork into a folder.

"My clothes? The ones you took yesterday. Will they be returned to me?"

"When the lab has finished with them. Unless they become evidence, of course."

Connor got to his feet when the inspector did, and the constable stood, poised with his hand on the door handle. At a nod from the inspector, the young copper tugged handcuffs from his belt.

"Procedure, Doctor Sanderson, I'm sure you understand?" said Cavendish.

Connor obligingly presented his back and felt the cold steel close around his wrists. "Sorry, sir," the constable muttered quietly.

As Connor turned around again, Cavendish grinned. "See what I mean? Ted here has cuffed more suspects than you've had hot dinners, and I've never heard him apologize for it. That is the power of doctors and lawyers." Turning his attention to the flushed constable, he said, "Take Doctor Sanderson to our nicest cell."

The man looked confused for a moment. "They're all the same, Inspector."

"So, they are." As if he'd suddenly lost interest, Cavendish left the room, not bothering to close the door.

"This way, sir."

Connor followed the constable past the custody officer, who looked down from behind a counter set at shoulder height for his 'customers'. It gave the sergeant a psychological advantage when booking in suspects.

Beyond the door at the end of a corridor was a row of cells. At the first cell on the left, the constable swung open the door built into the grid work of iron bars, followed Connor inside, and removed the cuffs.

Connor sat down on the narrow metal framed cot just as the constable said, "I'm sorry."

Connor laughed gently. "I understand, Constable." He took off his shoes while still sitting, then stood, shrugged out of his jacket, unclipped his suspenders, and removed his neck tie. The policeman put everything inside a paper bag and wrote the cell number on it.

"Thank you, Doctor Sanderson. Can I bring you something to eat?"

Connor answered truthfully. "No thank you, Constable. I can't face eating anything."

The gate clanged shut behind the officer, and the key grated in the lock.

Connor studied the three walls painted dull cream. The toilet pan in the corner was clean, at least. It was almost dark outside, so the high-level barred window looked out on a charcoal-colored sky, still thick with cloud.

There was nothing Connor could do, so he laid out on the thin mattress, stared at the ceiling, and waited for morning.

He wondered if Reggie had received his message. Cranham Hall was an hour's coach ride from the hospital and Lord Cranham would be a powerful ally. This time, unlike Rice, Connor knew he didn't murder Ivy. He could account for every moment of last evening. Searching his room would not take the police very long, but he doubted anything would happen soon.

Falling into a restful trance, Connor considered reaching out to Malachi, but this was a problem for the *real* world. He needed to appear human, at least, although he felt sure breaking through brick walls remained an option, but only as a last resort.

Listening to the discordant soundtrack of London traffic, the night passed by before Connor heard footsteps approach and stop outside the cell wing door.

The door opened. "Inspector Cavendish has sent for you." It was a different officer this morning, but the same routine with the handcuffs and escort duty.

Facing Cavendish in the interview room once again, the inspector wasted no time. He placed a pile of damp clothes on the table. "Your clothes. Found in your bathtub."

"It was raining. I got wet."

Turning over a flap of fabric with the end of his pen exposed a label. "Anderson & Sheppard. Saville Row. Expensive."

"Indeed. They live up to their reputation of concern with easy movement and a natural body line. I would recommend them highly."

Cavendish let the flap fall back into place. "Expensive, and yet, you didn't use an umbrella, overcoat, or hail a cab. In the pouring rain? Very odd. Are you sure you weren't trying to destroy evidence?"

Connor shook his head. "Just as I say. I was late for rounds and the suit was too wet to hang. That is all."

Back in the cell, another hour passed, and Connor began to think he should hire a lawyer.

He stood and gripped the bars, contemplating calling out. But, would that make him look guilty? As footfalls echoed in the hallway beyond, he whipped back and sat on the cot as though he hadn't moved, resting back with implied nonchalance.

The custody sergeant entered, selected a key from his belt, and pushed it into the lock.

So, this is it. They are charging me.

Swinging the cell door open, he said flatly, "You're free to go, sir. Sign for your property at the desk on your way out."

"Free?"

The sergeant maintained a blank look, and Connor decided questions could wait. Minutes later, standing outside on the sidewalk clutching the damp paper parcel containing his crumpled suit, he lifted his chin skyward and took a deep breath. The polluted London air had never felt so good.

The warmth on his face began to sting as the clouds shifted across the sky, and, dodging carriages and a motor car, Connor crossed with forced casual efficiency to the shaded side of the street. Glancing back, he saw Reggie running up the steps of the police station and called out.

Changing direction, Reggie joined him on the opposite sidewalk, slightly out of breath. "Thank God. I couldn't believe it when Cartwright told me."

"Lester?" Connor frowned.

"Well, yes. The police were asking questions. They weren't very discrete when they searched your room, I'm afraid. Lester went into the local police station to tell them about your encounter with Rufus." Reggie took the crumpled parcel from Connor and hailed a cab as he spoke. "I can't believe you saved his life. They phoned Bow Street and Cavendish talked to Lester and Rufus at the hospital this morning."

Following Reggie and stepping up into the carriage, Connor said, "I never thought I'd be grateful to Rufus Clare." He slumped back into the seat, making the carriage rock.

Reggie glanced across the confined space at his friend. "You look frightful, by the way."

Chapter 19

The sheen of dewdrops on the sidewalk glittered in the moonlight as he rested against the wall beside the sweeping archway which framed the cemetery gates. He had followed his prey to the house opposite and waited with growing tension for him to emerge once more.

The incarceration in the prison cell had been shorter than I expected. The fun is in the game. Gaining trust and playing with shades of truth. The police are fools. Running his diamond hard nails over the stonework, he scored deep troughs and listened to the whisper of the fragments hitting the ground.

The condensation stiffened to frost, and still he did not move or breathe. He filled the time listening to the conversations playing out inside the row of houses. The problems and concerns of the occupants struck him as fatuous. There were many more serious problems in life than who to invite to dinner, when to visit the aged Aunt Agnes, and fussing over a child who has fallen and grazed a knee. *Pathetic.*

He hadn't decided the where and the when. He just knew the man inside one of those houses would not make it back to his own home tonight. With a smile, he listened to the 'goodbyes' playing out on the other side of the glossy black door opposite. The 'take care, old man' was followed by the muffled thump of the men inside slapping each other on the back.

The door opened and the human stepped out.

Light from the hallway sharpened the silhouette as, turning up the collar of his long-tailored coat, the man made a final gesture of farewell. The door closed, and he turned away and bounced down the stone steps. Immediately, he set off along the sidewalk at a brisk pace. The distant glow of a busier street up ahead beckoned. The reassuring brightness of shop fronts and a stream of passing humanity, both on foot and riding in carriages and motor cars, waited for him there.

The man's footfalls rang out in a steady, determined tempo. He paused beneath a gas lantern while struggling with his gloves. He moved onwards, increasing speed again until his stride checked as he made sure it was safe to cross a side street. A gusting breeze blew his hair over his eyes. He pushed it back, still concentrating on scanning for traffic, and then his feet left the floor. His body hurtled through the air and slammed into a wall of brick.

The loud crack of ribs breaking shattered the silence. The coarse masonry ripped the skin from his cheek as he slid down and crumpled onto the cold sidewalk.

Appearing beside the body, his attacker bent to grab a handful of hair and examine the bleeding features. A crushed cheekbone sunk inwards and dark shadow filled the crater in the once handsome face.

Unbuttoning the dead man's coat, he reached inside and went through the pockets. He pulled out a money clip, a set of keys, a handkerchief, and a pack of cigarettes. *Such a filthy habit.* The hunter shook his head.

Dropping everything else onto the ground, he pushed the money from the clip into his pocket. From inside his own coat, he pulled out two glass vials with cork stoppers. Resting a knee on the sidewalk, he studied the bleeding face and licked his lips. Turning the corpse's head with a bony finger, he pushed a sharp nail into the carotid artery and filled both glass containers with the reluctant crimson flow. Standing up, he pocketed the vials. With no heart to pump it out, obeying the laws of gravity, the blood flowed until it resembled an oozing pool of black tar in the darkness.

Taking a final, intent look, as though committing the scene to memory, the dark stranger turned and disappeared. The dead man's copper bright hair shuffled in the breeze, blowing across his eyes.

Chapter 20

Connor crossed the room and washed his grubby hands at the vanity stand. He sat down at his desk and took stock. The evening shift had been uneventful.

Pretending he felt tired represented the biggest challenge for him. He tried not to take on more than his share, but it became harder when the nurses, easing their aching shoulders, had literally just sank into a chair to write up patient notes, and a call button bleeped at the ward station.

Once or twice, when alone in the hospital corridor, he heard the groan of distress in a patient and attended to them before their hand found the call button. That made him feel slightly better. He was off at eleven p.m. and try as he might, he couldn't persuade the night sister to swap shifts, even though the dark circles under her eyes were purple.

Instead, Connor used his time usefully. He joined Malachi for another hunting session. Rats, rabbits, badgers, and foxes all tasted intriguingly different. *Anyone who thought 'blood is blood' is a fool.* Meat tasted different so why shouldn't blood, but his biggest discovery was that fear ruined the taste. He learned the value of a fast kill, cloaked in surprise. If the creature had no time to react, then their blood remained untainted by adrenalin.

He heard police sirens wailing along the streets when he left Malachi and was on his way back. It served as a reminder that the streets of London had other predators too.

A few specks of blood marked his clothes, so he had come in through the window. Although he moved too fast for a human to see, ghostly swinging doors in corridors might raise alarm.

Rousing himself from his meandering thoughts, he set the blotter on the desk straight, and focused. He felt as human as he could, these days.

Opening the top draw, he pulled out a sheet of note paper and dipped a pen nib into the inkwell set in a wooden block. He poised it ready to write. Turning quickly, as if he heard a noise, he twisted and inspected the closed window. *Was it already open when I came back in?* He frowned. He couldn't remember if he had checked it. He made a mental note to be more careful.

Focusing back on the paper, he wrote 'Dearest, Lavinia', and then frowned. Unease crept along his spine. He detected an unfamiliar odor in the room. It smelled like Malachi, but that could not be. Getting up, he prowled around the space, sampling the air. His bed looked undisturbed. Running his fingers over the mattress, he found the smell grew stronger. Dropping to his knees, he peered under the metal frame, scanning the floor and the chain-linked fabric of the springs.

A scrap of white cloth poked through. *There's something underneath.* Connor stood and lifted the mattress. Reaching into the space, he pulled out a piece of torn fabric. It looked like part of a dress shirt. *How the hell did that get there?* The stench of blood radiated into the room, and the dried-in stain struck dread into Connor.

The sound of footsteps on the stairs broke his concentration, and he knew there was a decision to be made. *Is running going to help me? I need to catch the creep doing this.* The window being unlatched and the musky odor added up to a vampire. *Malachi? Playing games?* The only way to know what he was up against was to stay put and face whoever came through that door.

The voice shouting outside in the hallway almost drowned out the urgent pounding on the thick wood.

"Police. Open up."

Opening the window and tossing the cloth outside took milliseconds. Connor answered the door and stepped back as two policemen and Cavendish pushed their way in.

"You're under arrest, you murderer," blurted Cavendish.

Connor cooperated, letting an officer cuff his hands behind his back.

Cavendish glared into Connor's face and then his eyes dropped down to the front of Connor's shirt. The specks of blood he saw fuelled the inspector's aggression. "Friends in high places won't help you this time, you sick bastard."

"What am I supposed to have done?" Connor asked.

Ignoring the question, Cavendish beckoned three more officers into the room. "Search every square inch." Jerking his head towards the door, he said, "Take him away."

As Connor allowed himself to be bundled down the stairwell, he tried to piece together the puzzle. He knew the police didn't need a warrant this time. They could search his room because he was arrested there. A creeping sensation of dread filled him as he realized he had not searched the room himself.

◇◇◇

Connor had been stripped of his clothes yet again, but wore a standard issue prison tunic and pants this time, with his cuffed hands resting in his lap.

"You left a witness." Cavendish grinned.

Connor felt confused. *A witness?* He didn't remember murdering anything other than some wildlife last night. *So, who?*

"Where were you at midnight last night?"

"In my room." Another lie. But a calculated one, given he left and returned by the window.

"Wrong answer."

Is he bluffing? He has to be. "You have me at a disadvantage. Your witness is mistaken. Someone with a grudge would lie, of course."

"Who holds a grudge against you, Doctor Sanderson?" Cavendish's agitation had evaporated when he entered the interview room. He reminded Connor of a hunter stalking prey.

Instinct told Connor to remain silent.

"Let's run through some names, shall we? You can just nod. Reginald Cranham? Lester Cartwright?" Cavendish held Connor's gaze. "No? How about Rufus Clare?"

Everything screamed 'trap' to Connor, so he said nothing.

"Oh, come now, Doctor-"

A knock on the door interrupted the flow. The tension broke when Cavendish got up and went to answer it. Stepping out, even though he closed the door behind him, Connor heard what was being said, and had some answers, at last.

139

"We found blood on a torn shirt shoved behind the tallboy chest… Mr. Cartwright is still in shock… Cecil Clare has identified his son's body. Nasty business, sir."

So there was more 'evidence' planted.

Cavendish returned and sat. "Silence won't help you this time. I am charging you with the murder of Rufus Clare. You will appear in front of a magistrate and be remanded in custody." Conversationally, Cavendish added, "You'll ask for bail, but we will oppose on the grounds that people around you drop dead and we have a witness to protect. Do you understand the charge?"

Connor nodded.

"Humor me, Sanderson. Let me hear you admit to it. Save us all a lot of time."

"I understand the charge. As to the rest, no comment."

Cavendish stood up and called out to an officer. "Put him in the cells after the custody sergeant has completed the paperwork."

"Inspector, what did the witness say?" Connor asked, quietly.

"All in good time, Doctor."

Connor got up and followed the police officer out, wishing he could talk to Lester. None of this made any sense.

"Sanderson?"

Connor recognized the gloating tone. It was the best thing he could hope for. That Cavendish would want him to squirm; human instinct at its best.

"Here's something for you to sweat over. Lester Cartwright witnessed your vicious attack. He went out to catch Rufus, because he'd forgotten to tell him about an appointment. He is sedated and catatonic. We are waiting for him to recover. But, you're a doctor. You know he may *never* recover, but don't worry. We have enough to bury you anyway."

Chapter 21

The police were in no hurry, Connor knew. He lay on his back in the same cell as before, with his forearm covering his eyes.

A drunk snored rhythmically in the next cell.

Connor also gave the impression of being asleep, but his mind was in overdrive. Even though suspicion about Malachi had taken up lodgings like a maggot in his brain, he deliberately didn't think about that.

Malachi, where are you?

He sent out the call every few minutes. He sensed Malachi heard him, when a picture of his mentor's grinning face solidified inside his head, but Malachi remained stubbornly silent.

Connor hoped the decrepit vampire had a plan which did not include leaving him there to rot in jail. His feeling of optimism originated from somewhere, and it certainly wasn't from Connor himself.

As lists of pros and cons went, the cons side of things was heavily weighted. He might not be convicted, but laboratory tests were tediously slow and it would take time to determine the blood on the shirt he wore was animal blood. *And that opens another can of worms, in any case. Try explaining that away without sounding like a lunatic.* It could not alter the fact they found a blood-stained shirt in his room, and he knew the blood would be Rufus Clare's. What he couldn't work out was who put it there and why. Which led him back to the scenario he couldn't think about.

His current situation held no real fear for him. As a vampire, he could easily escape and disappear. Leaving London and starting again would be simple. But, leaving Reggie, Lavinia, and the Cranham family, thinking he was a murderer did not sit so well with him.

He heard Malachi approaching long before he arrived. Connor frowned. His mentor's progress resembled the vampire equivalent of a lumbering elephant. Every footfall sent shockwaves which bounced around Connor's cell. *What is he doing?*

Connor's imagination had not reached as far as formulating what Malachi would come up with to get him out of this fix. Swinging up to sitting, like a look-out at a robbery, Connor kept an ear open for human footsteps inside the police station.

The snoring next door stuttered, resuming once-more on a loud snort. The sting of alcohol seemed to be a whisky and bitter ale cocktail, which Connor knew the man would regret in the morning.

A shadow filled the high-level window, and a waterfall of debris rained down onto the concrete floor as the iron bars disappeared one by one.

"Malachi?" Connor whispered, even though it could not *be* anyone else.

Of course. The words melted into a grinning face.

What's the plan? Even though, Connor felt relief at finally hearing Malachi's voice inside his head, his patience was paper thin.

Escape and misdirection.

With all the bars removed, Connor stood back and watched with interest. As though it leapt from a trampoline, the body of a man appeared in the aperture and slumped forward onto his belly. His slack hands swung gently for a moment before he toppled over into the cell.

Connor had already decided the man was dead, but, to keep the noise down, he whipped forward and caught the body. Malachi landed soundlessly beside Connor.

What now?

Malachi grinned. *Now? A fire.*

What! Jerking his head towards the snoring coming from the other side of the wall, Connor frowned.

The walls are seven inches thick. The police are two minutes away. Do you want to get out of here, or stay and rot?

Malachi had a point. Connor stripped off his prison tunic and in seconds, the dead man and he swapped clothes. He laid the corpse on the narrow cot bed and watched Malachi pull out a box of matches. Holding a hand out to Connor, Malachi said aloud this time. "Whiskey. His coat pocket."

Slopping the contents over the man's face and chest, Malachi lit the match, dropped it and both vampires leapt up and out through the window. Wedging the four bars back into place, two for each, took seconds.

Just before Connor dropped to the ground again, he yelled, "Help. Fire!"

The sound of pounding feet and a shrieking alarm siren made him feel better as he followed the distant figure of Malachi along the streets, and across London to Kensal Cemetery. It seemed so much more than three days since Connor had first seen 'The Butcher' and come face to face with the reality of eternity. If he was honest, in many ways it still felt like a dream he would wake up from at any moment. Or rather, a nightmare.

Connor caught up with Malachi and said, "Who was he? You didn't kill him for me?"

Malachi exposed his yellow teeth in a macabre grin. "And if I did?" Before Connor could reply, his mentor said, "No, I didn't kill him. But it was good fortune rather than choice. He literally keeled over in front of me. Bad heart."

Connor didn't want to split hairs, but given Malachi's hideous appearance, if he appeared suddenly, as if from nowhere, he most likely *did* kill the man now burning in Connor's place.

Exasperation built inside, but with a long expelled breath, Connor let it go. He couldn't control everything, and worrying about the possibility of the man having a family? That route led to insanity.

The rusted gates of the mausoleum were draped in fog this evening. Malachi had already scaled them and taken on the quality of a ghost, as wisps of vapor drifted around him. Connor followed quickly and accepted, that as macabre as it seemed, taking refuge in the tomb alongside The Butcher would keep him safe until they worked out a course of action.

Inside the tomb, sitting at the far end of the chamber which contained the sarcophagus, the two conspirators were able to talk.

"I need to find out what, or who, Lester saw," Connor said, watching Malachi closely for a reaction.

"And how do you plan to accomplish such a thing?" asked Malachi.

Connor thought for a moment and then said heavily, "Reggie. I don't want him involved, but he can visit Lester at St Thomas'. If I can persuade him, that is. Can you deliver a note to the Hall without being seen?"

He nodded. "We don't have too much time. The body will fool the police for a while, but a medical examiner will know it isn't you."

Malachi got up and paused in the stone archway. "Stay out of sight. I'll be back soon."

The silence settled like a blanket over Connor's senses. Sitting without breathing enabled him to really listen. The Butcher's silence was equally profound, and Connor understood the true meaning of being undead. Would he turn back the clock if he could?

He thought of the kiss Lavinia stole outside the tea room and whispered, "Yes. I'd exchange this endless nothingness for a day of loving her."

Chapter 22

Settled in the mausoleum and locked inside his own head, inactivity was difficult to bear. All the things he wished he could do for himself preyed on Connor's mind like circling vultures. He shifted position on the ledge of cold stone which, after three hours of sitting, was the same temperature as his hard flesh.

Breathing in and expelling air noisily, to refresh the stale air inside, he grinned wryly. No tell-tale plume of vapor gave him pause. Flexing his hands, each tendon grated through its sheath; the connection to bone and fiber so stiff it could be read as pain. The sticky juddering was new, though. *Am I dehydrating?* Malachi would know. Connor recoiled at the thought, and it was then he realized that becoming dependent on Malachi could be a dangerous path. *What if he is using me?* How or why, Connor couldn't imagine, but worms of distrust ate away at his brain.

Closing his eyes, Connor reconnected with the Malachi of that first meeting – reliving his gloating 'survival' speech, but this time, Connor had the luxury of hindsight. It was like, having read an instruction manual in a foreign tongue, he now had a translation.

He laid out on the stone slab, and sluggish dryness filled his head, slid like lava into his throat, and swallowing couldn't shift it. The abrasive feeling made him yearn for the thick sweet taste of blood, and suddenly his eyes shot open.

Only human blood feeds the three compartments of the vampire brain. As the thirst drove him to distraction, he rose and began circling the tomb faster and faster until he knew the chamber could no longer contain him. *This is my body, my brain, telling me I must feed.* Even though his lip curled in distaste at the thought of killing a human, he erupted from the gates of the mausoleum and out into the night air.

He knew London well, and the 'decent' part of him still vying for control pleaded for compromise. *Not an innocent.* Connor headed across the green cultivated gardens of the Royal parks and into the shabbier, more-grimy district of Whitechapel.

Death of Connor Sanderson

The brick built dwellings bore the soot streaks of decades of London fog, made thicker by the coal fires which belched smoke from the chimney of every home in the city. The narrow side streets created claustrophobic wind tunnels. Humans hurried along, heads bent and hands gripping their collars tightly around their necks. Connor wove from one side of the street to another, like a heat-seeking missile. He searched through the pack, looking for the runt of the litter.

Finding a busy public house in Whitechapel wasn't hard to do. The emblem of Truman's Ale was a siren call to the locals of the East End. Even through the clouded etched glass of the windows, Connor picked out the dancing bobbing shadows of the drunk, uninhibited warm bodies in the glow of yellow light. Raucous laughter spilled out each time the door opened to welcome newcomers, or to release those taking their leave.

He'd once attended a lecture on 'description of class'. The disparaging label which best fit the heaving mass of humanity inside the cheap, dirty tavern made them a good hunting ground. *'Class A',* according to social cartographer, Charles Booth, *'were the lowest class, which consists of labourers, street sellers, loafers, criminals. They live the life of savages, with vicissitudes of extreme hardship and their only luxury is drink.'*

Connor's interest lay in the 'savage criminals' element.

A young woman fought her way through the wooden swing door and froze on the threshold when the wall of bitter cold made her gasp.

Connor rested back against the brick wall ten yards down the street, standing midway between two gas street lamps.

"Good Lawd," the girl muttered, "brass monkey weather out 'ere." Pulling her shawl tighter around her shoulders, but without covering her comely wares. The shiver that rattled through her soft scented body raised goosebumps across the rounded swell of her breasts.

Connor's mouth watered and his fists tightened until he felt each fingernail digging into his palms. Images flashed through his mind like blades of searing heat; the pale skin tearing as he bit into the succulent flesh. The red gash of her lips forming a perfect circle of agony until blood flooding into her throat smothered the sound.

Still fighting against the wind trying to rip the shawl from her black-lace gloved hands, she suddenly grunted. Grabbing the heavy brass handle on the door, she pulled it open. "C'mon, Aggie. Mum'll be 'ome soon. She'll 'ave me guts for garters if she knows I took you down the pub."

A young girl on the cusp of womanhood, but reeking with scent of childhood, emerged and linked arms with the older woman.

They set off at a scurry, huddled together so closely they lurched from side to side. Their strides were small and fast to keep the cold draft from penetrating their rustling skirts.

Connor turned his face to the wall and closed his eyes. He tracked the thick thud of their heartbeats – the childlike girl's pattering much faster. He detected the scent of alarm and knew she was scared of the dark. *And so she should be. No, not this one.* He thought each word forcefully, as if having an argument with someone else. And he was. The lunatic inside his head rattled louder on the bars of his cerebral cell.

He knew he couldn't hold back the blood thirsty tide of malice much longer. Swinging away to put distance between himself and the girls, he broke into a run and accelerated until his dehydrating muscles tightened in protest. The sand inside the hour glass in his head clattered loudly, like boulders – *time is running out.*

Stopping short, a dull weight dragged his shoulders down. If he didn't hunt, feed, kill, then he would die. In the last three days, he had witnessed pain and suffering he had no stomach for. What gave him the right to take away the lives of humans? Deciding who should live or die was a burden too heavy to bear. *If I die, the pain is over.*

He heard the gentle lullaby of lapping water. The River Thames flowed just beyond the row of factories and warehouses which served the London Docks. The hulking constructions cast dense shadows and using the concrete walkway which ran alongside one, dressed Connor in an ink-black cloak.

Death of Connor Sanderson

He rounded the corner and looked out over the slate-gray body of water. Ripples tore the surface like a seething mass of sharpened blades. The cranes rose into the sky; metal fingers stripped of flesh. Connor took a step forward, contemplating the pathway through the quayside clutter of coiled grime-stained ropes, greased chains as thick as a man's thigh, and splintered wooden pallets and crates. The wind snatched at his jacket and, without thinking, he shook it off and dropped it onto the ground.

The hypnotic shushing of the water had him entranced, until a grunt over to his left, out of sight, but very close, made him falter.

Switching direction when the scent of blood hit him, he wiped the back of his hand across his mouth and, nanoseconds later, he rounded the corner and looked down at the dying man. A glint of silver up ahead caught his eye; a dark figure walking quickly away, his footfalls echoing like the clap of applauding hands. Connor gathered the puzzle pieces in the seconds it took the man to wipe the blood from the knife and hide it inside his coat.

Drowning in the sweet scent rising from the victim at his feet, Connor dropped to his knees. Holding the rattling cell door of the psychopath closed a little longer, he inspected the slicing wound in the man's stomach and took his pulse, feeling it slowing with every second.

"Catch 'im. 'E's robbed me. Gripping Connor's forearm with surprising strength, the man whispered again. "Catch 'im, please." With a rattling sigh, the man's grasp slipped away and his head fell back onto the concrete with a thump.

Before Connor's conscious mind admitted defeat, the demon inside filled his senses with blood-red craving, and hot human blood flooded his throat, warming the ice cold pit of his stomach and sending a sizzling trail of heat up his carotid arteries; his brain lit up in a flash flood of ecstasy.

He felt the skin on his face flush as the thirsty capillaries soaked up the lifeblood of his victim. *No, not my victim.* Consciousness broke the surface like an iceberg rolling in a swelling tide. *No, NOT my kill.*

Pulling back sharply, Connor stared at the dead man – his mouth hung open and his hands flopped over beside him – and rested him back into the pool of his own blood. Passing a hand down over the slack face, Connor closed the dead man's eyes and stood up. His shirt was smeared red, but not enough to soak through to his skin. *I must be getting better.* Even his hands were *almost* clean.

Washing them quickly in a bucket of rainwater, he retrieved his jacket from the ground and shrugged back into it. Moving fast enough to become a blur of scattered light rays, he retraced his path, intending to return to Central London and the Mausoleum, but the man with the knife taunted him. 'The wrong man died tonight' was the only thing going around in his mind. *It doesn't matter.* But it did.

Moments later, the realization he was racing along a street he didn't recognize made no sense, until he heard that same weight of footfall. It wasn't just the noise, it was the gait. One foot dragged a little. He must have stored the information without knowing it. The mile between them reduced to yards within seconds, and the villain with the knife glanced over his shoulder at the sudden hurricane which whisked the dry autumn leaves into a cyclone.

The lunatic inside barely stirred this time – he was replete. *This* kill was for the human remnants of Connor, although, common sense said he should not *waste* a meal.

The man ran, and flinging himself forward, he became dangerously unbalanced.

Connor used the forward momentum, grabbed the man by the collar and redirected him face first into a tree trunk.

The man spun around clutching his face, blood trickling from his bruised nose.

Connor held his victim up against the tree by the throat and plucked the knife from his coat pocket. Connor ran the blade under his own nose as though it supported a line of cocaine. He grinned, revealing teeth smeared with the same blood residue still on the knife.

"What did you steal, hmm?"

"I-"

"Shhhh. Don't tell me. I'll guess," he said, and stared through the curtain of greasy hair into terrified, but weasel sharp eyes. He laughed. "You still think you have a chance. Tut, tut. Let's see what you're hiding."

He patted down the filthy coat and something clinked inside a pocket. Dipping his cold white hand inside, Connor's fingers closed around a ring. He pulled it out and found it was suspended on a broken length of twine. It rotated slowly when he held it up. Still looking at the wedding ring, clearly too small for a man, Connor mused, "So, you ripped this from around his neck. Why would a man wear a woman's wedding ring around his neck?" Raising a brow at the man he thought of as a 'murderer', Connor squeezed the hand he had around his throat tighter.

The man's boots thumped against the tree as he kicked out.

"My guess is, his wife is dead. What do you think?"

"It was an accident." The man grimaced.

Connor shook his head. "I don't think so. But, this is your lucky day." Connor let go so quickly, the man staggered. "I've already eaten."

Throwing the knife until it was buried to the hilt in a nearby tree, Connor turned away. The metal spike the thief drove into Connor's side skidded off hard skin. In a reflex, he whipped his hand back and hit the man full in the face.

The crack of his spine snapping echoed through the trees. He hit the ground in a heap of tangled limbs, like a puppet with cut strings.

Damn. The smashed face and shattered vertebrae were not injuries easily explained away. *Damn.* With a sigh, he hoisted the body up over his shoulders and took off at vampire top speed back to the Mausoleum.

Ducking down into the tomb, Connor dropped the body onto the stone ledge and covered the victim's face with his greasy coat. He had the feeling Malachi would have some stern words.

Chapter 23

Listening to the whispering sounds of spiders and beetles in the tomb distracted Connor from the consequences of his impetuous actions. He indulged in guessing, by sound alone, which bug or insect was busily creating lairs, and wishing his life was that simple.

A rushing wind blasted a shower of dust in through the entrance. It cascaded down over the stone steps and Connor knew Malachi had returned.

The elder vampire materialized beside where Connor sat and, as if he'd merely stepped out of the room for ten minutes, he handed over a large envelope with sheets of paper and a pencil tucked inside.

"Your friend Reginald is returning to Cranham Hall. He took your death badly. He will be there for the next two days." Malachi said.

Shutting out the guilt rising inside him, Connor asked, "How do you know this?"

"I know where everyone is, Connor. Humans are simple to track and eavesdrop on. Their voices carry even when they try not to. Tuning them out is the more common problem in vampires."

Is that true? Connor emptied his mind and heard streams of ghost like whispers. "I miss you my dear" – an unsteady voice, vocal chords slack with old age, was easy to pick out. *That* human was in the cemetery, or just outside it, walking past but sending out a muttered prayer to his lost companion. There were others, now he had found their wavelength he teased out individuals like separating strands from a twisted rope. The idea that Malachi knew where his friends and family were unsettled him, although he couldn't say why.

"I can deliver a note to the-" The smell of coagulated blood interrupted Malachi's train of thought and his head whipped round. He stared at the body, and the soles of the worn pair of boots pointing in his direction.

You left the tomb? Malachi's snarling face appeared half an inch away from Connor's and made him start. The dry crinkled skin covering his mentor's skull became more gruesome viewed up close. The old vampire scoured Connor's irises, his intensity almost a tangible pressure inside his student's cranium. *Grave sleep.*

Connor had heard the words before, somewhere in the distance, but he couldn't quite grasp their meaning.

Malachi laughed harshly. *You were lucky. Letting the lunatic from his cell to rehydrate the killing centre inside your brain could have left you insane.* Malachi cocked his head and muttered aloud, "I chose my protégé well. You can resist blood, and that means you control your destiny."

"The restlessness and agitation were real? Originating from brain starvation?" Connor asked.

"Yes. Preoccupied with guiding you through the murders, I almost let you sink into dementia." Malachi looked genuinely regretful. "Where did you go?"

"Whitechapel, and then the docks."

Glancing at the body again, Malachi sank back down beside Connor. I tried to groom another protégé in London once, in 1888."

Connor waited in silence, glad when Malachi descended into the form of communication he preferred; painting a scene inside Connor's head...

The darkness of the tomb became the crisp cold air of a moonlit night.

Connor saw a figure wearing a dark cloak moving quickly up ahead, the fabric flaring out behind him flipped back every few steps to reveal the battered, leather Gladstone bag he clutched in one hand. Connor recognized the area as Whitechapel. He followed the man past the church and entered the district where there was a public house every few yards. There were also alleys where the air seemed thick with darkness.

The musical lilt of female laughter floated through the night, and the figure changed direction. The speed with which the hunter dropped to one knee, extracted a blade and swooped down on his victim was terrifying. Connor felt disgust and despair as the man caught the girl by the hair – a prostitute judging by the low cut bodice and painted face – yanked her head back and slit her throat. Guiding her to the floor, with macabre care he arranged her on her back, cut open her bodice, and with devastating precision, cut out her liver. What am I watching? Connor didn't want to look, and he realized he was Malachi. The weight of sadness he felt was failure. The monster dipped his face into the warm cavity, vapor pluming into the cold night air as he drank her blood. The slurping noise made Connor's hackles rise.

But then, he did something worse, he bit into the liver, even though he retched; it was as though he was trying to choke on it.

The image faded and Connor looked at Malachi's still profile. "Your protégé? He went insane?"

Malachi nodded slowly. "Yes. Our worst fear was that he'd be caught and his 'undead' state would endanger the rest of us. You will have heard of his infamy. The newspapers called him 'Jack the Ripper', 'The Whitechapel Murderer' or even 'Leather Apron'."

"Did you kill him?"

"I planned to, but Principal Julian of the 'Undead Council' has to sanction executions."

"Even *you* fear this principal?"

Malachi chuckled. "We all do." Jerking his head towards the human corpse nearby, he added quietly, "*You* could be called up before Principle Julian if you bring our society to human attention. We've been here in London for many hundreds of years. Humans, thankfully, have eyes that look but don't see what is right in front of them."

Connor nodded. Having been at the hospital and living a lie, he knew that more than anyone. "So, 'Jack' still lives?"

"Yes, he disappeared from London. Until he returns, he is another council's problem."

Connor sat very still, struggling with the revelation that their species existed, undetected, side-by-side with humans, not *just* in London, but everywhere. "What made him become a monster?"

"The bloodlust of 'grave-sleep' is hard to subjugate. Some vampires lock themselves away in coffins or sarcophagi after one kill to curb the appetite. It prevents the psychopath inside becoming so strong that their own will cannot resurface and take back control. Exercising that control is what you did tonight." Malachi inspected Connor again, as if he had not seen him before, as if dissecting an insect under a microscope. "You are one of the strong ones. I made a good choice."

Connor could not agree. What he wouldn't give for the blinkered existence he had shared with Reggie, Lavinia, and even his enemy, Rufus. *But then, Rufus is dead, really dead, and that could have been me.* Confusion made Connor irritable.

"What happens now, Malachi? I'm undead, *and* a fugitive wanted for three murders. What happens now?"

Leaning back against the wall, Malachi presented a blank expression. "That is for you to decide. If talking to Reginald Cranham will help you, then you know where to find him, just be careful."

Picking up the envelope from the floor where it had fallen while Connor witnessed the fate which befell 'Jack', he pulled out a sheet of paper and prepared to write. With a wry smile he acknowledged that he had been a child in his playroom the last time he had used a lead pencil, but expecting Malachi to return with his 'Waterman' fountain pen and pot of blue ink was an unrealistic expectation.

He kept it simple, bearing in mind this was a letter from a dead man.

Reggie, please meet me in the stables at Cranham Hall at midnight. I am not dead, but I can explain, Connor.

Could he explain? He wasn't sure, not really, but he could try, and trust that Reginald would agree to visit Lester.

Folding the paper and putting it inside the envelope, Connor passed it to Malachi to deliver.

"I'll be only a few minutes. Please stay here." Malachi waited until Connor nodded, and then disappeared in a vortex of grit and stone dust.

Connor guessed what would be the next task. *We should get rid of the body.* The thought of meeting 'Principal Julian' intrigued him. Would meeting others help him understand his state of suspended being, more clearly? Would he feel like part of something, rather than an outcast? Getting answers from more than one undead soul satisfied the researcher in Connor. *I'll ask Malachi to take me before the Undead Council.* He ignored the little voice that asked, *'what if your sentence is real death?'*

In truth, he almost wished it was.

Malachi materialized a few minutes later, as promised, saying the words Connor expected. "Master Cranham will find the letter on the silver salver when he goes down to dinner this evening. If he is not hungry, the butler will take it to him. Now it is time to bury your mistake."

"I want to go before the council. Meet with Principal Julian."

"I know you do. All in good time. I have a feeling he would want to meet you too." Malachi waited until Connor picked up the body from the ledge, and then led the way out of the mausoleum. Connor expected to bury the body, however the solution was simpler. Drop it in the Thames and watch it float away. Connor didn't feel badly about that. He still had the wedding ring on a twine inside his pocket. Some people didn't deserve consideration.

Chapter 24

Leaving the cemetery at ten o'clock, Connor pulled up his collar and walked into the city center. He sensed the flutter of alarm, like an electric current, passing through the late-night travelers. Darkness made everything menacing. Noises echoed more loudly, visibility reduced, and everyone knew things that went bump in the night were always bad.

Connor heard what he hoped for, news about the 'Toffs Murders'. Ivy wasn't a 'toff', but she worked at the Hall. Three murders in three nights had everyone looking over their shoulder. Connor walked side by side with the fearful, and they had no idea he was the prime suspect.

"I heard the murderer killed himself. A journalist my father knows is writing the story."

That his 'death' was already public knowledge made things more difficult for the Cranhams. His thoughts turned to Lavinia. *I hope she has not heard the gossip.* The last thing he meant to do was cause pain to those he loved.

Heading to London Bridge railway station, he skimmed smoothly down the stairs to the platform just as a train pulled in. Choosing a window seat, he watched the rows of houses which lined the track pass by. The darkened windows bore the oily sheen of grime and the houses themselves were wedged together, filling every space along the route. Further out of London, the embankments were lined with tangled undergrowth and trees deformed by the unforgiving rush of endless carriages shuttling back and forth.

Connor alighted at Orpington. He had not taken a train in six months, and he couldn't account for the urge to travel on one tonight, except to say, he felt he was gathering experiences for the last time. Running lightly up onto the moonlit sidewalk, he walked until the shops and houses dwindled and greenery took over, and then, without a carriage or horse to ride, he ran.

He had an hour to kill before his meeting with Reggie. Whisking towards the imposing presence of the Hall, Connor's curiosity piqued when he saw the golden glow of lamplight in the window of George Cranham's study. Peering carefully through a gap in the drapes, Connor identified two other men. Sir Edgar Cranham and Cedric Clare.

Cedric Clare appeared to have shrunk since Connor's last encounter with him, and it wasn't difficult to guess why. The man's grief made his head drop and his shoulders slump. His red nose and puffy eyes bore witness to the emotional storm he struggled to control.

"Rufus was turning a corner." Cedric's voice was thick with tears. "The recent run-ins he had with Sanderson made him re-examine his future." The old man dragged a hand down over his face. "Why? Why would Sanderson do this? I don't understand. I don't understand any of it."

Cedric sunk further down into a brown leather wing-backed chair.

Uncle Edgar peered from beneath beetled brows and said, "I'm not convinced he did it. I know there was rivalry between the two, but murder, and *three* people, the police would have us believe. I'm sorry, I don't see Connor suddenly losing his sanity like that. Because that is what it would take."

His Lordship stood up from where he had sat behind his desk, drumming his fingers on the leather tooled surface. Passing in front of the window, he darted a glance at the drapes, almost as though he felt Connor's presence. He said evenly, "Connor must have felt bad about something. The police think he committed suicide because he couldn't face what he had done. It was the only way he could cope. I honestly don't know what to think. It all seems so bizarre, and the police have been wrong before." After circling the room, George Cranham sank back into his desk chair again. He sighed as though a weight crushed his chest and murmured, "Connor Sanderson may be dead, but I'll visit Inspector Cavendish in the morning. I want answers."

Easing away from the window, Connor withdrew to the deep shadow of the trees beyond the lawn. Seeing Cedric reduced to a fragile shell brought home what was at stake. *I have to clear my name. Cavendish is more than capable of labeling me a murderer. I can't let them think I would do these terrible things.*

At midnight, Connor made his way to the stables and waited. At least he knew Reggie would hear him out and had not called the police already. Lord Cranham, Cedric, and Sir Edgar, would not be in so somber a mood if Reggie had shared Connor's note.

Inside the stable, straw dust floated like flecks of gold to Connor's keen sight. Sabre snickered and his hooves scraped over the stone floor as he sidled away across his stall. The team of carriage horses, even though they were on the other side of the tack room, radiated nervous tension, blowing air through velvet nostrils.

"It's okay, boy." He silently entered Sabre's stall. The stallion's glossy black coat felt damp with sweat when Connor stroked the solid equine shoulder. Looking into the horse's terrified white-rimmed eye, he hummed softly under his breath until the animal relaxed and plucked at his coat with soft inquisitive lips.

"I won you over, boy. Now, I just need your master to be as understanding, hmmm?"

Sabre's head swung up when Reggie entered the stable and the wooden planked door swung shut behind him. Connor went back out into the hay store and waited for Reggie to notice he was there. It took human eyes time to adjust. Connor considered how easy it would be to surprise human prey before they knew what had happened. He thought like a hunter now.

"Reggie." He nodded in greeting when his friend eventually saw him.

"What the hell, Connor?" A cocktail of anger and confusion raged inside Reginald, until finally, the tension in his muscles eased into a rush of relief. "It *is* you. You're alive."

He smiled at the irony. "Yes. It wasn't my plan to fake my death-" Connor shrugged. "But I had to escape to find the real killer."

"How? And wasn't there a body? Burned?" Reggie's voice grew cold with suspicion.

"I can tell you the details. The body. Who helped me escape. But, Reggie, do you really want to know?"

Reggie's face gave nothing away, but the sudden rush of heat through his body and the heavy thud of a racing heartbeat gave Connor the answer he needed. *Better not to know.*

Connor swallowed down the rush of saliva that filled his mouth – Pavlov's dog theory held true with vampires too, it seemed – The plume of sweet nectar pumping through Reggie's veins was like a dinner bell.

"When all this is over, I will explain, I promise."

Pulling a grooming stool closer, Reggie dropped down onto it and rested his hands on his spread knees. "What do you want?"

"Lester. Cavendish says he is a witness."

"As much good as it will do you. You think he'll clear your name?" Reggie laughed bitterly. "Even if he does, you're dead, Connor. Remember?"

"But I need to know who did this. Don't you get it, Reggie? What do all the victims have in common?" Connor waited a heartbeat. "Me. If I'm dead, then the people I love are safe, for now, anyway." He wanted to believe that more than anything. "Lavinia. How is she?"

"The doctor administered a mild sedative. She took it badly."

"God, what a mess." Connor stabbed his fingers through his black hair. "Can you tell her I'm alive?"

"Is that what you want? It may be better to leave things as they are. If you can't clear your name then you'll have to leave, surely?"

He hadn't thought about that. Connor came face to face with the fact that he would have to leave, *whatever* the outcome.

"Perhaps you're right, Reggie."

"I just don't want to see her hurting again and again."

Connor nodded. "Can you get in to see Lester? He's in St Thomas' Hospital."

"And if I can get in?"

"I need a description. I know I wasn't there. If Lester was close enough to see what happened, and go into shock, he might have seen something important to identify the killer."

"Wouldn't the police think of that?"

"They would, unless they think the murderer was already locked in a cell, and is now dead. They won't be knocking down Lester's door."

Reggie digested everything Connor said. "Maybe you are right. Okay. It is worth a shot. I'll visit him first thing in the morning."

"Reggie, even if it doesn't make sense, whatever he says, write it down."

Connor gave Reggie a penetrating look. "No matter how strange what he says sounds, write everything down."

"Very well."

"Thank you. You're a good friend." Human slow, Connor walked over and placed his hand on Reggie's shoulder. "Thank you."

Connor turned to leave, but froze. Swinging back, he said, "Reggie, you should carry one of your father's handguns, for now, anyway."

Reggie frowned, his raised eyebrow filled with a hundred questions.

"I just want you to be prepared. 'Never underestimate your enemy', isn't that what your father says? Until the real killer is caught, you should take precautions."

The realization in Reggie's expression made Connor feel more comfortable. You, Lavinia, any member of the household, none of you are safe until we know who we are dealing with."

"Very well, I'll do that."

A second later, Connor had left Reggie alone with his thoughts. The weight of regret hurt. Like a broken glass, the events of the last few days had shattered so many lives, and things could never be put back the way they were.

Chapter 25

Connor couldn't talk to Lester himself, but he followed Reginald to St Thomas' Hospital and planned to gather clues from a distance. On his return journey the night before, he gave a beggar on a street corner at Orpington station money, and persuaded him to swap his coat and hat for Connor's. The vagrant took the Saville Row cashmere coat and scuttled away, as though scared that the 'gent' would come to his senses.

He didn't tell Reggie he would be there. He felt it better his friend didn't know. In the entrance foyer, Connor slumped into a wooden seat, polished slick by the thousands of backsides that had fidgeted while waiting to be called to the desk. Reggie shuffled forward each time the queue at the reception counter moved, then stood and waited. He adjusted his position every few seconds or so, staring at the clock on the wall as if it held the answers to the universe.

"Good morning, sir. How can I help?"

Reggie reached the front of the line at last. "Mr. Lester Cartwright? I'm a friend of his from The Royal Eye Hospital. I'm here to visit him."

The woman squinted over the top of her spectacles at Reggie, and then shuffled through a pile of papers below the counter. "Mr. Cartwright is no longer on the 'Observation Ward'." She smiled absently at Reggie, handed him a 'visitor' badge, and said, "Third floor. Ward C. He's in his own room in a side ward."

"Thank you, miss," Reggie said and headed towards the stairwell. If he noticed the funnel of air that chilled the space around him as he started up the steps, he didn't show it. Connor whipped up the stairs unseen, ahead of Reggie.

Connor felt reassured at the bulk disrupting Reggie's usual streamlined tailoring where a gun fit snugly against his side, tucked inside his pants waistband.

Looking for a position from where he could eavesdrop, Connor checked the other private rooms in side ward 'C', but found them all occupied. The tea station had nurses inside chatting between themselves, so in the end, Connor settled for the linen closet. He sat on the floor in his grimy coat and battered hat. *If an orderly comes in, they'll see a homeless guy.* They would throw him out, of course, but they wouldn't look at him twice.

Listening for footsteps, Connor sat still as stone.

Reggie arrived a few minutes later, puffing from the exertion of walking quickly up the stairs. Without being able to see, Connor heard Reggie knock quietly on a door, and then, hearing no reply, the door of Lester's room opened and closed again.

The voices were easy to tune into for Connor. The sluggish stream of garbled words belonged to Lester. Reggie asked how Lester was feeling. He offered condolences on the terrible events and let Lester know he had friends who cared about him. All these overtures were met by faltering, disjointed words.

Connor felt shocked at Lester's rambling narrative. *Whatever he saw must have been terrifying.*

Resting his head back against the wall, Connor concentrated harder. There was a light scraping sound on the waxed linoleum of the floor and Reggie lowered his voice. It was easy to picture the scene; Reggie sitting on a chair, now, at Lester's bedside. Listening for the low moan of bedsprings, Connor revised his perception. *Lester is sitting in a chair, too.*

"Lester, have the police talked to you, yet?"

A rattling sound filled the air, and then Lester blurted, "They don't want to listen. I told them. I told them. I told them." Like a gramophone needle which was stuck, Lester kept repeating those words.

"It's alright, Lester."

The creaking of a chair stopped, and Connor realized the poor boy must have been rocking in the seat.

"I'll listen. What happened? Can you remember?"

"Sanderson. Connor."

Connor's heart suddenly felt heavy. Did I do this? He rested his head against the painted bricks behind him. *No, I would know.* The human conversation beyond, began again.

"Connor?" The dismay in Reggie's voice was almost tangible.

"He was a decent man. He saved Rufus."

Reggie's confusion was evident, but he patiently walked Lester along the path his mind was taking. Lester recounted the drunken encounter when Rufus almost choked on his own vomit. "He said I could call him, Connor. Decent man."

Carefully, Reggie said, "And what about the night Rufus was murdered."

The blunt question set off a creaking of chair springs again. It settled into a steady tempo which matched the rhythm of Lester's words.

"Rufus came to dinner. He should have left earlier, but he had so many plans he wanted to share. He seemed euphoric, as if someone had turned on a light and he could see where he wanted to go. Such a waste."

A silence stretched until Reggie gently said, "So he left your house, late?"

"Yes, and almost immediately after I closed the front door, I remembered something I had to tell him." Lester's voice faded as he struggled to recall. "There was something he needed to know. What was it?"

"I don't think that is important, now, Lester. You went after him? Is that what happened next?"

"Yes." Lester's voice faltered. "I heard a thud. It was like a wet sponge hitting a wall. You know? That dull thump."

Reggie stayed silent.

"It was horrible. I wanted to chase it off."

"It?"

"It. Him. Whatever it was. The face was just a skin mask over bone. No hair, at least, not that I could see." Lester swallowed. "It bled Rufus like a hunter does to a stuck pig. The blood was everywhere."

"Take your time Lester. Anything you can recall will help catch this man."

"I don't think it was a man. It was a walking skeleton. I saw yellow stumps of teeth." Lester breathed in sharply. "It had something gold on its hands though. I remember a glint of gold."

The spaces between the sentences became longer and longer, and then Connor heard only breathing. Both men became silent and still for the longest time.

Connor no longer needed to listen. But couldn't help the final spurt of certainty when Lester took a shuddering breath and said, "It moved so quickly that at times it seemed to blur. You know, like a ghost. It was like a walking skeleton that appeared and disappeared. I should have tried to help Rufus, but I couldn't move."

Connor shot to his feet, and stopped with his hand poised on the handle of the closet door. The wait for Reggie to emerge seemed to last hours, but Connor needed Reggie's gun. After everything Lester had been through, Connor would not risk rendering Lester catatonic by rushing into the room, taking the gun, and leaving. If he registered on the human retina at all, then it would tip Lester over the edge, and so, he waited, impatiently.

The door opened and Reggie appeared, and froze on the spot. "You can't be here Connor," he hissed.

Even with the weight on his mind, Connor still could not help but laugh. "And yet, here I am."

Reggie spluttered and darted a glance at the closed door of Lester's room. "You can't-"

"Don't worry, Reggie. I'm not here to see Lester, but I do need your gun."

The look in Connor's eyes impressed the urgency on his friend, and wordlessly, he pulled out a Webley MK VI service revolver and handed it over.

"Thank you. I'll return it, you have my word." Pushing the gun into his own belt, Connor said, "You have to return to the hospital. Act normal. Attend lectures. Can you do that?"

"Yes, I can do that," Reggie replied.

Becoming a wraithlike ghost himself, Connor left the hospital. The journey back to the mausoleum was challenging, it took all his focus to stay in shadows. At one point he rounded a corner into a sunlit courtyard and danced backwards as, despite the speed he traveled at, the capillaries in the exposed skin of his hands and face pulled tight. He took more care after that. Even cloudy days deserved to be treated with respect.

He went over and over the things Lester said. Anger made his muscles tighten and his vision tint with red. Even though Connor having the gun would feel like aiming an arrow at a stone wall, David had felled Goliath. *Stranger things have happened, and everyone has a weak spot.*

He entered the tomb of The Butcher, and it was empty, save for the mummified remains which could not talk to him.

With a roar of rage, Connor punched the stone walls which felt as if they were closing in on him, and an explosion of shattered fragments hit the ground. *Where the hell is Malachi?*

He settled at the entrance and stared out over the sun-dappled grass. The shadows grew longer, their stains coalescing into a carpet of ink. When, an hour later, the grass flattened beneath the down draft of Malachi's fast approach, Connor observed his mentor objectively, as though through the eyes of a human.

Malachi's parchment-colored skin clung tightly to his bones.

When Malachi stopped beside him, Connor said, "Why am I getting the 'student' treatment? I am willing to wager that you disappear in a heartbeat – if you'll excuse the pun – on other humans you 'turn'."

Malachi assessed Connor's grim expression. "Maybe, I like you."

"And maybe you're amusing yourself by watching me self-destruct."

"Why would that amuse me? I broke you out of prison. You are safe here, are you not?"

"That depends. Is it safe, being inside the den with the lion?" Connor drew the pistol and pointed it at Malachi. "I believe *you* put me in prison. Lester saw you."

His mentor laughed aloud. He stared at Connor and in the depths of those yellow reptilian eyes, Connor saw something change. A dawning of something important.

"I know I can't kill you, but I can enjoy putting a dent in your smug face." Connor pulled the trigger and the bullet hit the wall where Malachi had been standing. It lodged in the space between two slabs of stone, excavating a crater. Once the sharp crack of the gunshot faded, Connor was left alone, with frustrating silence.

Chapter 26

Connor was reduced to hiding inside the mausoleum and waiting for Malachi to return. That look on Malachi's face unnerved him. Connor had lost a battle, but he knew his mentor well enough to know he would be back.

But as the hours ticked by, worms of doubt set up residence in his mind. "Is he out there murdering Lester? Reggie? Lavinia?" he whispered.

Even though the police thought Connor had died in the cell fire, he feared Malachi might do it anyway. *What did he say? It was only a matter of time before doubt would be cast on the identity of the dead man.*

Sitting and waiting became impossible for Connor. His doubts grew into monsters. He picked up a stone lying at his feet, and crumbled it into a handful of dust. He might not be as old as Malachi, but he had the strength of a newly turned vampire and he *could* protect what was precious to him.

In the gathering dusk, Connor took a direct route to Cranham Hall. The amber glow from a half-dozen windows created an illusion of peaceful warmth. Connor rested back against an elderly oak tree and scanned the surrounding woods for movement. He heard creatures rustling in the undergrowth, and peeling back the layers of awareness, he identified the soft shuffle of beetles moving over clumps of earth. The air around him remained still. *If Malachi is coming here, he has not made it yet.*

Once night fell, and the lights were dimmed in all but the servants' quarters, Connor jogged towards the house and scaled the wall of the east wing. Standing on the decorative stone cornice, he checked the room he peered into was empty, and then eased his way in through the second story window.

Walking silently across the thick wool carpet in Lord Cranham's den, he pulled the gun from his belt. He opened the chamber. Turning the remaining bullets out into his palm, Connor replaced them in their cardboard carton and set the Webley service revolver – a souvenir of the Second Boar War – into a velvet case, returned the weapon to its pride of place in Lord George's gun cabinet, and closed the door.

His good sense restored, Connor smiled wryly. David and Goliath could not be further from the truth. He and Malachi were more evenly matched than that, but it did not help him, he was still fighting shadows.

Will Malachi kill again? Connor realized he didn't know, and he didn't want to take a gamble. He returned to the window of the study and swung out onto the masonry ledge.

Instead of heading downward, he side-stepped further around the ledge and then climbed up another floor to where the Cranham family's bedrooms were. *Is this how the killer got to Rice?*

Anchoring his fingers into a crack in the stone wall, Connor applied persistent force to the window frame until the latch slowly bent out of shape and disengaged. He caught sight of his own reflection in the oily sheen of the glass. The ghost white cast to his complexion shocked even him. He had changed so much in the last three days, and the feeling of control continued to evaporate. But this, he could control. Easing open the window, he dropped inside and for three hours, he stood like a silent sentinel in the corner of Lavinia's room.

A slight turn of his head allowed him to scan the woodlands. The dead leaves he laid out carefully on the outside window ledge remained still and lifeless. If they shuffled or lifted, he'd know the pressure wave of an approaching vampire could be responsible. Fighting to the death felt apt. No one would get past him without ending his existence as an undead.

The lilac fingers of dawn bled into the sky before Connor began to relax. He put his hand on the window ledge, getting ready to leave, but could not. Turning back, he approached the large four poster bed and gazed down upon Lavinia's soft features. Tracks of dried tears marked her cheeks. Her black hair spreading across bronze-colored pillow shams created an intricate web of glistening dark threads. Leaning closer, Connor could smell the scent of her warm skin and the thud of her heart rate caught his attention like a siren call. Dropping to his knees beside her, he wound a silken rope of hair around his fingers. If he could freeze this moment and stay here beside her forever, he would. If he could take away the pain she felt, he would. Reggie's advice to 'stay dead' to Lavinia became harder to do with every moment he stayed.

He wanted to kiss her tears away, but knew that would be selfish. Standing, in one fluid movement, Connor headed for the window, bent the catch back into shape, and swung his legs out over the ledge. He dropped like a stone to the ground below, absorbing the shock through his body in an effortless crouch.

The trees wore a golden halo as the sun drove night away, and Connor sought the protection of their cover.

A truck trundled up the driveway at a leisurely amble. The signage on the side declared the owner as 'purveyor of fresh fruit and vegetables'. Mrs. Burnham would be up and about lighting the stove to prepare breakfast for her master's household, and checking the days' delivery and planning the dinner menu. The servants' world revolved around making sure the hospitality of the Cranhams was envied by all who visited them. The truck stopped at the servants' entrance, and the driver hopped out and banged on the door.

As the door opened, the man blurted, as though delighted at being the first to bring the gossip, "You heard the latest? That body ain't Doctor Sanderson at all."

It was enough to galvanize Connor into action. Going back into London, he whipped a newspaper from a stand outside the railway station and, like an animal retreating to his den, he didn't stop until he was once more in the mausoleum.

Just as Malachi predicted, the medical examiner found evidence which proved the body in the cell was not Connor. The newspaper report said the occupant of the police cell had a gold tooth. Other than that, the deceased had teeth missing, an old fracture to the eye socket. The clincher for the ME was the reason for the disruption to the teeth formation; a cleft palate.

"This man was clearly disfigured. The body in the fire was not that of Doctor Cornelius Sanderson.", was the expert findings of the autopsy.

The quote from Cavendish contained an underlying note of glee. 'We have launched a man hunt for Doctor Sanderson. He remains the chief suspect in three brutal, macabre murders. Evidence suggests he is responsible for a fourth death, perpetrated for the most diabolical of reasons, to cover his tracks and escape justice. This man must face trial for his crimes. Please come forward if you have any information of his whereabouts.'

The police search did not worry Connor unduly. *I can easily evade the police, and I have a search of my own to perform, for Malachi.* But first, Connor decided Reggie and Lavinia must be kept safe. He checked his pocket watch. *Reggie will be arriving at the hospital for lectures.*

Connor intercepted the Cranhams' coach and four. It was the first time he had tried it, and, when the horses sensed his approach, the whites of their eyes flashed as panic disrupted the synapsis in their brains. The odor reminded Connor of singed flesh as the unity of the team dissolved into chaos. Each horse became desperate to break formation and bolt. The team gave Harker a challenge he could barely manage, trying to prevent them injuring themselves and overturning the carriage.

As the carriage rocked wildly, Connor pulled open the door and swung inside. A terrified Reggie clung to the door handle with one hand, bracing the other against the roof.

Reggie's face was as white as a sheet. "Where the hell did you spring from?"

Beads of sweat stood out on Reginald's face. Connor knew the fear had nothing to do with the runaway coach when Reggie remained in the braced, muscle burning pose, even after Harker had regained control and the carriage rolled along at its usual sedate pace.

"What are you?" Reggie said.

"You deserve an explanation, I know that." *How the hell I'm going to do that is another matter.* Connor leaned back and spread his hands in a reassuring non- threatening attitude. "The papers have revealed I'm still alive, and Lavinia will be hurting even more, but listen to me Reggie, you could both be in danger."

Reggie snorted, but then said, "Danger? What kind of danger?"

"I didn't murder Rufus. Or Rice. Or Ivy. But whoever did, is still out there. You heard Lester. He wasn't describing me, was he?"

Reggie shook his head.

"So, I need you to bring Lavinia into London and check into The Strand Palace Hotel. I can't protect you both at Cranham Hall, and search for Malachi."

"Who?"

Connor shook his head. "I'll explain everything when you are both together, at the hotel, and safe. Will you trust me?"

Reginald stared at Connor. "You'll tell us what has happened to you?"

"Everything," Connor said quietly.

"Okay. What time should we expect you?"

For a beat, Connor entertained the idea that Reggie could betray him to the police, but his friends' steady regard told him otherwise. "Just after dusk. Five o'clock. I'll book you both into suite 310."

Chapter 27

Connor's attention was divided between searching for clues of Malachi's whereabouts and overseeing the wellbeing of Reginald and Lavinia. He had retraced his steps during the afternoon, and visited every place Malachi had shown him, and all to no avail. Connor began to wonder if Malachi could have left London for good.

If that turned out to be true, Connor would be the only suspect the police searched for, and, as the evidence pointed to him burning a man in his cell to affect his escape, his fate as a murderer was sealed. The police could write off Lester's testimony as trauma induced rambling. *Malachi has left me with no choice but to run. Perhaps that was always his plan.*

At three minutes to five o'clock, he abandoned his search and raced through central London to The Strand Palace Hotel. The entrance foyer, lined with ornate panels which also decorated the high curved ceiling, glinted with gilt and the sheen of polished marble. It had been open one year, and attracted peers, Lords, and prominent politicians.

The doormen created a flesh and bone barrier between the rich and scoundrels lying in wait.

Those same doormen didn't see Connor, however, when he whipped past them and headed up the wide staircase framed by carved stone balustrades. Of all the events of the past three days, this confrontation with Reggie and Lavinia was the most terrifying encounter Connor could imagine. *He* barely understood what he had become, so explaining it to people he loved, loomed as a huge mountain to climb.

He paused in the wide cream-painted hallway, and listened at the doorway of suite 310. Subdued human sounds beyond confirmed it was occupied. Connor did not wait to count how many hearts were beating inside the room. If the room contained the whole constabulary of Bow Street police station, then he would deal with that in his own way.

172

He knocked on the door, and waited for what seemed an eternity as human footfalls made their way across plush carpet. The door opened to reveal Reggie, his necktie hung loosely around the neck of his white dress shirt and a glass of whisky sat in his free hand.

With a brittle grin, he said, "Dutch courage. Cheers." He tossed down the remaining amber liquid and stepped back to allow Connor to enter. One deep inhalation reassured Connor that the alcohol levels in Reggie's body were minimal. He had consumed only one drink.

He walked past Reggie and stopped dead. Lavinia rose from her seat on a caramel and gold brocade couch. She smiled, and the act of smoothing creases from the jade colored silk skirt of her dress turned into convulsive plucking at the fabric.

Connor crossed the room, captured her hand and raised it to his chest. "I'm sorry."

Tears welled in the deep brown pools of her eyes and ran slowly down her cheeks. "I thought you were dead."

"I'm so sorry." He kissed her hand, and held it until the tremble shuddering through her body eased. With a sad smile, he said, "Please forgive me. I tried not to hurt you."

"You didn't kill Matthew Rice, or Ivy, or Rufus. I know you didn't."

Connor felt the tension in his shoulders dissolve. He had a tale of madness to relate, but at least Lavinia didn't believe he could murder. He hadn't realized how much that meant to him, until now.

Lowering himself carefully onto the couch, Connor drew Lavinia down beside him. Reggie, as if he knew this was the 'and now I'll begin moment', settled into the armchair opposite.

"This will sound insane. I know that, but hear me out. Three nights ago, I had an encounter-" Connor grimaced. *There is no point dancing around the truth.* "I was attacked in the morgue and I died."

Lavinia's mouth fell open, and Reggie snorted with laughter.

"I know. I have been through hell trying to get my head around this, but it's true. Watch." Connor deliberately breathed out, clamped his mouth shut, and sank into eerie stillness. He did not even blink.

The seconds ticked away and Reggie's gaze shuffled from Connor to Lavinia and back again.

Connor realized it would take more, so he got up from the couch and went into the bedroom. He heard the gasps when, to Lavinia and Reggie, he simply vanished. He walked human slow back into the room, holding a decorative quartz paperweight. When he had the attention of both humans, and they jumped to their feet, he slowly crumbled the ball of stone into a handful of dust.

Reggie took Lavinia's hand and pulled her behind his back. "Stay away, Connor."

Wriggling her fingers from his grasp, Lavinia pushed past Reggie and moved closer to Connor. "No, Reggie. It's okay."

The ocean of despair Connor felt inside was reflected back in her gaze.

"He won't hurt us." Shooting a pleading look over her shoulder, she said, "He wouldn't be here if he didn't care about us."

"Lavinia is right, Reggie. I would never harm you." Connor tried hard to keep eye contact, trying not to think about the dying man he drank from, and the thief he killed. He had not planned it, but the man died anyway.

Connor sat down on the couch once again and stared at his polished shoes. He waited for Reggie to decide what he wanted to do.

Both Reggie and Lavinia returned to their seats. Lavinia took Connor's hand, turned it over, and inspected the smooth hard white flesh. Without saying a word, she reached out and pressed her palm to his silent chest.

Connor expected questions, but he got acceptance as she whispered, "Who is killing people? Ivy? Rufus? Who wants to ruin your life?"

"I don't know, not for sure, but Reggie talked to Lester, and I think it's Malachi."

"Who the hell are you talking about, Connor?" Reggie leaned forward and braced his arms on his knees.

"He is the one who 'killed' me. I know it sounds crazy, but he's thousands of years old, and looks like a skull covered in dried out skin." Connor looked at Reggie. "Does that sound familiar?"

He nodded.

"What?" Lavinia looked from one man to the other, frustrated at being kept in the dark. "What? Tell me."

"Lester saw Rufus die. He told Reggie the killer looks like that. Skeleton covered in skin. Who drank Rufus' blood."

Lavinia sagged backward on the couch. "And he could come after us?"

Connor said slowly, "Malachi has disappeared. He may have gone. He has caused a lot of trouble and left me facing charges as a serial killer. Perhaps that is how he passes the decades. I don't know. But until I can be sure, I don't want either of you to leave London." Connor rubbed his temples, feeling a sensation like a rodent scratching inside his skull. "In London, I can keep an eye on you. The Hall is too far-"

"Do you-" Lavinia's teeth snapped shut as she changed her mind.

Do I drink blood? Connor could read her mind, and was relieved she decided it was better not to know.

"As soon as I know what Malachi intends, I'll come back. It should only be a day or two." In Connor's experience, Malachi tended to move fast. He couldn't imagine the elder vampire staying under the radar for very long, not if he was still in London.

The scratching inside Connor's head became whispered words, and he smiled. It looked like it would be faster than he imagined.

-Connor, I'm waiting in the morgue- As Malachi's words appeared inside his head, Connor wondered at the location. *Where we first met.* It seemed a fitting place for a showdown, somehow.

Getting to his feet, Connor said quietly, "Thank you, Reggie, for listening to me. And you, Lavinia. I'd do anything to turn back the clock. I've got to go, but stay here tonight, and stay together. I'll be back soon."

Death of Connor Sanderson

As though to impress upon them what they were up against, he left the room at a speed which left them both buffeted by his wake and staring at a door they could not have seen move.

Chapter 28

As Connor raced across London's dark wet streets to St George's Circus, he mulled over Malachi's choice. Like Morse code, his mentor's voice played the message over and over inside his head, as though he was unsure Connor had received it. Connor grinned. If he had learned one thing during his hours alone, it was how to retreat into his own head, enter the safe room he visualized, and lock others out; it worked with the human voices drifting through the cemetery. Apparently, it locked his own thoughts inside just as effectively. *Malachi doesn't seem to know I'm coming.*

Malachi's thoughts became insistent, banging on the door, but Connor felt safe. *Why does he want to go back to our beginning?* Everything Malachi did had a reason.

Entering the hospital and breezing through the corridors, Connor heard the soft shoe shuffle of the night nurses checking on patients. The deep breathing of slumber created a calming atmosphere which seeped into Connor. It felt as though nothing bad could happen here, not under the watch of those inspired by the teachings of Florence Nightingale.

Pushing quietly through the door marked 'morgue', Connor descended the stone steps and paused. Even *his* cold skin detected the drop in temperature to well below 'preservation of the dead' cold.

Malachi is here. Connor entered and noticed immediately the deeper texture in the shadow at the end of the room. A gleam of twin yellow-tinted jewels instantly focused Connor's mind. Stepping outside the safe room in his head, he asked the question which burned inside.

Why here, Malachi? Connor laughed harshly. *I thought you achieved your aim to destroy me. Have you come to gloat?*

Malachi moved into the blade of moonlight cutting through the room, from a street-level letterbox shaped window to the ceramic tiles underfoot. Motes of dust pirouetted around him like fireflies as he pushed the flowing ash-gray robe he wore back from his shoulders. Connor recognized it from their first night-time encounter. The fabric brushed the floor, and could shield a face in sand storms or shut out the sunlight, Connor guessed.

It seems you are dressed for a journey? You are leaving, then? Connor resented the sadness he felt.

"I have spent enough time here." The older vampire's thin smile revealed yellowed teeth. "I yearn for home."

It was the first time Connor considered that Malachi had an emotional attachment to a place. "What brought you here, to London? It's a long way from Egypt."

Thin bony fingers rubbed over the creased parchment of skin on his forehead. "I travel. There are others like me whose paths I cross along the way. It is a reminder I am not alone. You, for example, will always feel an affinity for London. Even when the city changes into a place you no longer recognize. In the decades to come, you'll be drawn here. It is the way of things."

Connor nodded. It made perfect sense. *When are you leaving?*
-That depends on you-
On me? Connor peered into the impassive features. *Why me?*
-I have a conscience. You are being hunted by the police. You can't stay here, but you can't run. You have to end it, here, first, or they'll never stop looking- "You don't want to be looking over your shoulder whenever you come back."

Malachi's gaze exuded a zealous gleam Connor had not noticed before. As though he held his breath, feeling tension. *As though my answer means something to him.*

The bony hand plucked at the necklace hanging around his scrawny neck. The serpent ring clinked against the glass vial. Connor watched the movement, and the glint of the emerald eyes on the gold coiled serpent caressing the skeletal hand.

"What do you suggest I do," said Connor quietly, his muscles tight with the unease trickling down his spine.

Dropping both hands and shrugging, the old vampire replied, "You have to die. Publicly."

Connor waited and watched.

A picture emerged from a mist inside his head, of him stood on the gallows in a bleak yard at the Old Bailey. At his shoulder, stood a celebrity of sorts. *Ellis.* He held the sackcloth hood which would go over Connor's head. Everyone knew Ellis, the famous executioner of London, who had put to death the most notorious criminals in the city.

Connor felt his neck muscles ache with cramp as he watched the scene Malachi played out for him. He even stopped breathing and experienced a moment of vertigo when the 'Connor' he watched through the misty veil of second sight, dropped through the hatch door and swung by the neck.

"You think I should give myself up to the police? Face a trial and the death sentence?"

-Think about it. You are already dead. They cannot kill you again, and once you are buried, I'll be here to dig you out. Once we are in Egypt, you'll merely be another face in the crowd-

The more Connor listened, the more it began to make sense. He nodded. He walked towards Malachi, studying the expressions playing across the thin slack features.

Quietly, Connor said, "You haven't changed your mind, then. You still think we should go to Egypt, together."

Through rusty dry vocal chords, Malachi said, "No, I haven't changed my mind. England is too risky for you. Egypt is the better option."

Connor absently ran his fingers over the metal autopsy tables. "I can see the logic. So, I go to the police station and give myself up. Plead guilty, perhaps? To speed things along?"

Frowning in thought, Connor rearranged the surgical implements he found inside a folded linen cloth on an instrument table.

-Precisely. The police stop looking for you, and you're free to learn how to survive decades unshackled by your human existence-
Malachi drifted closer. His sharp ridged taloned nails tapping out a mesmerizing rhythm on the glass vial necklace again. He leaned in until Connor felt the cool breeze of stale breath. "You'll be free."

Jerking his head up and glaring at the skeletal presence at his shoulder, Connor spat, "But you taught me survival depends on staying fit." He lunged to grab hold of the scrawny neck, but the aged vampire disappeared, materializing across the room. Connor ran full tilt at the cloaked figure, crashing into the wall, just as he expected to. Bracing his boot against the slick tiles, Connor launched himself quickly after the swift moving shadow. His peripheral vision picked up the accelerating movement easier, and like a pin ball ricocheting around the enclosed space, Connor began to guess where his mentor would pause next.

The aged skull hit the wall and cracked porcelain cascaded to the ground when Connor's hand finally closed around more than fresh air, and vertebrae creaked in his grasp.

Clawed hands struck out at Connor's eyes, and in one swift move, he snapped the old vampire's wrist, leaving a hand hanging limply. The other, he dragged from his throat, hearing fingernails score across his quartz-hard skin. Pressing his face in close, until the jaundice yellow eyes were out of focus, Connor said, "New vampires are stronger. You taught me that. And this time, I'm smarter than you, too."

Malachi hissed like a scalded cat. His flailing bony knees caught Connor in the thigh muscles. -*You have no idea what I can do to you*-

Agony swelled inside Connor's skull like a swarm of bees stinging over and over until his thoughts dissolved into a soot black cloud. Blinding streaks of white hot pain darted behind his eyes and the wizened face before him became wreathed in a halo of light.

Staggering back, Connor no longer felt the ridged bone of Malachi's spine in his grasp, and every instinct screamed 'protect yourself'. Folding his arms across his chest and dipping his chin, he protected the vulnerable cage of life. His blood network, as Malachi always said, was of paramount importance. Diving to the floor, Connor collided with the autopsy tray, scattering instruments across the ceramic tiles. He rolled under a metal table, feeling the knots of steel beneath him grinding into his flesh.

Closing his eyes, he sampled the air; his skin and sense of hearing on red alert for a shift in pressure. *Will a broken wrist, a useless hand, stop him?* Connor knew it wouldn't. The whine of rushing air closed in fast, and Connor braced for impact. His body skidded across the floor and he hit the wall side on, like a freight train. The lumps of steel beneath him screeched across the slick tiled surface, scarring the glaze with gouged lines. The crushing blow would come next. Twisting and reaching behind his shoulder, Connor's scrabbling fingers grabbed a cranial drill bit and raised it up, level with his face. Bracing the back of his hand on his forehead, he locked every muscle tight and closed his eyes.

The crunch, when it came, as Malachi slammed hard into Connor's body, made every rib creak. But Connor didn't notice that. The back of his hand crushed the flesh on his forehead and the blunt metal shaft dug into his palm with the impact. Connor felt the sharp crack vibrate through his own head as the drill bit pierced Malachi's skull, between those manic gleaming eyes.

The thin scrawny body went slack and, when Connor dared to look, there was a crumbling void where Malachi's face should be. *So much for the hangman's noose.* Connor had smelled a rat when the old wizened vampire related the plan. Even a vampire can't survive a broken neck. Severing the blood network between his head and body would have put Connor in the same place as The Butcher.

Rolling the body away, Connor rose to his feet. His shirt hung in tatters and the gouges in his face seeped pink-colored chalky ooze, but other than that, he had survived. Lifting the bundle of bones from the floor, Connor placed the inert form onto a cadaver drawer bed and shut the door.

Malachi, where are you?

Closing his eyes, Connor opened up his mind, searching for his mentor's voice. The silence felt heavy, thicker than air. His vision clouded, but the weight on his chest told him this came from somewhere other than his own despair.

He tried to breathe in but couldn't. Reaching out a hand, his fingers grazed over a rough splintered surface even though, when he looked, Connor's hand stroked nothing but the polished steel of a cadaver drawer.

As though a zip line of concentration called to him, he left the morgue and headed out of the hospital by the shortest route. He shivered as if he felt cold and gathered the sensation as another clue.

Thick weighted atmosphere. Splintered wood. Bone chilling cold. The graveyard?

Connor set off at a run towards the cemetery, but the picture inside his mind melted and lost its sharpness. The graveyard was the wrong choice.

Help me, Malachi. Where are you?

A flash of silver resolved into shimmering bodies swimming around, passing behind Connor's eyes as if his head was an aquarium. *A shoal of fish.* Puzzle pieces slotted into place.

The Thames. Connor swung around and headed back through the city and onto the embankment. The slate-gray river boiled lazily before him, the tumbling currents churning in an endless, slow rolling motion. The length of the river bank bore landmark statues and benches. Cleopatra's needle drew Connor as if it was a real needle of steel and held a magnetic force within.

He arrived at the base of the monument and looked down over the wall at the promenade below. In a smooth movement, he vaulted over the side and landed lightly on the paved concrete path. Walking along close to the edge, he peered into the soot gray depths.

He stopped suddenly and retraced his steps ten yards. A pale circle shimmered a hundred feet below, at least.

Shedding his coat, Connor stepped off the path and plummeted into the water. His dense body took him effortlessly downwards until the moon and gas lights above no longer penetrated. The currents buffeted his body and his hair billowed, becoming a spiked cloud of coal black strands.

The black hanks obscured his vision until he dipped his chin and peered down the wall of wood which lined the river bank far below the water level.

He glimpsed a pale oval with ink-black holes where eyes would be, and realized it was a face. Diving into a faster descent, Connor felt his muscles tighten with mindless fear. He was not breathing, so why would Malachi drown? Why would he be down here at all?

His mentor finally sent words splintered by frozen thoughts: *Trapped- not strong- iron-*

Trapped by who? How? Connor gave up asking questions. His fingers finally tangled into the saturated fabric of Malachi's coat. The thin angular bones beneath it seemed fragile, brittle even. Connor took a moment to dissipate the haste and alarm. He felt as though he would snap the old vampire's bones if he let panic take hold.

Trying to gather Malachi's slack form into his arms, Connor discovered chains were wrapped around both his ankles. No, not *around*, metal stakes were driven through both feet. The chain wound around his scrawny neck was secured to the wall, and prevented Malachi reaching down to free himself.

But why is he so weak? Connor knew the elder vampire's feeble appearance disguised incredible strength. Reaching down, Connor extracted the steel pins carefully. He felt the bones grate, but the metal had pierced only flesh and none were broken. The chain around Malachi's neck was easier to deal with, although, beneath the icy water, Connor found channeling his own strength required more concentration. But still, he managed to grip the links and distort the metal until it fractured.

Holding onto Malachi, bracing his foot on the riveted wooden barrier, Connor launched them both upwards. As their heads broke the surface of the water, the old vampire's unresponsive features caused more concern.

"You need to hold on, old man." Folding the bony fingers over a ledge, Connor anchored Malachi to the concrete wall. Barely noticing the water-logged weight of his clothes, Connor scaled the embankment and then reached down and pulled Malachi up after him. Supporting his mentor, Connor guided him into the deep shadow below a bridge over the river, and sunk down with Malachi beside him.

The silence stretched as they both rested back against the concrete wall and gathered their thoughts and let the consequences sink in.

Finally, Connor rolled his head to the side and peered at Malachi's gray translucent skin. "Why couldn't you free yourself?"

Malachi's breath rattled in weak laughter. "Of all the questions, you start with that one. Let me ask you, how did you know it wasn't me in the morgue?"

Resting his forearms on his bent knees and gazing out over the ripples racing over the water, Connor said quietly, "I sensed something different about him, but it was the serpent ring. His had emerald eyes, yours are rubies."

"Ah," said Malachi, "The devil is in the detail."

"I asked him about our plans to return to Egypt. We never made any such plans, and then I knew for certain." Connor looked at the smile which etched creases into Malachi's face. "It was Numu? The killer? And you have been protecting him, so what happened? What changed?"

"What changed? He knew I considered you my protégé. That was what tipped him over the edge into the killing spree. He wanted to bury you, one way or another."

"So, I was supposed to suffer a broken neck and rot away like The Butcher, and you and your brother disappear back to Egypt?"

Malachi nodded. "That was what he worked towards. Everything led to removing you."

"Was it you that attacked me in the morgue that night?"

Malachi shook his head. "No, it was Numu. I found you soon after and I just had a feeling about you. You should have been dead, but you were fighting to survive. I saved you. Numu didn't like that."

"This brings me back to my first question. Why couldn't you free yourself?"

"I was stupid. Numu finally revealed himself. We've been playing cat and mouse until now. Me protecting you, and him hiding from me. But then he came out of hiding. I underestimated him." Pulling the folds of wet fabric from around his neck, Malachi revealed tears in his flesh. "He hugged me like a brother, and then drained my blood. He wanted me out of the way until he finished you."

"So much for brotherly love."

"He would have rescued me. But by anchoring me there, below the water, when I was so weak, he knew I'd stay there rather than tear the pins through my feet and suffer decades of not being able to walk. Vanity, but he knew I couldn't risk that."

"I can understand that. Immortality is daunting, but as a cripple, it would be unbearable." Digesting all he had learned, Connor finally asked, "So, what now?"

"I assume Numu is dead?" Malachi's voice rang hollow with the regret.

"Yes."

"Then we have our murderer. Your name can be cleared if Lester Cartwright identifies Numu. Did you search him?"

"No."

"I know my brother well. He will have trophies from his victims. Something from Rice, and Ivy. Usually a sample of their blood. Smelling it transports him back to the thrill of his kill."

"Will you recover?" Connor asked.

"I will. It will take a short while, but what I need now is rest while my flesh dries out."

"I'll take you back to the cemetery, and then I'll go and see my favorite police inspector."

Chapter 29

"Take a seat, Doctor Sanderson." Cavendish smiled, the light of glee in his eyes hard to miss. "You look remarkably well, for a corpse."

Connor nodded. "Thank you, Inspector. It has been a trying few days." Connor's dried disheveled clothes pulled tight across his shoulders when he shrugged. "I will answer any questions you have. As you know, I found the murderer, the real murderer, and I just want a normal life again." Connor knew that 'normal' could never be restored to him, but for now, he'd settle for getting Cavendish off his back once and for all.

Cavendish flipped through the papers and photographs on his desk. Skin samples which were taken from Connor when he walked into the police station, and photographs of wounds he sustained in the fight to the death with the 'John Doe' now lying in the police pathology lab were spread out before him.

"You have no idea who your attacker is, was? You've never seen him before?"

"No," answered Connor. "But from what Lester Cartwright has said in his statement, I believe the man could be described as a psychopath who, for some reason, fixated on me."

Connor knew, from searching Numu's body himself that the police would have found a vial of blood which, from what Lester said, Connor suspected came from Rufus. A scrap of a cotton apron covered in blood spots and Rice's epaulette bearing his regimental insignia were tucked into the folds of a fabric belt tied around Numu's waist.

Connor also planted some evidence of his own; brick dust and rust flakes from the prison bars Malachi loosened when he helped Connor escape. He dipped Numu's slack fingers into the residue then wiped them over the folds of his robe.

"Tell me, Doctor Sanderson, how did you escape from your burning cell?"

Connor looked at Cavendish and said, regretfully. "I wish I could help you. I really do, but I woke up down on the embankment with a bump on the head. I don't remember how I got there."

"But you didn't come forward when you came to your senses?"

Connor leaned back in his seat. "Inspector, put yourself in my shoes. I know I am not a murderer. How can I hope to prove that from inside a cell? I'm not proud of myself, but I wanted the chance to clear my name."

Cavendish frowned as he flicked through the sheaf of papers once again. "It is all very convenient, but, for now, it seems, you are no longer implicated." Pushing back his chair and standing up, Cavendish said, "Good day to you, Sanderson."

Connor rose from his seat and shook hands with the inspector. "Thank you, Inspector. I'm glad you found your man and we can all sleep easier tonight."

Connor left the room and walked slowly down the corridor. The smell of sweat and starch reminded him a little of the hospital wards. The scent of blood was more subtle here. Although nurses were as calm as their law enforcement counterparts, the patients at the hospital were generally anxious with hearts pumping blood faster in a more alluring beat. And there were the cannulas. A smear of blood was like a drenching of heroin to Connor's senses.

He glanced towards the closed door, beyond which he had been held prisoner. The blood he could smell pluming from *that* area probably came from grazed faces, black eyes, or other drunken brawl induced injuries.

Some people really were their own worst enemy.

Nodding at the desk sergeant and pushing his way through a glass paneled door, Connor's smile was genuine when he spotted Reggie's profile through the open window of the Cranhams' carriage.

Reggie waved as Connor opened the door and climbed into the shadowed interior. The evening sun appeared to stage a protest at the chill of dusk chasing her away, and the golden glow scattered bright coins of light across the sidewalk.

"I thought you'd appreciate the safety of a carriage." Reggie's half smile expressed quiet acceptance.

He knows all there is, and is still a good friend. No, more than that, a brother in all but blood. "Are there many guests this evening?"

Reggie chuckled. "Lavinia will be there, and Uncle Edgar. Even Cecil Clare begged for an invitation. You have delivered a serial killer to the police and Rufus' family are very grateful."

"It was nothing. Not really."

Connor had told Reggie everything, and his friend had protested when Connor put the blame for the deaths squarely on his own shoulders. 'You were stalked by a monster. It could happen to any of us. Now I'll hear no more of it', had been Reggie's viewpoint.

Despite the no nonsense delivery of Reggie's words, Connor detected the suppressed glee of a man who feels safe once more, and thankful that Lavinia, and the rest of his family, no longer had to look over their shoulders.

Reggie rapped his cane on the roof of the carriage. "Harker, if you please."

From behind, Connor heard William hop down from his seat and perform his footman duties. He tuned out the shouts of London street sellers and the cacophony of chatter which fell from shop doorways, from the public houses, and on the bustling streets themselves.

Resting his head back against the leather upholstered wall, he relaxed for the first time in what felt like an eternity. The rolling of the carriage diminished as the four horse team picked up speed and found their stride.

The journey unfolded in an oasis of silence. Reggie's air of comfort meant more to Connor than he thought it could. He had the feeling others, if they knew the truth, would view him as a monster almost as terrifying as Numu. *Of course, Reggie has never laid eyes on Malachi.* His mentor embodied every child's nightmare. *Will I end up looking like that, I wonder?* But Connor already knew the rules of the game. Look after your raw material, and you stay young and healthy.

Connor opened his eyes and watched the passing flashes of street lamps strobing over Reggie's content face. Friendships and relationships with humans would be the hardest thing to lose. He acknowledged an inevitable truth, he would have to say goodbye to the Cranhams, for their sakes.

The gas lights faded to the thick darkness of tree-lined country lanes. The city smells of coal, soot, and rotting garbage gave way to earth, flora, and evening dew, and very soon, the halo of light shrouding Cranham Hall became a beacon which lifted the spirits. Even the horses appeared to stretch their stride in joyful abandon.

The horseshoe driveway afforded a view of the entire ground floor, and Connor felt flattered to find most of the household staff lined up outside beneath the portico. Connor alighted from the carriage before William could disembark and open the door, and the staff, led by Mr. Phelps and Mrs. Burnham, burst into a rousing chorus of 'For He's a Jolly Good Fellow'.

Connor's laughter held genuine delight.

"Thank you, sir. You caught Ivy's murderer and we'll be forever grateful." Mr. Phelps shook Connor's hand and the rest of the staff beamed smiles of adoration upon him. If this was to be his last night at the Hall, then at least he would take away a wealth of precious memories.

"Thank you, Phelps. You'll never know how good it feels to make sure such evil met a fitting end."

Reggie joined Connor on the top step and taking his arm, he led him into the Hall. The high ceilings and gilt-edged mirrors refracted prisms of light which Connor's mature vampire vision saw as glittering strands cutting through the air. These prisms of light cast a warm glow over each of the figures waiting beyond the open double doors of the drawing room.

Lady Isobel, dressed in a sleek gown of blue silk stepped forward and reached for both Connor's hands. "My dear boy, it is wonderful to see you."

He bowed and brushed his lips over the lace on the gloves she wore. "Lady Isobel, I am relieved normality has been restored. I just regret the terror you all suffered."

"And you too, Connor. You suffered as much as we, and you showed great bravery."

Connor smiled. He knew the family were privy to everything Inspector Cavendish had reluctantly accepted as true, and Lester Cartwright added weight to Connor's hero status.

Connor tuned into the number of heat signatures in the room beyond, and swallowed down the salivating response to the chorus of succulent cantering heartbeats. The odor of each person resembled notes in a symphony, and if his own heart could beat faster, it would have when he detected Lavinia's delicate aroma.

Lester appeared behind Lady Cranham and, with red smudges staining his cheeks, he murmured, "Anything I can do for you, Sanderson, just say the word." Rufus' ghost sat on the youngster's shoulder as surely as the guilt Connor shared at sealing the unfortunate man's fate.

"Lester, you were a good friend to Rufus. Never doubt that." Clasping the young man's shoulder gently, Connor turned to the next well-wisher.

Cedric Clare's complexion bore the gray cast of a tortured soul. "Sanderson-" The elder man swallowed and his throat clamped shut. The flush of blood burning beneath his starched collar threatened to end in an undignified sob until Connor stepped in.

He looked at Cedric and said quietly, "Rufus had turned a corner. You can be proud of him, and I'm just sorry I was too late to save him."

The shame Cedric felt fell away like a weighted shroud. "Thank you, Sanderson." He met Connor's steady gray regard and said, "Connor. Thank you."

Turning away, Connor smiled and acknowledged compliments from the other members of the Cranham household. Reggie's youngest sister, Tilly, gazed at him with the unabashed glee of hero worship, and he made the girl blush when he gave her a chivalrous bow.

Connor's own smile died when he glanced over Tilly's head and saw Lavinia wearing a stunning crystal blue gown and smiling at him as though he was the only person in the room. The noise of subdued conversation faded and the only sound Connor heard was the shallow excitement of Lavinia's breathing.

He allowed himself the indulgence of pretending, just for a moment, that a future existed in which he could love Lavinia in the way he wanted to, and crossing the room, his feelings were written clearly on his face.

The lull in conversation meant others were watching, and Lavinia moved away with a bright smile. "I think I need some fresh air. Take a turn around the garden with me, Connor." With a glance his way, she drifted away across the room.

"Don't be too long, you two," Lady Isabel said lightly, "Mrs. Burnham has prepared a feast fit for a king."

Collecting a throw from the back of a leather couch, Connor said, "It's chilly out, Lady Isabel, we will be back directly."

He followed Lavinia's lead, leaving by the French doors and running lightly down the steps. It took him one second to locate her. She stood beneath the shade of a tree in the center of the meticulously clipped lawn.

Connor silently crossed the grass and stopped a hair's breadth away from her. He pushed his fingers into the silky black tresses of her carefully dressed hair and kissed her. He kept his eyes open at first, watching her deep brown gaze melt, before the black crescent of her lowered lashes stole the mesmerizing image away. Her perfume intoxicated him. The incandescent heat of her body tortured him as he closed the distance and his hand spanned her waist.

When he broke the kiss, time stood still and he wanted to stay there, in that moment, forever. Her hand on his cheek felt like a fiery brand. Her skin glowed with iridescence, and Connor savored and absorbed every detail.

Her smile said all the words he could not find as the light in her eyes flooded with sorrow. She knew he wanted more than they could ever have. 'If only' resounded inside his head as a forlorn lament.

"I love you, Connor. That is enough."

Laying his forehead gently on hers, his fingertips still stroking through her hair, Connor whispered, "I love you, too, my heart."

"Where will you go?"

"I'm not sure. I just know I can't let myself become a monster."

Connor felt the smile on her lips as she raised her chin and kissed him. "Oh no, Mr. Sanderson, you'll never become a monster."

Connor chuckled. "Okay, well perhaps I mean, I need to help people." His gray eyes glinted in the gloom. "You know what I am? That I need to drink b-"

"Shhh." Lavinia put a finger on his mouth. "I *do* know." Taking a deliberate breath, she said, quietly and clearly, "You need to drink blood. Animal *and* human."

Connor nodded.

"But that's not all you are. I know you. You'll find a way to do something good."

Lavinia's faith in him lifted a weight from Connor's shoulders. Malachi, too, had faith in him. All he needed to do, was to find a way of living with himself.

Taking Lavinia's hand, he led her back towards the Hall. What was it Malachi said? Connor's control in the face of human blood made him exceptional. Entering the drawing room once again, Connor embraced the buffeting sensation of a dozen hearts beating. He inhaled and passed the alluring nectar of blood-drenched aromas over his palette, and even though a blade of hunger dragged its way through his gut, he controlled it.

In that moment, he knew that he had a choice, and he chose not to be the monster.

With Lavinia at his left side, and Reggie at his right, Connor made a show of sampling some of Mrs. Burnham's pies, pastries, and fruit compote. He found that he could eat the odd mouthful, but his body did not enjoy it. The food he discarded, he and his two accomplices folded into napkins which would be found by the perplexed maids when the family retired for the night.

Reggie accompanied Connor out into the courtyard to where the carriage waited.

He echoed Lavinia's words. "Where will you go?"

Connor felt relief that the truth needed no explanation. He could not stay, and he would probably never see any of the Cranham family again. Connor laid a hand on Reggie's shoulder and smiled. Turning away, he climbed into the carriage and waved goodbye as Reggie's lonely figure faded into the distance.

Where will I go?

~~~THE END~~~
~~~

194

I share now, a **bonus** short story, part of the ice-berg of hidden
backstory that lives inside every author's brain…

Julian and Connor began a ninety-three-year friendship here, in
1918.

Doctor Connor Sanderson was called before the Undead
Council,
and the rest, as they say, is history.

Connor Sanderson Meets Principal Julian

The Death of Jack the Ripper

The City of London, 1918.

Connor held his tongue when Malachi materialized in front of him in the morgue at the hospital. The tracing paper tight mask of his mentor's face and the fish-scale sheen glistening in his eyes had lost their horror. Connor was now well acquainted with his two-thousand-year old companion.

As he had on the day their paths first crossed, Malachi raised a hand and crooked a bony finger that begged Connor to follow.

Connor immediately turned on his heel and left the cold basement, passing silently up the glittering quartz treads of the staircase. He moved briskly along the white ceramic-tiled hallways, but was careful not to exceed the limits of human sight. If he became a blur, it frightened the nurses. In a deserted hallway, he got to push his speed up and disappear through the door which led to the students' quarters. Entering his own rooms, he peeled his white doctor's coat quickly from solid shoulders, stripped off his white shirt, and redressed in black and charcoal-gray garb.

Though he considered blending into shadow a challenge when he was six-feet and three-inches tall, he had yet to realize that concealing the mesmerizing edifice of hard muscle covering his powerful frame was impossible. And the raven-black sweep of hair that held sapphire fragments trapped in each glossy strand would always be arresting. He wheeled around, bowled back out of the door, and, minutes later, was standing on the sidewalk outside the hospital.

Malachi appeared soundlessly at his side. Connor was not surprised when his mentor's arrival more closely resembled a drive by shooting. He barely broke stride as his bony finger poked Connor in the shoulder and he took off along the dark sidewalk.

He watched Malachi dash beneath the lamp-posts lining the route, his putty colored scalp glistening with cobweb strands of hair. *He should wear a hat.* But then Connor realized he was the only creature who could see the weaving figure.

It took barely ten minutes for the pair of vampires to skim through the moonlit streets, heading north from the hospital through Hyde and Regents Parks, until they finally came to a halt before the impressive arched entrance to the gatehouse of Highgate Cemetery. The glowering presence of tall, blackened leaded-glass windows scarred the ethereal beauty of the pale-gray granite turrets. Connor could almost conjure a ghostly face pressed up close to the panes. *It is no wonder humans find graveyards at night the place of nightmares.*

He sliced a steely-gray glance across at Malachi's hawkish features, and found him staring back. With a sharp nod, Malachi surged forward, pushed the gates open, and vanished inside. Connor followed, moving wordlessly in concert with Malachi's meandering flight as they negotiated the maze of mausoleums and gravestones.

At the rear boundary of the East cemetery, Malachi dug his fingers into a seam in the wall, and a low grating noise rumbled through Connor's head as an eight feet tall slab of stone slid smoothly aside. Stepping over the threshold, Malachi sank downward out of view, and Connor discovered that, rather than a hole through the wall, a flight of roughly hewn steps descended into inky depths.

Connor's shadow swelled to fill the space as he tracked Malachi's path. The slick greasy surface of the moss-covered rocks underfoot and the thick damp air settled over his features like a smothering mask, but they barely registered as he set off at a hair-raising speed.

Malachi moved ahead down steep slopes which took them beneath the sewer system of London. Connor curiously trailed his fingertips over glacier smooth walls glistening with a flowing river of moisture. Only the dripping of rain water trickling through fissures in the rocks broke the silence. And, they whipped along the potholed surface where the decades of running water had eroded the bedrock of the maze of manmade passageways.

Where are we going? Connor asked, writing the thoughts inside his head and waiting for Malachi to read them.

"You will see." Malachi's crystal clear words were less than a whisper.

Connor grinned into the darkness. Eight years and counting, and he still found the supernatural senses of being a vampire fascinating. Malachi was still an enigma. He had been a priest in ancient Egypt, and a clairvoyant. But, Connor would never know how much of his mentor's talent in reading Connor's mind was because he had drank from Malachi's sliced vein as his human form was dying.

-Better my *thoughts than my twin's-* Malachi laughed gently, reminding Connor that all his thoughts were there to be plundered, although the older vampire did show restraint. *At least, that is how it appears, but how would I know for sure?* As the years passed, Connor's awareness of the spectrum of vampire consciousness became more acute. He usually sensed Malachi tiptoeing through his mind before his mentor spoke.

You're right. I wouldn't want Numu inside my mind, not even for an instant. Connor grinned in the darkness, knowing Malachi would feel the laughter lighting up the synapses in his brain.

He almost barreled into the stationery scrawny figure when Malachi stopped dead – although a full-scale collision would have hurt Connor more. He had found that bony elbows and knees forged in steel should be respected.

"What?" Connor studied Malachi's grim mask.

"There are worse things than Numu's mind." Malachi spoke aloud this time too, before turning and whipping away again.

"And that's it?" Connor's trailing hand gouged a trough into the wall as frustration bit deep.

Malachi's laughter rippled through the dead air. "Patience, Doctor Connor. Principal Julian has summoned you. You are very young, not yet reached your first decade of immortal years, so it is an honor. The rest will become clear in time."

Mention of Principal Julian shocked Connor into movement, as though Malachi held a leash and yanked it tight.

Just when the stagnant, iron-oxide tainted atmosphere in the tunnel coated Connor's tongue and rippled a sneer across his face, the space suddenly opened out into a huge underground cavern. An imposing stone altar dominated the far end of a rectangular chamber.

Darkness hung overhead like coal dust. The flames of the candles, cemented to the alter by the spiny embrace of dried wax, could not reach the high ceiling.

Three ghostly-pale ovals which appeared to hang in midair resolved into the faces of the council jurors as each one turned in Connor's direction. Their rigidly set bodies rested in the stiff embrace of throne-like seats carved from the darkest oak, and even when Connor and Malachi approached, they did not stir.

"This is the one." Malachi's voice shattered the silence, and, as though they were jolted from a trance, the three vampires assessed Connor with watchful eyes.

He could almost feel their intent inspection crawling over his skin. He was drawn to the commanding tilt to the strong jaw of the blond vampire seated center stage. In silence, his penetrating ice-green regard raked over Connor's tight features.

The burn in his throat, urging Connor to cough, became harder to resist with each passing second, but Malachi had told him countless times, you wait; you do not speak until spoken to. He suspected that applied to any noise, at all.

Finally, fabric rustled, and the principal of the Undead Council was ready to speak.

"My name is Principal Julian." He lifted a hand to indicate his fellow jurors. "Juror Raymond."

The vampire with hair the color of wet sand and eyes the pale blue of limpid pools inclined his head slowly.

"And Juror Marius."

The dark glowering features did not move, and the hard stare in the glittering black eyes flickered for the briefest second.

Principal Julian folded his perfect complexion into a smile, stroking long pale fingers over his square jaw as he said quietly, "Play nice, Marius. I'm sure Doctor Connor will earn your respect, in time."

Marius raised a black-winged brow over his hooded gaze and said slowly, "We shall see."

A sense that their bark would be worse than their bite seeped into Connor's mind. *Would it be like looking behind the curtain to discover the Wizard of Oz was merely a man?* He studied the jury, stood quietly at ease, and waited.

"Malachi has brought you before us by my request," said Principal Julian. "He says that you are a surgeon."

"That is true."

"You were turned in 1910. Tell me about yourself... how have you passed your immortal years?" Julian sat back and adopted a relaxed pose.

Connor considered his words carefully. "I was twenty-four years old. I'm a surgeon and I returned to London three months ago. I spent the war in France, in the trenches, operating on injured soldiers in the mobile army surgical hospital."

"Operating? You can cut into their flesh... and not feed?" Juror Raymond's tone was skeptical, and the half grin didn't reach his eyes.

"It took greater effort at first. Not breathing and locking the air inside my lungs helped. But yes, I can do that."

Without taking his eyes from Connor, Julian said, "You have done well, Malachi."

Malachi grinned widely.

Julian leaned forward and laid his palms on the cold stone table. "Doctor Connor, we are in a state of emergency. The status quo of vampire secrecy is under threat. Do you remember Jack the Ripper?"

"I was only a two-year-old child, but yes, I heard the stories. He murdered half a dozen prostitutes back in 1888."

"Well, let's just say, he is back."

Light dawned in Connor's eyes, and he resisted the knee jerk reaction of looking at Malachi. "I seem to remember hearing that he's a vampire."

Julian gave a bark of laughter. "Malachi told you with good reason. You really don't want to become like Jack. Of course, we do not know for certain his real name *is* Jack, but it is the name he earned thirty years ago. He is back, and the Metropolitan Police are talking about Copycat Jack."

"Why are you telling *me* this?" asked Connor, and this time, he did shoot a glance at Malachi's frozen profile.

"Why indeed." The principal took a deep breath. "Although we have a vampire placed in the police service as a night constable, and he provides information on where Jack prefers to hunt, sadly, he does not have the skills to solve our problem."

"Skills?"

"Come now, do I have to spell it out?" Julian indicated Connor's tall, muscular physique and said, "You are a formidable vampire, Doctor Connor, and you have the expertise to terminate Jack, and cover your tracks... our tracks. The humans must not discover he is a vampire."

Malachi's tone was persuasive. "Jack's killing rate is accelerating. He's in a feeding frenzy and neglecting grave-sleep. As each night passes, his brain becomes more dehydrated and it has shredded his sanity. He can no longer be ignored. This time he has killed fifteen women in three months, although the newspapers have only reported the deaths of the eleven who were prostitutes, *those* he left lying in the back-street alleys of London."

Julian watched Connor closely, waiting until Malachi finished speaking.

"Usually, we would haul Jack up in front of the council, but he is beyond reason. He leaves us no choice. We know where he will be... and you will stop him."

It was not a request. The atmosphere was deathly still while the three jurors waited.

Connor inclined his head. "How will I know him?"

"Malachi will put his picture into your mind. And it has to be tonight." Julian glanced at his watch. "You have one hour... and a trap to bait."

Connor's hackles rose as the meaning sank in. Feeding and sacrificing were not the same thing, but, as regret settled over Principal Julian's resolute expression, Connor realized they did not have the luxury of morals. Knowing this powerful blonde vampire shared his distaste of offering up a human life lit a fire of curiosity inside him.

"Very well," he murmured.

Julian nodded slowly, and as though the assembled vampires shared one mind, the three Jurors rose instantly from their seats and flowed across the floor. They melted into the darkest corner at the rear of the cavern, and disappeared.

Connor fixed his eyes on the spot, but couldn't see them.

"The clock is ticking," Malachi said quietly, touching Connor's shoulder. In seconds, both vampires turned on their heels and left.

So, thought Connor, summing up his current situation with bitter irony, it is 1918, the war has just ended, the men are back, the women are grateful, and Jack is insane. *A recipe for disaster, Jack the Ripper is vampire Jack, and he has lost it again.* Turning the words over in his mind could not make the next act he had to play out any more palatable.

He checked his watch. Half an hour had passed, during which time he and Malachi had not spoken, not out loud, in any event. Connor did, however, have Jack's face etched into his brain. The network of alleys behind the respectable gas-lit facades of the music halls and theaters were a favored killing ground, and Connor had much left to do in barely thirty minutes.

He knew the mechanisms of the vampire brain better than most. Jack had delayed grave sleep *too* long this time. And when Jack had finally succumbed to it, not only had his sanity been dissolved in the blood rush, but the hungry vessels in his brain, being starved and then drenched in the sudden surge of blood, had compressed the medulla oblongata. Messages were now barely detectable above the brainstem, and the temporal lobes no longer registered a personality.

Connor waited, impatiently, outside the gates of the Whitechapel Cemetery. *The living have no respect for the dead in early twentieth century London.* The cemetery was a popular place for men of good standing to have sex with prostitutes, and he needed bait.

It was hard not to feel repulsed by what he had planned. But, he had a job to do, and stage one was to launch a seduction of his own. Malachi had melted into the shadows somewhere along the way, and as Connor pulled up the collar of his dress coat, and tapped the brim of his top hat further down his brow, he became a coal black statue exuding an aura of dangerous fascination.

He heard voices floating on the evening breeze; a male and female. The pair emerged through the cemetery gates. The clinking of copper pennies was accompanied by a rustling of taffeta as the man indulged in one last grope of the girl's plump rump, slapping it hard as she yelped playfully.

"'Ere, cut it out, cheeky blighter," she cackled.

The male doffed his hat and turned away to the right, and Connor's victim turned left.

He drifted along the railings, tracking her silently, willing her to notice him. He was dressed in opera attire. *Ridiculous to think that prostitutes, even on alert with all the killings, are so easily disarmed. One whiff of "a toff" with a billfold of crisp white pound notes would be enough to make her lie down in the street and spread her thighs.*

He had drawn the line at the opera cape Malachi had produced with a flourish.

Laughing aloud, he had said, "I might as well put a placard around my neck saying, I'm a vampire, and I bite."

Malachi had tilted his head and said, "You may well be right."

Looking at the girl's bright orange hair, disconcertingly beige powdered face, and the crimson-painted lips, Connor doubted that the cape would have been out of place, after all. *Perhaps she is an actress.* For a moment uncertainty surfaced. *It will not do for her to be missed too soon.* The looming prospect of finding another target shunted a wave of irritation through him, and then he relaxed.

His confidence returned as the girl tugged on her bodice, arranged her décolletage, and slipped her shawl from her shoulders.

Reassured that her stage was certainly the cobbled streets, and not the theater, he ambled closer. Baiting a trap of her own, then, he thought. Connor smiled invitingly as the girl's sashaying saunter faltered and she turned to face him.

He suppressed the sneer that tugged at his lip as the scent of her unwashed, sweat-stained skin enveloped him. This was certainly not going to be pleasant... for either of them.

Predictably, Pearl was very obliging. "'Ello, me darling. Me name's Pearl." She smiled, and blackened teeth spoiled the effect of an otherwise passably presentable face. The breasts were a distraction, spilling over the bodice and jiggling with every inhaled breath. Connor had not been dead *that* long, and he reached out a finger to stroke along the swelling flesh.

"Blimey, lover, you is colder than a witch's tit! You need an 'ot toddy." She batted thin eyelashes upon which scurvy had taken its toll. "C'mere. If you want, I got 'anover way to warm yer 'ands, if yer git me drift."

Taking the tart with heart to almost comic proportions... but then we are both acting. Connor sighed inside his head, arranging a tight grin on his white face, and making an effort to warm it a little when he noticed a spark of alarm light her eyes. "Well now... Pearl, was it?"

She giggled with girlish charm, and then ruined it with a consumptive cough.

"I'd be 'appy to 'elp, I'm sure," she responded as Connor decided subtlety was a waste of time and flipped open his coat to indicate the button fly of his high-waisted breeches.

Pearl's triumphant grin turned Connor's stomach. He allowed her fingers to walk like bony spider's legs down over the cotton fabric of his dress shirt.

"My," she breathed in a sickly-sweet tone. "You looks after yerself. Rock 'ard those muscles."

Connor smiled as her hands snaked up under his waistcoat and she reached for the waistband of his pants. Closing his long fingers around hers, trapping them, he said, "Not here. I have a theater box... if you fancy?"

Pearl's eyes glittered with beads of jet. "Never been in a theater, not even up in the gods, let alone the stalls."

He smoothly turned away, letting her fingers slip from his as he set off along the sidewalk, jerking his head for her to follow. "Come along, Pearl. You only live once." He laughed to smother the bitterness in his tone.

The artificial light spilling out from the theater foyer onto the sidewalk captured the first glimmer of suspicion crossing Pearl's rouged face as Connor walked past the doorman, touching his hat in greeting, and disappeared around the corner.

"'Ere," Pearl spluttered in protest, hurrying along at the doorman's scowl.

"We don't want your sort here, miss."

"Alright, keep yer 'air on," she muttered, rushing around the corner as though Connor and his wallet were slipping from her fingers.

She collided with Connor's chest and his hands closed over her arms as he steadied her.

"Well, here we are, Pearl." Connor bent to breathe seductively into her ear, chasing goose bumps over her dry skin, "Wait here, I'll be back, directly."

Pearl turned her face and her lips grazed Connor's cheek. Her heart rate quickened as he stopped breathing to keep her stench at bay, and kissed her.

Poor girl. Even the string of her sticky saliva clinging to his lips could not turn the feeling of regret to revulsion.

"Wait here," he whispered, and then he vanished.

Pearl had time to turn her head and wonder before a crow-black form collided with her chest, breaking three of her ribs as it slammed her into the wall, yanked her rag doll-floppy stunned body forward again, and threw her down onto the ground twenty yards further along the dark alley.

Straddling her hips and staring into her petrified face, in three seconds, Jack had used his thumb to burrow into her voice box, killing the scream rattling inside her throat.

Ten yards away, buried in the deepest shadow, Connor wondered why his heart felt like it had doubled in size, or weight, at least. He felt like shit. *Why the hell can't the Undead Council do their own dirty work?* He sighed, having gone this far, the very least he owed Pearl was that she not have died in vain.

He waited for Jack to finish the kill. Having used a blade to slice open her abdomen, Connor understood the hard bite Jack made into the belly, near her womb. *The tissue there is always plump, always at some stage of preparing for the joy of life, and Jack's tastes are for the iron enriched parts of the female body.* Thin arterial blood could no longer satisfy his deformed brain cells.

Watching until Jack left the scene, Connor faced what he had done.

The weight in his chest dropped him down to his haunches as his eyes roamed over the body. Taking out a handkerchief, he took a moment to clean the blood from Pearl's blank face, the desiccated tissue already shrinking to cling tightly to her skull. Dragging his cold fingertips down from brow to cheek, he closed her eyelids, veiling the black pools of her blown pupils which glistened with accusation.

"I'm sorry, Pearl," he murmured.

Rising swiftly, he set off in pursuit of Jack, and found him, within seconds, vomiting in the alley behind the Astoria Theater, of all places. *Certainly a well chosen spot.* Puns tumbled over in Connor's mind as a distraction from the deed he had yet to perform.

After encore number sixteen, Jack's final curtain call. Connor was about to enter stage left.

The metallic stench of regurgitated liver shrank Connor's sinuses in disgust, curling his lip in a sneer. Jack had returned to eating; a classic sign of vampire dementia. Connor had seen it once before. *The craving for blood is so overwhelming the vampire's instincts step over the line into addiction. They still drink the blood, but in desperation, are compelled to eat the flesh.*

Of course, absorbing fluids as rehydration was one thing. *Digestion is an altogether different process, and vampires do not have that function.* So, here knelt Jack, vomiting up the indigestible pulped liver of Pearl like a bulimic regretting every last mouthful.

Connor as an executioner was an ironic choice. Firstly, because the newspapers had Jack down as a surgeon because of the clinical disemboweling of victims, and secondly, because Connor *was* a surgeon and the butchery he had just seen was an insult to his profession.

Jack dropped to his knees, retching, his hands massaging the offal, trying to reinsert it into his mouth even as it flooded out. Connor materialized as an ethereal face floating above a body of shadow. The moon glinted on the stiletto blade in Connor's hand, sharpened to a needle fine surgical implement. Unseen by hapless Jack, Connor pressed the tip into the space at the first vertebrae, where the curve of the skull ends. With the heel of his hand, he hammered hard on the hilt and drove the knife up into Jack's brain stem, severing the spinal cord. Jack collapsed face down into his last meal, and lay stone still.

Connor ignored the blood seeping into the knee of his black gabardine pants where it rested on the floor beside Jack. He pushed the knife deeper up into the skull and stirred it through the jelly of his brain. Crushing his skull would cause suspicion, but death was only a word for vampires. The devil is in the detail, thought Connor. Death was the termination of brain function, anything else was just an eternity of mistakes replaying behind a frozen inanimate facade. *Even Jack does not deserve to be buried alive.*

Rising smoothly to his feet, Connor slipped back into the shadows, and whisked away along the dark streets. Being a cold night, Jack's chilled firm tissues would be attributed to the freezing temperature, so for now, vampire society could heave a collective sigh of relief.

Buttoning up his long coat as he moved hid the blood-soaked fabric at his knees from view. It was a simple act to saunter towards the wide promenade along the embankment of the River Thames, and to hurl the blade into the middle of the gunmetal-gray boiling current.

A shrill shrieking sound sliced through the night air, and Connor smiled.

Nothing conveyed panic and mayhem as surely as the repeated blasts of a policeman's whistle. Connor could almost see the flushed face of the copper, blowing hard, and trying to keep his own rising panic under control.

Who have they stumbled across, I wonder? Pearl or Jack? Connor hoped it was Pearl. She deserved that, to not be left lying in the alley until frost bit into her as spitefully as Jack had.

Connor headed home. He had done everything Principal Julian and Malachi had asked of him. He could not be happy about it, and he hoped that vampires such as Jack were rare.

But for now, their secrets were safe.